The M...

by A...

"You're not g... ..., but when I ca... here today, I had no intention of dragging you off to bed like a sex-starved caveman," he said.

"'Kay."

"Are you angry?"

"Don't have the energy."

He chuckled and the sound echoed beneath her ear. "Do you want to go out for lunch?"

She lifted her head as her stomach growled. "Sounds good."

"Since I interrupted your shower earlier, why don't we shower together?"

"If my knees will hold me up."

He turned to his side, holding her in place against him. "Don't worry. I'll be there to catch you if you fall."

It was too late. She'd already fallen.

Devlin and the Deep Blue Sea
by Merline Lovelace

"Permission to come aboard, Captain?"

At Devlin's question, Liz pulled in another breath. She could think of a hundred reasons to refuse his request. She didn't really know this man, wasn't sure she believed everything he'd told her.

Yet she couldn't deny he acted on her like a damn spark plug. Every time he got this close, he transmitted an electrical energy that made her pulse rev faster and her skin get hotter. Still, she was pretty sure she would have denied his request if the rig had remained stable.

Well, it didn't pitch much. Just enough to send Liz staggering forward a step, smack into Devlin's denim-covered chest.

"I'll take that as a yes," he said, his voice edged with a husky note that had Liz's toes curling into the deck.

Available in February 2007 from Silhouette Desire

Engagement Between Enemies
by Kathie DeNosky
(The Illegitimate Heirs)
&
Tycoon Takes Revenge
by Anna DePalo

The Man Means Business
by Annette Broadrick
&
Devlin and the Deep Blue Sea
by Merline Lovelace
(Code Name: Danger)

Baby, I'm Yours
by Catherine Mann
&
Her High-Stakes Affair
by Katherine Garbera
(What Happens in Vegas…)

The Man Means Business
ANNETTE BROADRICK

Devlin and the Deep Blue Sea
MERLINE LOVELACE

SILHOUETTE®

Desire™

DID YOU PURCHASE THIS BOOK WITHOUT A COVER?
If you did, you should be aware it is **stolen property** as it was reported *unsold and destroyed* by a retailer. Neither the author nor the publisher has received any payment for this book.

All the characters in this book have no existence outside the imagination of the author, and have no relation whatsoever to anyone bearing the same name or names. They are not even distantly inspired by any individual known or unknown to the author, and all the incidents are pure invention.

All Rights Reserved including the right of reproduction in whole or in part in any form. This edition is published by arrangement with Harlequin Enterprises II B.V. The text of this publication or any part thereof may not be reproduced or transmitted in any form or by any means, electronic or mechanical, including photocopying, recording, storage in an information retrieval system, or otherwise, without the written permission of the publisher.

This book is sold subject to the condition that it shall not, by way of trade or otherwise, be lent, resold, hired out or otherwise circulated without the prior consent of the publisher in any form of binding or cover other than that in which it is published and without a similar condition including this condition being imposed on the subsequent purchaser.

Silhouette, Silhouette Desire and Colophon are registered trademarks of Harlequin Books S.A., used under licence.

First published in Great Britain 2007
Silhouette Books, Eton House, 18-24 Paradise Road,
Richmond, Surrey TW9 1SR

The publisher acknowledges the copyright holders of the individual works as follows:

The Man Means Business © Annette Broadrick 2006
Devlin and the Deep Blue Sea © Merline Lovelace 2006

ISBN-13: 978 0 373 40228 1
ISBN-10: 0 373 40228 7

51-0207

Printed and bound in Spain
by Litografia Rosés S.A., Barcelona

THE MAN MEANS BUSINESS

by
Annette Broadrick

ANNETTE BROADRICK

believes in romance and the magic of life. Since 1984, Annette has shared her view of life and love with readers. In addition to being nominated by *Romantic Times BOOKclub* as one of the Best New Authors of that year, she has also won the *Romantic Times BOOKclub* Reviewers' Choice Award for Best in its Series; the *Romantic Times BOOKclub* WISH Award; and the *Romantic Times BOOKclub* Lifetime Achievement Awards for Series Romance and Series Romantic Fantasy.

To Ralph and Betty Carruthers,
who believe that family comes first,
for which I'm extremely grateful.

One

"Man your battle stations! Incoming! Incoming!"

Jodie Cameron grinned at the innovative way the receptionist notified her that the man she worked for had finally arrived at the office on this gloomy winter day in Chicago.

"Thanks, Betty." Jodie cleared her computer screen, brushed a wisp of hair that had escaped the tidy knot at the back of her neck away from her face and waited for him.

Jodie knew something was up with Dean Logan. In the five years she'd worked for him Dean had never come to work this late in the morning. He generally was already there when she arrived.

Earlier she'd checked his calendar to see if he was scheduled to go out of town, but he had nothing written down. She had wondered if he'd decided not to come in since it was Friday and he planned to go on a week's vacation starting on Sunday. But that didn't seem likely. He would have called to let her know.

This would be the first vacation he'd taken since she'd been his secretary, and she looked forward to having the time to clean out files, set up subfiles and work uninterrupted.

At least Betty had warned her that he wasn't in the best of moods. Dean was moody at the best of times, but no matter how cranky he was this morning, she could put up with him for one more day.

She waited at her desk for him to enter her office.

Dean was an astute businessman and he'd worked hard to build his electronic security business. She had no idea why he didn't appear content with what he'd accomplished during the past fifteen years.

The man looked more like a football player than the head of a multimillion-dollar corporation. Too bad he rarely smiled. As far as she could recall, she'd never heard him laugh.

He was not the jovial type.

His face looked as if it had been carved out of granite and his nose had been broken at some point. His heavy brows and piercing silver-blue eyes would never get him selected to a list of America's sexiest bachelors.

Not that his looks stopped the bevy of beauties who flocked around him. Each hoped to have the distinction of becoming Mrs. Dean Logan.

From what Jodie could tell, he neither encouraged them nor discouraged them. Rachel Hunt was his latest arm candy. He'd been seeing her for almost three months now, which was close to a record for him.

Jodie knew when he started seeing someone new because he had her take care of sending flowers, ordering gifts, obtaining tickets for various events and, at times, listening to his comments about the women who came and went in his life.

He knew that most of the women were more interested in his money and connections than in him. He listened cynically to confessions of undying love and a yearning for a commitment he refused to give.

Hence the number of women who came in and out of his life.

There were times when Jodie saw the loneliness in his eyes. At some point, long before she'd come to work for him, Dean must have made the decision not to allow anyone to get close to him. She found that to be very sad. Not that she'd ever let him know that she pitied him. No, she listened when he needed to talk and kept her opinions to herself.

Of course, her sister would never believe that, since Jodie was known for expressing her opinion on myriad subjects at any given moment. She smiled at the thought.

Dean moved silently, and she had grown used to his suddenly appearing in her doorway. As he did now.

"Good morn—"

"No, it definitely is not a good morning." Dean stopped in front of her desk, pulled an envelope out of his coat pocket and handed it to her. "I won't need these." He started into his office. "Would you mind getting me some coffee, please? I have a hellacious headache."

"Sure," she replied absently. She picked up the envelope and looked inside. The envelope held the airline tickets to Hawaii that she'd ordered for Dean and Rachel. Had Rachel changed her mind about going?

She stood and walked over to the coffeepot, filled one of the large mugs she kept nearby and followed him into his office.

Dean stood with his hands in his pockets looking out the window. She set the cup on his desk and sat in her usual chair.

"What happened, Dean?"

He didn't answer right away. Instead he stared out at the spitting snow and occasional ice blowing against the glass. She waited.

After several minutes of silence, he turned and sat down behind his desk, reaching for the coffee. "Do you have any aspirin?"

"Certainly." She went to the small bar behind a sliding door and poured him a glass of water before she picked up the aspirin bottle and set it in front of him.

He really was in a ferocious mood. His frown, always intimidating, was firmly in place. No wonder people were wary of him. She didn't think he realized how gruff he sounded…and that was on one of his good days.

When she'd first gone to work for him, Jodie knew she had replaced a string of four women who had attempted to work for him and left after only a few weeks. So she'd been warned.

However, she was made of sterner stuff. She'd been raised with three brothers and she and her sister had learned to hold their own with the boys.

After several minutes of silence, Dean looked at her with a puzzled expression. "Why are you here?"

"I work here," she replied with a straight face.

He closed his eyes. "Sorry. I'm not in the best of moods."

No kidding. And he'd actually apologized! She must mark the day on her calendar.

"How long have you worked for me?"

"Five years."

"Why?"

"Why what?"

"If I'm such a disagreeable person, why do you put up with me?"

"Who said you're a disagreeable person? I find you extremely agreeable as long as you get your own way," she replied lightly.

"Rachel says that everyone in this office is intimidated by me. But you aren't."

"I wasn't aware that was part of my job description. Is that what's bothering you this morning?"

"No."

"Do you care what people in the office think of you?"

"No. Well, except for you. What do you think of me?"

She sat back in her chair and considered her answer. Finally she looked him in the eye and said, "I think you're a brilliant man who is impatient with people, a man who has single-handedly built this company into a thriving corporation by ignoring the naysayers and following your own vision."

"Hmph."

He took the aspirin and drank the water. Then he picked up his coffee and sipped.

They sat in silence for several more minutes.

Finally Dean said, "Rachel broke up with me last night."

She couldn't hide her surprise. That must be a first for Dean. He was generally the one who broke things off any time a woman wanted more from him than he was willing to offer.

"Because you wanted her to go to Hawaii with you?" she asked, her disbelief plain.

He grimaced. "Actually she didn't give me a chance to surprise her with the tickets before she informed me that she never wanted to see me again."

Jodie was caught off guard by his admission. "Oh? I didn't realize you'd planned the trip as a surprise."

"Well, I did. Turns out I was the one surprised."

"What in the world happened?"

"I forgot we had tickets to the opera last night. I worked late to clear my desk and I'd forgotten to put the opera on my calendar."

"Oops."

"By the time I checked my cell phone messages on the way home, I was an hour late picking her up."

"Uh-oh."

"She was furious when I arrived at her place. I pointed out that we could still get there before intermission. It wasn't as if we didn't know the story, after all. However, the opera no longer mattered as far as she was concerned." He scrubbed his face with his hand. "She handed me a sack with the things I'd left in her apartment since we've been seeing each other and told me to get out."

"Rachel was obviously upset at the time," Jodie said. "Why don't you call her today and tell her about the trip you've planned? I'm sure you'll be back in her good graces once she discovers your surprise."

He was shaking his head before she finished. "I'm not going to do that. She made it plain she wanted no part of me, so why should I bother?" His mouth turned up at the corners. "I'll admit my ego might have been bruised a little and I went home to sulk, but she made it clear that we were through. I can accept that."

He nodded toward the envelope she'd placed on his desk. "So," he said with a shrug, "I won't be needing those."

Oh, dear. She'd promised herself never to offer her opinion unless he asked for it—and then any question he asked invariably had to do with business.

She wrestled with her conscience for a long moment but could no longer remain quiet. "I disagree," she said bravely, bracing for his response. "I believe you need the time away whether Rachel is with you or not. You know you love Hawaii and it's been three years since you acquired the condo there. I think you should go and spend some time on the beach. Forget the business for a few days. Catch up on your sleep. Once you're there, I know you'll enjoy it."

He leaned back in his chair and stared at her. She waited for his salvo telling her to mind her own business. Jodie was surprised when instead he asked, "Do you think I'm married to my job?"

She eyed him uncertainly. This man had never questioned himself in front of her before. Now that he'd asked her opinion, she wondered how candid she could be while he was in this unusual mood. "Maybe," she said cautiously.

He lowered his brows and stared at her. "Gee, thanks."

She might as well continue. "Look at it this way. You needed to put in long hours when you first started the company and you got into the habit of spending most of your time here. Now you've hired people you can rely on to take care of the day-to-day business. Maybe it's time for you to discover other things you might like to do with your life besides work."

He rubbed his chin. "I suppose." He shook his head. "I still can't get over how angry Rachel was when I arrived. What did I do that was so bad, please tell me? She could have called a cab when she couldn't reach me and been able to see the whole thing."

"Did you by any chance call her after you listened to her messages?"

"Why? I was on my way to pick her up by that time."

She coughed to hide her amusement. "My guess is that her irritation was the result of an accumulation of times when you've been late or forgotten to call or gone out of town without notice. Some women can find that sort of behavior off-putting."

"You don't."

"You pay me quite well not to notice. Besides, I'm your secretary, not your girlfriend."

He studied her in silence for a moment. "That's only going to last another few months," he said, not sounding at all pleased. "You'll be moving over to Frank's department in June."

She grinned. "All thanks to you."

"You caught me in a rare moment of gratitude for your hard work. You graduate with your degree in business this spring, don't you?"

"That's right. I wouldn't have been able to take the night classes without your paying for my tuition."

"I didn't pay it," he growled. "The company did. It was strictly a sound business decision. With your knowledge of the company and your quick grasp of things, it would be foolish to hold you back from exercising your full potential."

He rubbed his forehead as though the headache was hanging on. "Of course, that means I'll go through hell finding someone to work for me."

"No, you won't. I'll do the screening. If I think someone—male or female—will be able to work with you without running the first time you raise your voice, I'll set up an appointment for you to meet them."

"I suppose that might work." He didn't look happy at the thought.

His decision to promote her had been quite a sacrifice for him and she knew it. Beneath that tough, gruff exterior was a very fair man.

Of course, he was clueless about women, but what man wasn't?

"Do you socialize much?" he asked, surprising her again. He'd never shown any interest in her personal life. He was definitely in a strange mood today.

"I date occasionally. Of course, going to school three nights a week and studying takes up most of my spare time."

"I work you too hard."

She offered him a cheerful smile. "Comes with the territory."

"The only reason I planned the trip was to appease Rachel, even if I was a little late in doing so. However, there is a man I'd like to meet in Honolulu. Steve Furukawa owns several businesses in the islands, and I'd like to offer our services to him." He studied her for a moment. "In case he's interested, I'd need you to help me make a presentation to him. I think we should both fly out there. We'll spend a day or two on business and the rest of the time we'll be on vacation."

"Me?" She almost strangled on the word. "I can't do something like that!"

"Why not?"

She stared at him in disbelief. Didn't he understand? Obviously not.

"I'm in the middle of classes, for one thing. And it just doesn't look right, our going to Hawaii together."

"It will be a business trip."

"You've never needed me on one before."

"Jodie, you're a very competent secretary and level-headed. As for school, I doubt missing a week's worth of classes will cause you to flunk. Will it?"

"Well, no, but—"

"Then I don't see a problem." He ruffled through the stack of files on his desk. "Would you check with accounting and see if they have the latest figures on the Malone file? I'd like to see them before lunch if possible."

Two

"What did you say to him?" Jodie's sister, Lynette, asked her that evening after dinner.

Jodie had a standing invitation for dinner at Chuck and Lynette's home every Friday, but she'd never had such earthshaking news to share as she did tonight.

Chuck had called earlier to say he'd be home later than normal and for them not to hold dinner for him. Jodie hadn't mentioned Dean's plan when she'd arrived. Instead she'd helped with dinner and then made certain that her nephews, Kent and Kyle—seven and six respectively—got their baths and were ready for bed.

It was only after she'd joined Lynette in the living room while she nursed eight-week-old Emily that Jodie dropped her bombshell.

"I think I muttered something but don't remember what. I was reeling."

"You're going, of course."

"He practically ordered me to go," Jodie wailed with a laugh.

"When are you supposed to leave?"

"The tickets are for Sunday morning. Early Sunday morning."

"So his latest darling finally had enough of your romantically challenged boss, did she? She lasted longer than the others, though."

"I think what got to him was that she was the one who broke things off. He usually has the privilege of doing that. At least he got a taste of what rejection feels like."

"I can't believe she turned down a trip to Hawaii. I would have gone and then broken up with him," Lynette said with a grin.

"She didn't know about his plans. He'd kept the trip a surprise."

Lynette shook her head with disbelief. "Doesn't the man know anything about women? The anticipation of going is part of the excitement."

"We're talking about Dean Logan. Of course he doesn't know anything about us. For a brilliant businessman, he's unnervingly obtuse about the opposite sex."

"Well, who cares, if you get a free vacation out of it?"

"I'll be missing three classes."

"So? You've aced all your tests, you can easily catch up."

The door opened between the garage and kitchen, and Lynette peered over her shoulder. Chuck was home.

"Good evening, all," he said, sauntering into the room.

He was a police detective for the city and looked good in his sports jacket and slacks. "How are my three favorite women doing?" He leaned over Lynette and gave her a leisurely kiss that made Jodie's toes curl to watch.

When he straightened, he brushed his lips across the top of Emily's head. Emily ignored him. Dinner was more important at the moment.

"Your dinner's in the fridge. Just put it in the microwave."

"How are things going for you, Jodie?" he asked casually as he turned to go back into the kitchen.

Before Jodie had a chance to answer, Lynette said, "Her boss has invited her to go with him to Hawaii for a week."

Chuck stopped in his tracks and spun around. "Are you serious? Logan asked you to go away with him? Wow. Aren't you the sly one? I had no idea you two were an item."

"We're not! Believe me, there is nothing going on in a romantic sense. The girl he's been seeing broke up with him. He had the tickets. I suggested he should take the vacation anyway, and he decided to meet with a prospective client while he was there. He said he could use my help. So it will be a working vacation."

Chuck grinned. "And you believed him."

"Of course. Why shouldn't I?"

Chuck, his dinner forgotten, sat down next to Lynette. "Jodie. Honey. Let's get real, okay? A man doesn't invite his good-looking secretary to go away with him to a tropical isle without some strictly male motive. He's going to do his best to get you into his bed. Count on it."

"Chuck!" Lynette kept her voice soft but emphatic. Jodie wondered how she did that. "Not every man has sex on the brain like you do."

He gave her an intimate smile. "Oh, yes, they do. Some just hide it better than others."

Jodie said, "You're probably right, Chuck, but Dean is a definite exception. I've worked for him too many years not to know that he doesn't notice me as a woman. I'm an efficient machine to him and that's fine with me."

"If you say so. When do you leave?"

"Sunday morning."

"Have you ever been to Hawaii?"

"No."

"Then go and enjoy yourself. I would guess he's picking up the tab for your accommodations."

"Actually he acquired a condo there a few years ago. It was part of a business deal he made. He went over to check it out and that's the last time he was there. There are three bedrooms and three baths. I think the company he bought it from used the condo for the executives to, quote, get away, unquote, for some relaxation."

"So he'll have you right where he wants you for a leisurely seduction," Chuck replied, twisting his imaginary mustache with a grin.

"Nothing wrong with your imagination, that's for sure," Jodie replied, laughing. "If you'd ever met him, you'd see how far off base you are."

"Why? Is he some kind of monster?"

"Let's just say he takes some getting used to. Once his business is completed he'll probably forget that I'm there."

Lynette said, "Now that's carrying the platonic bit too far, sis. There's bound to be a middle ground between what you've imagined and what my crazy husband came up with."

"So you two think I should go ahead and plan to go?"

They answered in unison. "Yes."

"But what about the talk around the office?" Jodie asked. "Won't that give everyone the wrong idea?"

"So what?" Chuck answered. "It will give them something to gossip about. Probably improve morale. The office employees will start a betting pool as to when you'll announce your engagement."

"You're a big help," Lynette said, shaking her head at her spouse. "The idea here is to give her reasons to go, not make up stuff."

"Well, since it looks as though I'm going, I'll need to go shopping for beachwear tomorrow."

"Great idea. Buy some things that are colorful and tropical. No business suits." She eyed her for a moment. "You've said you never have time to get your hair cut. Why don't you get it trimmed tomorrow, as well?"

Jodie nodded. "I could do that."

"And get plenty of sunscreen. You know how easily we burn, thanks to our Scandinavian ancestors."

Jodie looked at her arms and ruefully shook her head. "I hope to come back with at least a little more color. I'll slather myself with the stuff and see what happens."

Lynette lifted Emily to her shoulder and rubbed her back until she gave a very unladylike belch, causing the three of them to laugh. "I need to put her down," Lynette said. "I'll be right back."

"I need to go, you guys. It's been a long week," Jodie said, rising. "And it looks like I'll be spending tomorrow shopping."

"Poor baby," Lynette consoled with a grin. "That's your favorite hobby in the entire world, and we both know it."

"True. And buying summer things in the dead of winter will be just the thing I need to get into the spirit of the trip."

Later that night while Jodie prepared for bed, she thought about the comments she'd heard tonight from Lynette and Chuck. She scrubbed her teeth and removed her makeup before looking in the mirror.

"Are you going to be brave and treat this as a chance in a lifetime to see Hawaii with all expenses paid?"

Here image stared back at her with sparkling eyes.

After a long pause, she sighed and said, "You're no help. You want to see Hawaii. Will the trade-off be worth it? Hawaii with all its pleasures weighed against a week with a man who's a workaholic? Knowing Dean, he'll have us working the whole time we're there.

Then again, we're bound to find some time to enjoy the sun and sand.

She smiled as she crawled into bed.

Three

Dean stood in front of the mirror shaving early Sunday morning and wondered what he was doing. Had he lost his mind?

What had possessed him to invite his secretary to go with him to Hawaii? She was a great secretary. In fact, she was a great human being, but he didn't need to spend a week with her to be reminded of the fact.

Of course, if he planned to meet with Furukawa, he could use her presence there to help him make a presentation and to help formulate a contract. She was very conscientious and did her work without a complaint.

But to take her to Hawaii with him?

Had his midlife crisis arrived sooner than expected? Why else would he have considered taking her? He knew nothing about her outside of the office. Well, he knew she was single, but that was about it. Did she have family close by? Would they warn her about going with him?

He could get in trouble for harassment.

Well. Maybe that was a little extreme. She'd had the option to say no. When he'd called her at home last night she'd sounded agreeable enough. He certainly hadn't coerced her. At least, not much.

He finished dressing and picked up the bag he'd packed. He'd had trouble knowing what to pack besides his business clothes. The only other time he'd been there, his business suits had been expected, but then he hadn't been on vacation. He'd spent the three days in meetings, ironing out the conditions of the merger with the parties involved.

He'd tossed in a few shirts and khaki pants this morning and even remembered to stick in a pair of tennis shoes, which was a laugh. He hadn't played tennis in years, but it was the idea that counted.

Maybe he *was* a little too focused on business. Working hard had become a habit, and he wasn't certain that he could break it.

Or that he wanted to.

He'd really let Rachel's comments get to him, which was ridiculous. What did he care what she thought about him? He'd just been surprised, that's all.

He and Jodie would get along well enough for the few days they'd be there, he was fairly certain. He'd treat the trip as a bonus for Jodie in appreciation for her years of service.

He smiled at the thought, pleased that he'd found the correct category for the trip.

* * *

Jodie had almost reached the door into the airport before Dean recognized her. She looked different, but why? Then he realized that she was wearing her hair down. He'd never seen her wear it any way but pulled back into a knot on the nape of her neck. It danced around her neck and shoulders in the wind. She certainly looked different this morning.

He glanced at his watch and frowned.

As soon as Jodie stepped out of the cab, she spotted Dean waiting for her just inside the door to the airline check-in counters. She hurriedly crossed the sidewalk toward him.

The wind-chill factor must be in the teens. Hawaii sounded better and better to her. At least she'd be getting away from the wonderful winter weather of dear old Chicago for a few days. She looked forward to soaking up some sun.

Just as she reached the door, he opened it and took her bag. "You're late," he snapped. "Security is tight and I don't want to miss the flight."

Actually she was forty-five minutes earlier than the airline recommended, but she wasn't going to start their trip together disputing his words. Instead she smiled at him and said, "I'm here now and good morning to you. Have you checked your luggage?"

"Yes." He glanced down at her suitcase. "Is this all you're taking?"

She looked down at her bag and then back up at him. "We're only going to be gone a week," she replied.

"I thought women packed three or four suitcases wherever they went," he mumbled.

"Not me."

"Well," he said awkwardly. "That's good."

She walked over to join the line to the counter and he followed her. "I might as well stay with you. No sense losing you in this crowd."

Jodie realized that he was nervous! She found that hard to believe, considering how much traveling he did. Was it because she was along?

She hadn't spotted it at first, probably because she'd been shaken by his accusation that she may have caused them to miss their plane. There was no way she would lose him in the crowd. As tall as he was, she'd spot him in any group.

She circumspectly checked out what he'd chosen to wear for the trip and was pleasantly surprised to see him in black pants, a black turtleneck sweater and a black leather jacket that fit snugly at his waist.

The wind had ruffled his dark hair and the leather jacket made him appear dangerous and very masculine.

He looked downright swashbuckling.

Now if he'd only smile once in a while, he could be attractive.

They reached their plane with time to spare, which Jodie wisely did not point out. Dean stopped and bought himself a paper and a couple of magazines. Jodie found the newest book out by one of her favorite authors, as well as a crossword puzzle book in case she got tired of reading.

She watched Dean as he paced the concourse. Was the man ever still? She placed her parka on her lap and started reading.

When it was time to board, first-class passengers were seated first. Not too bad. Dean waved her to the window seat before settling down beside her. A flight attendant checked to see what they would like to drink and handed them menus for breakfast.

Once they gave their orders, Jodie settled comfortably into the luxurious depths of her seat and looked around her.

The only time she'd seen first class on her flights was when she'd walked through to the tourist section. What a way to travel.

"Are you nervous about flying?" he asked after several minutes of silence.

She'd been peering out the window when he asked, and she straightened. "A little perhaps. Why?"

"I noticed your fingers gripping the armrests, and the plane hasn't moved."

She jerked her hands away and folded them into her lap. After a moment she dug into her purse and pulled out the book she'd been reading but gave up a few minutes later because she couldn't seem to concentrate. Maybe she'd work one of the crossword puzzles.

After another prolonged silence—were they ever going to leave the terminal?—Jodie asked, "How long is the flight, do you recall? I've forgotten what the reservations said."

"About thirteen hours, depending on a headwind. We change planes in Los Angeles."

"Oh."

"We should reach Maui by midafternoon local time."

"But we'll still be on Midwest time."

"True."

Well, she'd exhausted all her skills at social chitchat

with him. Jodie picked up the airline magazine and began to thumb through it.

After what felt like hours, the plane finally taxied out to the runway for takeoff. Then it stopped. The captain apologized for the delay. There were nine jets ahead of this one. Great. That gave her plenty of time to rethink this whole idea.

Dean cleared his throat. "Jodie?"

She'd just peered out the window again. "Yes?"

"I'm a little embarrassed to mention this after you've worked for me so many years, but I really don't know much about you besides your work ethic, which is outstanding, and your determination to get your degree, which is admirable. I'd like to learn more about you. Why don't we use this time to get acquainted?"

"I'm sorry, but I really don't want to talk right now. I need all my concentration once we're ready for takeoff to make absolutely certain the plane's wings are firmly attached." After all, there was a lot of thrust by the jet engines, and everyone knew that takeoffs and landings were the most dangerous times during a flight. Unless they happened to fly into the side of a mountain. They had to cross the Rockies, didn't they?

Or if they went down over water…say, maybe the Pacific Ocean?

"Jodie?" She jerked her head away from the window and looked at him inquiringly.

"We're perfectly safe, you know."

"Of course we are," she promptly agreed. "As long as we sit here on the runway." She glanced back out the window to continue to check the wings.

Dean made some kind of noise that sounded as if he was either choking or coughing. She looked back at him in concern. His lips were compressed and he wore a frown. His shoulders shook and suddenly, like Mount St. Helens, he erupted into laughter.

Laughter? She had rarely seen him smile, much less heard him laugh, and she stared at him in amazement. What a difference it made in him. He looked much younger than his thirty-eight years. Who would have believed it?

He immediately attempted to quell the sound, but then he looked at her again, recognized her bemusement, shook his head and continued to laugh—a deep-throated sound that finally made her smile.

He reached for his handkerchief and wiped his eyes, blew his nose and finally, after what seemed like forever, managed to stop.

But he continued to smile and she still hadn't recovered from the change in him. Dean was smiling and, miracle of miracles, his face hadn't cracked into a thousand little pieces. Who would have believed it?

"Care to share the joke?" she asked. She smiled her pleasure at this unexpected peek into the man she thought she knew so well.

He touched her arm and slid his hand down, lacing his fingers between hers. "I'm sorry. I shouldn't have laughed at your nervousness. You're going to be just fine, I promise."

"From your lips to God's ear," she muttered.

He chuckled again. He was certainly getting a great deal of amusement out of her fear of flying. Then again, maybe it was worth it to see that the man had a human side. A decidedly masculine side at that.

The brackets around his mouth had revealed dimples. She bet he hated them.

In fact, the man bore little resemblance to her stone-faced boss. Same hair and eyes, same strong jaw, and yet with his silver-blue eyes sparkling and his teeth flashing he was actually handsome.

Okay, she was losing it. When she looked at Dean Logan and saw a handsome man she knew she'd lost her grip. Fear could certainly do crazy things to a person's perceptions.

"I was born in Indiana," he said in a casual voice as though answering her question. "Came to Chicago to attend Northwestern and never left. How about you?"

She cleared her throat. "We're from Wisconsin originally."

"Who is we?"

"Mom, my three brothers, my sister and me. My parents got married way too young, but they were in love and didn't want to wait until after they finished school to get married. My brother came along not long afterward, and Dad dropped out of college to get a job. He took good care of all of us, but I think he pushed himself too hard for too many years and he died of a heart attack when he was forty-five.

"Mom had to get a job but had trouble finding one since she'd never worked before. Without training or an education, it was tough going for her. She ended up as a waitress. Both Mom and Dad really stressed the importance of an education when we were growing up. All three of my brothers worked their way through college so they could take care of her."

"Where does your family live?"

"All over the place. Mom's in Phoenix. That's where

they lived when Dad died. One of my brothers is an attorney in Oregon, one is career Navy and based out of Bremerton, Washington, and one lives just outside of D.C. doing who knows what. If anyone asks, he says, 'I work for the government' in a vague way and changes the subject. My sister, Lynette, and I live here in Chicago."

"Do any of them have children?"

She smiled. "Chuck and Lynette have two boys and a brand-new baby girl. The boys are pleased as little boys can be that they have a baby sister. My sister had two miscarriages before Emily came along."

"Are any of your brothers married?"

"Not a one. Too busy with work or too busy playing the field." She waited, and when he didn't ask any more questions, she said, "It's your turn. Tell me about your family."

She wasn't sure at first that he was going to answer her, but eventually he said, "My mother lives in a nursing home here. I had an older brother, but he and my dad were out on Lake Michigan at the wrong time years ago. A storm blew up and they didn't make it back."

"How awful. How old was your brother?"

"Twelve. I was eight and had a cold, so my mother wouldn't let me go with them." He looked away. After two or three minutes he added, "I haven't talked about them in years."

She wondered about the emotional scars he carried from that time. No doubt he'd been upset, probably angry, that he didn't get to go. Then to lose them like that. Survivor's guilt probably played a part. She knew him well enough not to say any more by way of sympathy for his loss.

"Why aren't you married?" he asked bluntly.

She looked at him in surprise. "Isn't that a rather personal question to ask?"

"Probably. But if I'm going to drag out all my personal stuff, I figure you can, too."

"Mmm. I don't think it's quite the same, unless you want to discuss why *you're* not married."

"That's easy enough. I have no intention of getting married. I was engaged once, but she found someone who had more money and broke the engagement six weeks before the wedding." He shrugged. "She's on her third marriage now, so she did me a favor. After that I decided to devote my time and energy to building my business, which was much more important to me than getting too involved in a relationship."

"You know, Dean, one of these days you're going to meet the woman you've been waiting for your whole life. And when you do, you'll be a goner."

"Somehow I doubt that very much." He studied her for a moment in silence. "So," he finally said, "have you ever been married?"

She shook her head, feeling a little exasperated with him. His persistence was one of his strongest traits. It made him an excellent businessman. But she didn't particularly like it when he aimed his curiosity at her.

Before she could decide how much she wanted to share with him, the captain's voice came over the speakers and said they were next to take off.

She immediately tightened her seat belt.

"Any tighter and you'll cut off the blood flow to the rest of your body," he said drily.

She took a deep breath, held it briefly and slowly exhaled. She was being an idiot. She adjusted the strap around her and forcibly relaxed her shoulders.

"No," she finally said in a strained voice. "I have never been married."

"Why not?"

"Because I haven't wanted to be, obviously."

"Any particular reason?"

"I feel like you have me under a microscope."

"Why? We're going to be together for the next week. I just want to get to know who you are when you're away from the office."

"Oh, all right. I had one serious relationship when I was nineteen. I shared a tiny apartment with one of my co-workers. We were both secretaries in a law firm and that's where I met him. He was a law student working at the firm part-time.

"We dated for more than a year and we talked about marriage once he finished law school. We spent most of our free time together. Everything was perfect...until I came home early one night and found him in bed with my roommate."

"Ouch."

"Yeah."

"Did he explain why?"

"To hear him tell it, he'd left school early and thought I might be home. When I wasn't, my roommate suggested he wait there for me. I'm sure she planned everything to work out the way it did. His explanation was that she was there and one thing led to another and it didn't mean anything. He apologized. Said it would never happen again."

"And you said?"

"I was very dignified. I told him if he ever made an attempt to see me again, I'd severely injure a delicate part of his anatomy."

He made a strangling sound but didn't comment.

"He pretty much left me alone after that. He and my ex-friend/roommate got married a few months later because she was pregnant. I don't know what happened after that because I accepted the job I have now and moved closer to work."

"You took it hard."

"That I did. There's something about finding out that someone you considered a friend and the man you thought you were going to marry betrayed you that dampens the spirit."

"But that was—what?—five years ago?"

"About that."

"And you haven't had a relationship since?"

"Not a serious one, no," she said, knowing she sounded defensive. "I just don't intend to get hurt again. So I don't allow anyone to get too close."

He looked at their hands, still entwined. "Then I feel honored."

She lowered her brows and glared at him. "We are not close. I work for you. Just because you think I'll try to get out of this plane before we take off doesn't mean we're close." She pulled her hand away just as the plane began to roll.

"Actually you work for the company."

"You are the company. Like I said, I work for you." Faking nonchalance, she picked up the book and determinedly began to read, hoping his questions were at an end.

Four

Jodie was glad to get off the plane in Los Angeles and walk around. She'd finished her book and decided to get more reading material.

"We have time to get something to eat if you'd like," Dean said as they walked past several small restaurants located along the concourse.

"I'm not really hungry. They'll feed us on this next flight, won't they?"

"Yes."

"Then I'll wait."

She glanced out the glass walls and saw sunshine, blue skies and palm trees. What a difference from Chicago. "I've never been to L.A. before. I guess this doesn't count since all I'm seeing is the airport."

"Don't you like to travel?" he asked. He motioned for her to go into one of the coffee shops with him.

"I haven't done all that much. I've flown to Phoenix several times to see my mother. One Christmas the family gathered in Oregon at my brother's place. Otherwise, my schedule keeps me too busy."

They got their coffee and found a small table near the glass wall overlooking one of the runways. "Then I'm glad you've come with me this week."

"Thank you."

"I hope this isn't out of line, but I can't get over how different you look with your hair down."

"Ah. You have no problem asking why I'm not married but hesitate to make a comment about my hair?"

"You have a point. Is it too late to apologize for my earlier questions?"

"Much too late since you listened to the entire tawdry story." She spoiled her solemn reprimand by chuckling at the expression on his face. "Do you like my hair shorter?"

"Oh. You had it cut."

"Yesterday." She ran her fingers through it. "I'm still getting used to it myself."

"It's, uh, you look very, uh—" He stopped. "Yes, I like it."

"Why, thank you." She looked around them. "Are you ready to find the gate for the next leg of our trip?"

He stood and stretched, briefly causing a gap between his sweater and pants. His stomach was flat and toned. She wondered what he'd look like in a bathing suit.

On the way to the gate Jodie picked up a couple of magazines. She was a little more relaxed for this second flight.

In fact, she was getting sleepy despite the coffee. Perhaps she'd be able to nap once they got into the air.

Jodie stirred as the captain announced that the plane would be making its descent into Kahului Airport, Maui, and that they would be landing in forty minutes.

She couldn't believe she'd slept that long. She glanced at her lap and saw the magazine she'd been reading when she'd fallen asleep.

She looked over at Dean. He wore his horn-rimmed reading glasses and seemed engrossed in a technical manual. No murder mysteries and thrillers for that man.

"I see you found something light and entertaining for your vacation reading," she said.

He lowered his chin and looked over his glasses at her. "Each of us relaxes in his own way. Did you sleep okay?"

"Surprisingly so." She covered her mouth and yawned. "I could get used to traveling in style." She waited a beat and said, "If you'll excuse me, I'd like to go freshen up before the seat-belt light comes on."

Dean moved promptly out of his chair and stepped back. She walked to the front and saw that the lavatory was unoccupied, thank goodness. She went in and locked the door. After she washed her hands, she found her comb and ran it through her hair.

The haircut really did give her a different look. The waves fell around her face and called attention to her eyes. She was surprised that Dean had not only noticed but commented on her appearance.

She felt that she'd been on the plane for at least a week and wondered if she'd ever get the constant drone of the engines out of her head. When she opened the door, she found another first-class passenger standing there. She smiled. He returned her smile with interest.

Jodie felt herself blush and hurriedly returned to her seat. Dean had seen her coming and was standing in the aisle out of her way when she arrived.

"Thank you," she said hurriedly and slipped into her seat.

He sat down beside her and closed the manual he'd been reading.

During the next fifteen minutes he asked her a few more questions about her life—her hobbies, favorite movies and television shows—and she gave him brief answers, at least enough to satisfy him. After that he left her to read her magazine.

She still felt strange about traveling with him, but she'd no doubt get over that once they arrived at the condo and she set up a routine of sorts.

Once they landed, she and Dean methodically checked around them for their belongings before getting off the plane. Anyone seeing them would think they were a couple who'd been married for years. She had no idea why the thought made her nervous.

Once in the terminal, Jodie noticed that many of the people on departing flights wore leis. She smiled, looking forward to getting one for herself. Dean found an available taxi and he and the driver put their bags in the trunk of the cab.

Dean settled into the seat next to her. "So what do you think?"

"I'm amazed. The scented air is refreshing."

"Beats the heck out of car exhausts and diesel fuel."

She glanced at Dean while he gazed out the window and asked questions of the driver. He already looked more relaxed than she'd ever seen him. That was good. She had hopes that the rest would do him good.

The scenery was breathtaking, with towering mountains on one side and the ocean on the other. They followed the coast for several miles until the taxi slowed and turned onto a lane that led to security gates.

Dean gave his name and the gates swung open.

Once inside the gated area, the lane wound through tropical foliage that looked green and lush. When they reached the building, she felt that they'd burst into sunshine with a panoramic view of the sea and the sand.

She sighed with pleasure.

Dean helped her out of the taxi, and while he went to get their bags and pay the driver, Jodie looked up at the building. Balconies jutted out, all facing the water. There would be a fantastic view from each one. The scent of lavish blooms wafted all around her, and she took several deep breaths for the pleasure of soaking up the aromas.

"Ready?"

Jodie turned and saw Dean waiting by the door, their bags in hand. "Sorry," she said. "I'm awestruck." She walked over to the door, opened it for him and then followed him across a large lobby to the elevators.

She pushed the button and the doors silently opened. Once inside, she asked, "Which floor?"

"The top one." She nodded and pushed the fourth-floor button.

When the doors opened, Jodie discovered there was only one set of double doors on the floor. Dean put their bags down, reached into his pocket for a key and opened one of the doors.

He stepped back for the bags and nodded. "After you, Ms. Cameron."

She hurried inside only to come to an abrupt stop, causing him to drop the bags just inside the door. "Oh, Dean, I've never seen anything like this. It looks like the set of a Hollywood movie about the rich and famous."

He closed the door and followed her into the room. "Pretty impressive, I'll admit. Would you like a tour?"

The condo encircled the elevator shaft, with windows looking out in all directions. She saw the well-stocked kitchen, the formal dining room with a mahogany table that could easily seat twelve people and three spacious bedrooms, each with its own bathroom and balcony. She thought the word for them in Hawaii was *lanai* but wasn't certain.

"Pick whichever bedroom you like," Dean said after their tour.

"Which one would you like?" she asked, feeling overwhelmed with choices.

"Doesn't matter."

"Mmm." She paused in the doorway of one. The room seemed the size of a basketball court. The view drew her to the window. "This will be fine," she murmured, opening the door to the outside.

She could hear the sound of the waves rolling onto the beach, the rhythm soothing to her ear. When she turned around, Dean was no longer there. He'd placed her bag on the bed.

Jodie wandered into the bathroom, which was larger

than her living room in Chicago. She smiled. She could quickly become used to living like this. All she could think was, Wow.

Suddenly feeling energized despite the long trip, she quickly unpacked, changed into a pair of cotton slacks and a sleeveless blouse and went back to the main room.

Dean was at the bar, pouring himself a drink. "Want one?" he asked as she walked in.

"Water will be fine. I'm not much of a drinker. I thought I'd go down and wander on the beach for a while."

"Aren't you hungry? I thought we could go eat first."

She thought about it. "Yes, as a matter of fact, I am. I suppose there will be plenty of daylight after we finish eating."

The restaurant was next to the complex. One side was open with tables and chairs inside and out. Jodie noticed there were only a few people at the tables. She glanced at her watch. "I suppose it's a little early to be eating according to local time."

"Doesn't matter. They're used to customers coming in at all hours. They're open twenty-four hours a day."

Once seated, Jodie picked up her menu and started reading the items listed. She yawned and hastily covered her mouth.

Dean watched her for a moment in silence before speaking. "You're going to want to go to sleep early tonight despite your nap on the plane, but if you can manage to stay awake, you'll adjust to the time change quicker."

"The steady sounds of the surf are so soothing. I hope I don't fall asleep with my nose in the salad."

Dean picked up his water glass and held it out. "Here's to our working vacation together."

Jodie picked up her glass and lightly tapped it against his. "I appreciate the invitation." She yawned again. "The way I'm feeling now, I could sleep the entire week away."

Once their food arrived, there was no more conversation. Jodie didn't want to chatter; that wasn't her style. Since they'd already commented on the beauty surrounding them, she could think of nothing to say to him.

By the time they finished eating, the sun was low in the west. Dean walked beside her in silence, his hands in his pockets, as she made her way to the sandy beach.

As the sky darkened, they watched the lights appear along the shoreline before turning back toward the condo. Walking in the sand would be an adjustment, but if she walked like this every day, she'd be in great shape when she returned home.

She smiled at the thought.

"What do you find so amusing?" he asked, stopping as she did to empty the sand from her shoes. He followed her example.

"I was thinking what a workout walking in the sand is. If I'm not in shape now, I will be by the time we leave."

"Probably."

A man of few words. Not that she cared. Tomorrow she would be up with the sun and she intended to enjoy every minute she was here.

After Jodie went to her room, Dean took a shower, dried off and stretched out on the bed.

He thought about Rachel. His anger at the abrupt way she'd dismissed him had caught him off guard. He'd learned many years ago to keep his emotions locked down.

He considered himself to be a thinking man who wasn't swayed by irrational feelings. But when Rachel had blown up at him—*inconsiderate* and *unfeeling* were the nicest things she'd called him—he'd felt an anger he hadn't experienced in a long time.

She hadn't given him a chance to explain. And she'd made it clear she wanted nothing more to do with him.

He had no problem with that and he was thankful he hadn't told her about his plans. Jodie had been right. He'd needed to get away for a few days. Seeing her excitement and enthusiasm this evening had caused him to look at everything through her eyes.

He couldn't remember a time when he'd been that joyous about anything.

Yes, having Jodie here with him might teach him how to enjoy life a little better.

He bet she'd been protected from the harsher realities of life until her—what? boyfriend? fiancé? she hadn't said—pulled his stupid stunt.

He smiled at the way she'd handled the situation. She'd faced the clod and gotten rid of him. But she'd suffered. Why else would she now be too busy to date much?

He turned and adjusted his pillow, willing himself to sleep. Instead his thoughts circled around Jodie. She'd looked so different today when she'd arrived at the airport, wearing formfitting jeans, a sweater, ankle boots and a parka.

The cold had turned her cheeks and nose a rosy hue, and he couldn't help wondering why he'd only noticed today how attractive she was. She was more than attractive, actually. *Beautiful* was an overused word and it didn't quite fit her, but it came close. He liked her looks. He liked and had always appreciated her frankness and her refusal to be intimidated by him. Jodie worked hard and earned every penny of her salary. She was smart and he valued her judgment.

He'd be lost without her.

At least she'd still be with the company. He hoped she could find someone as efficient to replace her.

He wanted this trip to be special for her. He'd get in touch with Furukawa tomorrow to set up a meeting. Once they met, he'd know if he had a chance of setting up some security systems for him.

He settled into sleep, planning the next day's activities.

"So much for plans," he muttered to himself the next morning when he discovered Jodie wasn't still in bed. He'd ordered breakfast from the restaurant, and when it had arrived, he'd knocked on her door.

When she hadn't answered, he'd eased the door open and discovered her room to be empty.

He sat at the kitchen bar, sipped his coffee and ate some of the delicious fruit that seemed to come with each meal. He'd arranged to have several newspapers brought to him each morning, so he read them while he absently ate.

Eventually Dean wandered over to the window and looked down at the beach.

The water looked peaceful this morning and there were several people on the beach, some walking and some relaxed in recliners, reading.

He watched as a lithe young woman came out of the water and grabbed her towel. He watched her for a few minutes before he recognized Jodie.

Her blond hair clung to her head in a beguiling helmet. Her face glowed with pleasure as she quickly dried off and placed her towel on the sand.

Dean couldn't take his eyes off her. Why had he never noticed her trim waist and curvaceous backside. In a one-piece bright red swimsuit cut high on the thighs, she could have posed for the cover of *Sports Illustrated* magazine.

She slicked her hands over her hair before ruffling it with her fingers. She had a way of moving that was quite sensuous. Why had he never noticed?

Dean realized that he wasn't the only male taking notice of her. As he watched, one of the men walked over and spoke to her. Dean turned away. It was none of his business what she did or who she met. So why was he bothered by seeing another man come on to her? There was absolutely no reason for him to feel so possessive about his secretary. She was free to enjoy her vacation in whatever manner she wanted.

He looked back down at them. The male said something to her and she laughed and turned away.

She laughed.

She didn't laugh around him.

With fresh resolve, he turned back to the papers on the counter and scanned them. He looked at his watch. He felt restless and unsettled, and it was too early to call his prospective client. He wondered how things were going at the office. His second in command could handle anything that came up. He knew the business as well as Dean did.

Dean paced to the window and looked at the sea, the mountains and finally the beach. She was alone now, but that didn't seem to bother the men who noticed her. He hoped they got their eyeful.

Dean turned away. He could go down there, maybe do a little swimming...except he hadn't packed a suit. Well, he could walk along the beach, but then the sand would fill his shoes.

The clothes he'd chosen to bring weren't suitable here. Of course, he'd be working, so it probably wouldn't matter. But if he wasn't working, what then? He shook his head in frustration. What did people do on vacation? After a moment he picked up the phone and called the office.

The sun was high overhead by the time Jodie gathered up her towels and beach bag to go search for something to eat. She'd go shower and change clothes and wander down the beach. There was bound to be a place other than the restaurant that was nearby.

She'd had great fun this morning and had met several people who, like her, were there enjoying the warm weather and beautiful scenery with no regrets about missing winter on the mainland.

She'd met a couple on their honeymoon, another celebrating their thirtieth wedding anniversary and a young couple with two little girls playing in the shallows.

Two or three guys had stopped and introduced themselves. One of them said he was on the beach each morning and would probably see her again. Another told her that today was his last day there and he intended to enjoy the water to the very last minute.

When she let herself into the condo, Jodie knew Dean

wasn't there. She wasn't certain how he managed to do it, but his charged energy filled whatever space surrounded him. When he wasn't there, the place was peaceful.

She looked around and saw a pile of newspapers beside a chair and the remains of breakfast on the kitchen counter. He'd ordered for both of them, she discovered, lifting a lid. She ate a brioche and then grabbed a banana. Delicious. That should tide her over while she showered and dressed.

Peering into the mirror after her shower, Jodie touched her nose. Yes, she'd definitely gotten some sun. She was going to have to be very careful not to burn.

She rubbed more sunscreen into her skin before she went into her bedroom to dress.

Jodie had splurged on her new clothes, telling herself that a vacation in Hawaii deserved tropical wear. She chose a pair of sandals, walking shorts and a sleeveless blouse that matched her blue eyes.

She left the condo and waited for the elevator. When the doors opened, Dean stood there. He was the first to speak.

"Going down?" he intoned politely.

She laughed. "Yes, please," she said, stepping into the elevator.

"I came up to see if you were here and wanted to get something to eat."

"You read my mind. I thought I'd walk along the beach and get something from one of the little restaurants I saw earlier."

He put his hands in his pockets. "I take it you enjoyed your morning?"

"Very much. How was yours?"

"I talked to Furukawa this morning. He said he could see me day after tomorrow, so I guess I'll be hanging around here for the next couple of days." He glanced at her and then away. "I think I'm going to need some pointers on how to take a vacation. I hope you're up for the job."

Jodie smiled at him. "Oh, I'm sure you'll get the hang of it soon."

The doors opened and they stepped into the lobby.

"I've called the office twice in hopes of learning about some crisis that only I could handle," he said with a slight smile. "Unfortunately everything is running smoothly."

He sounded so disgruntled that Jodie laughed. "It's not that bad, I'm sure."

"I asked around to find out what people usually do here besides visit the beach." He reached into his shirt pocket. "I found there are all sorts of things to see, if you'd be interested."

They walked out toward the water and walked along the edge.

He offered her the brochures and she eagerly took them. She looked over the various places of interest.

"There's so much to do and see."

By mutual agreement they turned toward a small café that caught their attention. Once seated, they glanced over the menu. Jodie ordered a large salad and Dean had a sandwich.

She continued to look through the brochures. "I'm amazed. We could spend a month and probably not see everything." She pointed to one of the brochures. "We can attend a luau," she said hopefully. "Or have you already been to one?"

"'Fraid not. I wasn't here long enough to do any sightseeing. I'm game for whatever appeals to you."

"Mmm," she said thoughtfully, thumbing through the brochures. "We could explore the other islands, charter a helicopter to look around at everything, check out the mountains or turn into slugs and lie on the beach all week."

He couldn't seem to take his eyes off her. She glowed with enthusiasm, something he'd rarely felt. "Sounds like a plan." He glanced at his watch and reached for his cell phone. "I'll make reservations for the luau and then I thought I might rent a car so I can do some shopping."

Her brows lifted. "You want to go to a mall? Dean, you have hidden depths!"

"I'm embarrassed to say that I didn't really pack the right clothes." He glanced down toward his feet. "I'm going to need to go native and get some sandals, maybe a couple pair of shorts, as well. And no self-respecting tourist could leave the islands without owning an authentic Hawaiian shirt."

She laughed. "Good for you. Step number one—dress for the occasion. Do you want me to go with you?"

He froze. Of course he wanted her with him. He realized that he'd presumed she'd go.

He cleared his throat. "Unless there's something else you'd like to do."

"I love to shop. Stick with me, kid, and I'll show you a pro at work."

He touched her hand. "Thank you."

She grinned at him. "You may not feel so grateful after I drag you through a few stores."

"I'll take my chances."

As a general rule, Dean disliked shopping, but then he'd never before gone on a spree with Jodie Cameron. They wandered through one of the malls and listened while groups of the locals played ukuleles and serenaded the shoppers.

"I used to play one of those when I was a kid," she confided as they stood and listened.

"Were you any good?"

"Well, I won't go so far as to say that, but I learned three or four basic chords that worked for most songs. What I lacked in talent I made up for in enthusiasm." She looked up at him and laughed, wrinkling her nose.

She was adorable.

"You'll have to play for me sometime," he said.

"Oooh, nooo, I don't think so. I haven't touched one in years. I don't know what happened to the one I had."

"Then we'll add that to our shopping list. One ukulele for you to serenade me with each evening. There are all kinds of working vacations. Who knows? You may launch a new career."

"You have no idea what you're asking," she replied ominously before she ruined the effect with a chuckle.

Dean followed Jodie in and out of various stores, in awe of her shopping talents. She knew immediately whether something would work for him and wasted no time looking at the rest.

She finally sent him back to a dressing room to try on several of the items she'd chosen. While she waited, Jodie wandered over to the gift-shop section of the store. She cheerfully bought gifts for everyone in the family as well as several of her friends.

She'd just paid for them when she saw Dean come out wearing a pair of shorts that fit him like a glove and a short-sleeved shirt with a tropical print.

"Wow. You look gorgeous," she said without thinking. When he turned an interesting shade of red, she realized what she'd said. "Oh! I'm sorry. I shouldn't have—"

"Oh, no. Don't apologize. You've just made my day. I don't believe anyone has every applied that word to me."

"Turn around," she said, still feeling a little awkward.

She checked the fit of the shirt across his shoulders and tried to ignore the way the shorts curved over his muscular butt. "You'll do," she said in a croak. Jodie cleared her throat. "What about the others? Did you like them?"

"Yeah. I'm getting all three shorts and a few extra shirts." He glanced down at his bare feet. "I, uh, didn't think my black socks and shoes went with the outfit."

"Good thinking. It just so happens the shoe department is right over there. Let's see what size you are and we'll get you fixed up right away."

By the time they reached the condo it was late afternoon and both of them had their arms full of packages. Once inside, they dumped them in the middle of the floor.

"I think we bought out the stores," he said, staring at the pile in wonderment.

"I still can't believe you actually bought a ukulele. You must be a glutton for punishment."

"How can you be in Hawaii and not want to play some of their songs? Now you have the songbook to help you."

"Uh-huh," Jodie replied, sounding skeptical. She looked around. "All right. Let's sort them out."

"What did you sneak off and buy while I was trying on shoes?" Dean asked, sorting through and picking out his purchases.

"A dress to wear for the luau tonight. I thought as long as you're going native, I might as well join you."

They carried the packages and sacks to their respective bedrooms. Before going into hers, Jodie looked at him and said, "I'm going to need a nap if I'm going to stay up late tonight."

"I was thinking along the same lines. I'll set my alarm to ring in a couple of hours."

"Thanks."

Once inside her room, Jodie leaned against the closed door, dropping her packages. What in the world was wrong with her! She felt as though scales had dropped from her eyes. How could she ever have thought Dean wasn't attractive? Maybe it was the environment and seeing him away from the business. He seemed so earnest about learning how to vacation. She wondered if he'd ever done anything like this before. How sad if he hadn't.

What bothered her was the amused affection she'd felt for him all afternoon as they'd looked at clothes. When she'd run her hands across his shoulders, she'd felt the ripple of muscle beneath her fingers and had a sudden longing to continue touching him.

Without a doubt, she was in trouble. They'd been gone two days, and here she was getting all tingly whenever she looked at him.

Of course, she wasn't going to do anything about it. That

would be too foolish to consider. But there was no law against looking—if she could keep herself from doing something obvious, like drooling.

Five

His wristwatch alarm woke Dean and he was surprised how soundly he'd slept. He sat on the side of the bed and looked out the sliding glass doors. The sky was turning to a deep blue as the day faded. Checking his watch again, he went down the hallway and knocked on Jodie's door.

There was no response.

Finally he opened the door and saw her sound asleep, a cover thrown over her.

"Jodie?"

No answer.

He walked over to the bed. "Jodie, it's time to wake up."

"'Kay," she mumbled into the pillow without moving.

Giving in to temptation, he turned on the radio on her night table and turned up the volume, which certainly did the trick. She jerked up on all fours and looked all around in alarm.

"Sorry. Didn't mean to startle you," he said, trying not to smile.

She sat back on her heels. "Oh. Guess I should have warned you. I'm a sound sleeper."

"I gathered that. I'll let you get ready and meet you in the living room."

"Are you going to wear your new clothes?"

"Absolutely," he said and removed himself from the room.

"Wow," she said to him when she joined him later. "You've definitely gone native."

"When in Rome…" he said with a shrug, trying not to stare.

She wore a tropical print with a sea-blue background. It looked to be wrapped around her, revealing her shapely shoulders and hugging her delectable body. There was little evidence of the secretary tonight.

"What do you think?" she asked and slowly turned in a circle.

He swallowed. "Looks good. Fits nicely."

She laughed. "Actually it's a wrap. The clerk showed me how to put it on. I'm wearing an honest-to-goodness sarong."

That's when he knew he was in serious trouble.

She walked toward him. "I also bought this shell necklace to go with it." She took his arm. "This is going to be so much fun, I just know it."

He silently agreed—if he could survive the evening without grabbing her and kissing her senseless.

* * *

Jodie decided that the luau was everything she'd dreamed about and more. Foods—some she liked better than others—and mai tais, a drink she'd never had before and found delicious, all added to the occasion. The native dances called to her. She had no idea how the women moved their hips so rapidly to the beat of the drums.

It was the drums that kept her pulse throbbing. She glanced at Dean beside her, who seemed to be enjoying himself and the entertainment. She glanced back at the young women. They really were something. Every man there watched them with avid eyes.

She leaned against his shoulder and gave him a slight nudge. "Think you could dance and play the drums like that?"

He glanced at her. "I wouldn't attempt to try. Are you enjoying yourself?"

"Oh, yes."

"You might want to go easy on the rum drinks. They have a delayed kick."

She looked at her almost-empty glass. Was that her second one or her third? "Oh. They taste like fruit juice." She glanced over at his glass. "What are you drinking?"

"Piña colada. Want to try it?"

"No, thanks." She sipped on her drink. "There can't be much rum in this or I'd be able to taste it."

"You're not much of a drinker, are you?"

"Not really." She grinned. "But I'm on vacation, so I thought I'd indulge."

The drums came to a sudden stop and Jodie looked around. The dancing girls were carrying leis in their arms and placing them around each guest's neck.

She liked the way Dean looked with the flowers draped over his shoulders.

"Are you ready to go back to the condo?" he asked.

"Sure." They had walked along the beach to this location and would walk back. He helped her up and she realized that she was a little dizzy. Maybe Dean had been right about the drinks.

He slipped his arm around her waist and she naturally did the same to him. He looked good tonight. The shorts he'd chosen to wear showed off his muscular legs. She smoothed his shirt beneath her hand, enjoying the feel of him. She smiled to herself. This was definitely a romantic evening, and Dean was fulfilling her fantasy of a midnight stroll with someone she cared about.

As they ambled along the edge of the water, she looked up into the sky and said, "I've never seen the stars so bright."

"Big cities tend to put off too much light to see the stars."

"That explains it." She rested her head on his shoulder. The sound of the surf added a sensuous rhythm to the night. She'd never been this close to Dean before and she inhaled the scent of his aftershave.

His warmth radiated along her side, and her body tingled everywhere they touched.

"It's going to be hard to top this experience," she said dreamily to break the silence that had fallen between them. They turned toward the path that led to the condos. When he didn't answer, she lifted her head and looked at him. He looked grim as he stared ahead of them. She eased away from him and promptly stumbled.

He grabbed her arm to keep her from falling.

"I think you were right about the drinks," she said ruefully. "I'm beginning to feel the effects."

He opened the door to the lobby for her and waited until they were in the elevator alone before he said, "I'm afraid you're going to have a bad headache in the morning."

They stepped out of the elevator and he unlocked the door to the condo. Once inside, she replied, "Probably. But it will be worth it."

He nodded. "Hope you feel the same way in the morning." They walked toward their bedrooms. They reached hers first.

"Thank you for tonight. I hope you weren't bored," she said.

"Not at all. I don't think I gave the business a thought for, oh, at least thirty minutes." He grinned at her.

She smiled. "I don't know what I'm going to do about you."

"A good-night kiss would be nice."

His comment caught her off guard. It was the last thing she'd expected to hear from him.

"Of course," she said and leaned toward him. She closed her eyes, expecting a peck on her cheek. Instead he slowly drew her into his arms and brushed his lips against hers. What was happening to her? Was it the rum that suddenly made her melt against him...and put her arms around his neck?

By the time he loosened his grip, they were both gasping for air.

"I've wanted to do that all evening," he said hoarsely.

"I didn't know," she murmured and rubbed her finger

along his strong jawline and cheek. Jodie attempted a smile. "Well, good night," she managed to say before she stepped into her room and closed the door.

Dean closed his eyes and stood there. What had he done? Was he out of his mind? He'd taken advantage of the fact that she was there with him, which was unconscionable.

And why hadn't she slapped his face!

Now he knew exactly how she felt pressed against him, how she tasted as her soft mouth opened to his like a budding flower. He'd not forget it, nor would he forget the fact that they still had five days together before heading back to Chicago.

He shook his head and strode into his bedroom. He stripped off his clothes and headed for a much-needed shower and some stern self-talk. Getting involved with Jodie Cameron would be the height of recklessness.

Unfortunately for his peace of mind, he'd discovered tonight that he'd been involved with her for years.

The first thing Jodie knew the next morning when she opened her eyes was that Dean had grossly underestimated the effect of the mai tais. She didn't have just a headache; concrete drills were going off inside her head.

The second thing that registered was the heavenly scent of freshly brewed coffee wafting its way into her room. The thought of coffee was the call of the sirens that drew her out of bed. She put on the thick terry-cloth robe that was in the bathroom, carefully brushed her hair—even her scalp hurt this morning—and went in search of the elixir that might help her live.

Dean sat at the kitchen bar, next to the coffeepot, reading the paper. He glanced up when she moved carefully toward him.

"How're you feeling?" he asked, his voice low.

She almost whimpered. Even that much noise made her head hurt worse. "I should have stopped after the first drink," she whispered. She filled the large coffee mug sitting beside the pot to the brim and immediately lifted it to her mouth. It was too hot to drink, but she could live off the aroma for a moment.

"Aspirin will help," he said, nodding toward a bottle there on the counter.

She filled a glass with water, took a couple of tablets and sat down on the bar stool next to Dean.

He wore shorts, a shirt and sandals. He looked rested and fit. She could almost hate a person for that when she felt like something that had washed up on the shore. He continued to read the paper, and for the first time she fully appreciated his taciturn personality.

She sipped her coffee and squinted out the window. The sun had been up for hours, but at this particular moment she didn't care if she ever saw the sun again.

Dean laid the paper on the counter and got up. He walked over to the expanse of windows and drew the drapes closed.

"How did you know?" she asked with relief when he seated himself once again. He flicked on the small light near where he sat.

"I've overindulged myself a few times in my thirty-odd years. I know what it's like."

She placed her mug on the counter and rested her head in her hands. "The drinks tasted so innocent. I had no idea…" Her voice faded.

He raised his hand to rub her back in sympathy but thought better of it. He cleared his throat. "I know the idea doesn't sound appealing, but you'll feel better once you get some food inside you."

"You are absolutely right. The idea doesn't sound at all appealing."

He grinned and picked up the phone. After ordering them both breakfasts, he hung up and looked at her. "Nibble on some toast, drink some juice—"

"Are you kidding?" she asked in horror, dropping her hands from her head. "I'll probably never drink another glass of juice again."

"It wasn't the fruit juice that caused your pain."

She groaned. "You're always so logical."

"So are you, most of the time. You'll feel better as the day wears on."

"That's a relief. Right now I'd have to get better to die."

He chuckled but didn't say anything else.

When their meal arrived, he opened the door and took the tray, giving the waiter a tip before closing the door and bringing the food to the bar.

Jodie eyed the tray skeptically at the same time her stomach growled. Like it or not, she needed to eat something.

Did Dean always have to be right?

Miraculously by midafternoon she was beginning to feel almost human again. Not well enough to go outside just yet, but better. Anything was an improvement.

Dean had left after breakfast and hadn't yet returned. She wondered where he'd gone. Not that it was any of her business. He might have hooked up with one of the women they'd met at the luau last night.

She frowned at the thought.

What was the matter with her? He'd dated a number of women since she'd worked for him and she hadn't given the matter a thought. Until last night, she hadn't figured he had much passion in him.

She'd definitely been proved wrong there. She groaned at the memory of her response to him. If she hadn't felt so awful this morning, she probably couldn't have faced him.

At least he'd been a gentleman and hadn't mentioned what had happened last night.

Jodie finally went in and showered, the water having its usual soothing effect on her. By the time she dressed and returned to the living room, she felt human again.

She heard the key in the door and glanced around as Dean let himself inside. When he saw her, he grinned and said, "Ignore the ransom note, I managed to escape."

Six

Jodie jumped up and stared at him in shock. "You were kidnapped?" she asked, her voice going up.

He paused before closing the door. "Sorry, I was just making a joke. I was gone longer than I expected to be." She lowered herself back into the chair, feeling silly for overreacting. "How are you feeling?" he asked, making himself comfortable on the nearby sofa.

"Much better than this morning, thank you."

"Did you eat anything for lunch?"

"I ordered some soup. I wasn't up to going downstairs."

"I've set up sightseeing tours for the rest of our stay here. We'll meet Steve Furukawa for lunch tomorrow in Honolulu. While we're there, we'll see the Pearl Harbor Memorial and whatever else looks interesting. There are some great places to see while we're here. I think you'll feel well enough tomorrow to enjoy them."

"Oh. Well. That's nice. I mean, I'm looking forward to it."

"Do you think you're up to sitting out on the beach for a while? The fresh air will do you good."

She nodded. "Good idea. I'll go change."

He got up when she did. "I'll do the same."

As she changed into a two-piece suit she'd bought the day before, Jodie realized that she hadn't seen Dean in his swimsuit. He'd reported that it fit, and that was all that had mattered to her.

She just wished she wasn't so physically aware of him.

They rode the elevator in silence. Jodie wore the matching cover-up to the suit. Dean had on one of his shirts but hadn't bothered to button it. They both had large towels with them.

She did her best not to stare at his chest. Instead she trained her eyes on his face, only to discover that he was looking at her with a great deal of interest.

"New suit?" he asked as they left the building.

"Yes." She stopped and put on her dark sunglasses.

Once on the beach, Jodie carefully laid out one of her towels and slipped off the beach cover.

"Very nice," he said and she glanced around. He stood with his hands resting on his hips, obviously waiting for her to finish making her beach nest.

Dean stripped to his swimsuit was a Dean she'd never known existed. It unnerved her to have all her ideas about who the man was turned upside down. When did he have time to work out, which he had to do to be in such good shape?

She sat and he tossed his towel down and sat beside her.

She wished that she could forget the kiss they'd shared. It had been an aberration; certainly not the norm. However, every time she looked at his mouth, she remembered how his lips had felt touching hers.

The man certainly knew how to kiss!

"This is nice," he said several minutes later. "Is the air helping your head?"

"You're being nice to me," she finally replied. "And it's making me nervous."

"Why? Aren't I always nice to you?"

"Shall I be polite or honest?"

"You're talking about the office, aren't you?"

"That's the person I know—or thought I knew."

He leaned back on his elbows. "Well, we've moved past that, haven't we? After last night?"

She groaned. "I was hoping you'd forgotten about that."

He turned onto his side, propping himself up on an elbow. "Why? We'd had fun at the party and we ended the evening the way most dates are ended—with a kiss."

She slipped her shades down her nose and looked at him. "This is not a dating situation, Dean. I happened to be available to come here because my boss gave me the time off."

"Worked out well, didn't it?" He grinned. "You've opened my eyes regarding several things about my life. I'm hoping you can continue to teach me how to relax and enjoy myself. You've done a good job so far."

Jodie sat up and folded her legs into a yoga position. "What's going on, anyway? What do you hope to accomplish while we're here, other than gaining another client?"

"I want to get to know you better. I've already told you."

"Why? You've known me for years and have never looked at me the way you have since we arrived here."

He chuckled, and despite her practical nature, she was charmed by the sound. A week ago she would have sworn he didn't know how.

"I've never seen you in a swimsuit before...or a sarong, for that matter," he offered casually. Then his tone changed. "I find you fascinating. You have so many facets to your personality, and I've discovered that I want to learn each and every one of them."

"Dean. We'll be back at the office next week and none of this will have mattered. I don't want to make anything more out of our time together than it is."

"I guess that means we won't be sleeping together."

Chuck was right. All men thought about was getting an available woman in bed with them! Then she realized he was laughing at her reaction.

"You're teasing, right?"

"Actually I'm enjoying the expressions running across your face. Just so we're clear, I wouldn't say no if you decide to take me up on my offer."

She shook her head and stretched out on her towel once more. Her heart raced so fast she was certain he could see it pounding in her chest. She knew he was teasing.

He had to be teasing, hoping to fluster her.

Well, she was made of sterner stuff.

Her tone casual, Jodie said, "I'll think about it."

He gave a whoop of laughter and said, "You do that," and then trotted to the water's edge to wade out into the water.

She watched him dive into a wave and appear on the other side. Of course she wasn't going to sleep with him.

That would be the dumbest thing possible for her to do. Okay, so he wouldn't turn her down. So what? To him it would be a casual fling. But becoming intimate with him would change her life. Long after he'd forgotten about this trip, memories would haunt her. It would be impossible to work closely with him without recalling what they had shared.

No. The answer was no.

Jodie stood and walked toward the water.

The water felt good to her, cooling her overheated body. Jodie lowered herself into the water and began a leisurely crawl, feeling her muscles work as she glided through the water.

When Dean spotted her, he angled toward her, cleaving the water in strong strokes.

She smiled at him as he drew near. "I decided to see if the water felt as good as it looks...and it does."

"How's your head?"

"Still on my shoulders. From now on, I'll have one drink and stop, no matter how good it tastes to me."

They continued to swim parallel to the beach, Dean keeping pace with her. Eventually they waded toward the shore together and continued walking until they reached their towels. He quickly dried off and waited for her to gather her things.

"What would you like to do this evening?"

There was a provocative question if she'd ever heard one. "You don't have to entertain me while we're here, you know."

"True, but we've both got to eat and I'd prefer not to eat alone."

"That makes sense, I guess," she replied. "Do you have someplace in mind?"

"Actually I do. I ate there the last time I was here and the Polynesian food is well prepared. If you've never tried it, you're in for a treat."

They stepped inside the elevator.

Finally she nodded. "All right. Thank you for suggesting it."

That evening Jodie looked around the softly lit room, the hurricane lamps on each table making an oasis of light. "You're right," she said to Dean, "this is a great place with a distinct atmosphere."

"I'm glad you're enjoying it. Do you like the food I ordered?"

"It's different but really good. Thanks for bringing me." She sipped her iced tea. "How should I behave toward your prospective client tomorrow?"

He studied her for a moment in silence. Finally he said, "No striptease, no hula and no playing the ukulele."

"Striptease? I've never done anything like that in my—" She stopped. "You're teasing me again."

"Can't resist. You're so much fun to watch when you react."

"Fine. Just for that, I'll take my ukulele and sing all through lunch."

"You can sing?"

"No."

"A threat then."

"Very much a threat."

"You'll do fine tomorrow. You know our business very well. Speaking of which, once we get back, I'm going to talk to Frank Godfrey about putting you into his department as soon as possible rather than waiting until you graduate. We're only talking about a few months. So treat tomorrow like a training session as I present what we have to offer and answer Furukawa's questions."

"You're going to promote me now?"

"Not this minute, no. But when we get back to the office I'll start the ball rolling."

"That's wonderful news! Thank you so much."

"Don't thank me. Frank's a good supervisor and he'll work you hard learning how we go about providing the necessary equipment to keep our clients secure."

Over dessert and coffee Jodie asked, "Why are you promoting me now?"

"What do you mean?"

"Well, you don't have a secretary lined up to replace me, for one thing."

He groaned. "Don't remind me. But that shouldn't take too long."

"Well, um…"

"Why do you make such a point that I'm difficult to work for?"

"Because you are difficult to work for. Or have you forgotten how many secretaries walked out on you before I was hired?"

He pulled his earlobe and looked uncomfortable. "I've mellowed since then."

"I'll take your word for it."

"Haven't I?"

"You've mellowed because I learned how you like to work."

"That doesn't sound too hard."

"That's true. It doesn't." She looked around. "Shall we go?"

"Wait a minute. I'm missing something here, Jodie. Tell me."

"You want your office to run smoothly. I know your likes and dislikes enough to anticipate how and what you want, that's all."

"In other words, you can read my mind."

"Not at all."

"That's good to know considering some of my thoughts while on this trip."

A burst of heat engulfed her and she knew she'd turned a fiery red. Jodie picked up her water glass and drank. When she had emptied the glass, she studied it without looking up.

"I'm sorry. I didn't mean to embarrass you."

Why should he apologize when she certainly wouldn't want him to learn of any of her thoughts these past few days?

"It's all right."

He brushed his fingers across the back of her hand. "No, it isn't. I've made you uncomfortable around me and that's the last thing I want. You're right. It's time to go."

They drove back to the condo listening to music. Once inside the condo, Jodie said, "If you'll excuse me, I think I'll go to bed."

"Of course. Sleep well."

Dean watched her walk out of the room, still irritated with himself. What was the matter with him, coming on to her like this? He'd been off balance where she was concerned since he'd first seen her at the airport.

He wandered over to the window and looked out. The view continued to be spectacular, even at night. While he stood there, he thought about their trip to Oahu the next day.

In an airplane.

In a small airplane.

Of course, Jodie knew they would have to fly. From what he remembered, the flight was a short one. They barely got into the air before it was time to land. The small plane could make the experience a little bumpy since the pilot flew at a reasonably low altitude.

Perhaps the flight here from Chicago had helped to allay her fears about flying. He could only hope.

One look at her face the next morning and he knew his hope had been futile. Not that she said anything. However, despite the slight tan she'd gotten thus far on the trip, she was a pasty white. Not a good sign.

Without a word, he poured her a cup of coffee. He'd been up since dawn and had already had several cups.

"Thank you," she murmured, immediately picking up the cup and sipping.

He waited until she set the cup down and then casually asked, "How are you this morning?"

"Okay," she said quietly.

"I believe our flight leaves in a couple of hours."

She didn't comment.

"Jodie?"

Startled, she looked at him. "Yes?"

"Are you nervous about the flight?"

"How did you know?"

"I remembered you were a little nervous—" there was an understatement if he'd ever made one "—on our flights here."

She nodded. "I don't mind it once we get in the air and level out. It's the taking off and landing that bothers me."

"Unfortunately that's what we'll be doing this morning."

"Oh. Well, of course."

"Why don't we go downstairs and get some breakfast. Are you up for that?"

"Okay."

She didn't sound at all certain.

While they ate, he chatted about the office and some projects he was working on, trying to keep her mind off her upcoming ordeal. She responded in monosyllables.

Finally he said, "I thought we might go to the Big Island tomorrow. It will mean another short flight, but I've been told the volcano is something to behold."

She went from pasty white to an interesting color of green.

"Of course, if you don't want to go..."

"That's fine. Really. Whatever you want to do is fine with me."

Sure it was.

Dean checked his watch. "We should head for the airport soon. Do you need to go back to the condo?"

She shook her head.

Today she looked like the secretary he'd known for years. She had her hair pinned up—he hadn't realized how much he liked to see it down until now—and wore a lightweight suit. She looked like a business professional despite her pallor. Unfortunately for his peace of mind, he had the vision of her in a swimsuit and wearing a sarong. He would never view his efficient secretary in the same way now that he'd gotten to know her better.

She must have been hurt badly by the jerk she'd thought would be her husband. How else could he explain to himself the subdued person he'd known for the past five years?

Seeing her literally letting her hair down and enjoying herself had been a revelation to him.

Once in the car, he tried to make conversation by asking her about various subjects. She answered in monosyllables until he gave up and turned on the radio.

By the time they were seated in the smallish plane, he knew that the situation required drastic action.

He'd been on flights like this before. The plane took off at a steep angle. Since she'd admitted she'd never been on one this small, she probably would be startled.

"Jodie?"

"Mmm?"

He took her hand. "Do you know what I'd like to do right now?"

She turned and looked at him hopefully. "Get off the plane?"

He laughed. "Um, no. What I'd like to do is kiss you senseless."

Well, that certainly took her mind off flying. She stared at him in astonishment. "Why?" she asked starkly.

"Well, for one thing, you have the most kissable mouth

of anyone I've ever known." He looked down at their clasped hands. With his other hand, he stroked the back of her hand with his finger. "And you fit into my arms as though you were made just for me."

He felt her hand tremble and she turned a charming shade of red, which nicely replaced her ashen color.

The plane started moving. He lifted her hand to his mouth and kissed her palm, his tongue lightly touching her. She stiffened when they took off. He wasn't certain whether it was the kiss or the flight. So he leaned toward her and kissed her on the mouth.

Her lips trembled, and he took his time caressing her mouth with his lips and tongue. Slowly she responded and he forgot his reason for starting this in the first place.

An amused feminine voice spoke near his shoulder. "I'm sorry to interrupt you, sir, but I'd like to offer the two of you something to drink, if you like. We'll only be in the air for another twenty minutes."

Jodie pulled away from him and stared at her. "We're in the air?"

"Yes, ma'am." The flight attendant grinned. "I can understand your distraction."

Jodie looked at Dean. "You did that on purpose!"

Dean told the attendant to bring them some orange juice before he looked at Jodie. "I suppose I did. I've never accidentally kissed anyone."

She glanced out the window and blanched.

"From now on you'll sit in the aisle seat," he said briskly. We're doing fine."

She turned and looked at him. "You know what I mean! You deliberately distracted me."

Once again he lifted her hand and kissed her palm. "Did it work?"

"I know I'm being ridiculous about flying."

"You just need to do it more often so you can get used to it."

"That's your prescription, Dr. Logan?"

"Absolutely. And here in the islands is a perfect place to practice. We'll make certain to visit each and every one of them."

"Oh, joy," she muttered.

Their drinks arrived and he let go of her hand.

The landing was as abrupt as the takeoff. Jodie squeezed his hand so hard she must have been cutting off circulation. But he didn't mind. She was adorable when she was vulnerable.

Once on the ground, Jodie felt giddy with relief despite her embarrassment. When she had finally let go of Dean's hand, it still had the imprints of her fingers on it.

They took a cab to the address Dean had. Once they arrived, Jodie asked, "Is this his office?"

"No. This is a private club for local businessmen. He said to give his name at the door."

Jodie waited while Dean spoke to the man who met them at the front door. The man looked at a list he carried on a clipboard, found Dean's name and nodded. He escorted them to a double door that was ornately engraved.

When Jodie walked in, she looked around her. There was a large bar made of teak to the right of the entrance. A maître d' met them at the top of the steps.

"We're here to meet Mr. Furukawa," Dean said.

"Right this way, sir," the man replied.

The place was meticulously designed and elegantly decorated. The only sounds were the murmured voices of other diners, their voices muted by the thick carpeting underfoot. Pristine white tablecloths covered each table and they looked like islands floating on the deep red carpet.

The maître d' continued through the room until he reached an alcove that overlooked the water. Once they were seated, he poured ice water into glasses and said, "Your waiter will be with you shortly."

Once Jodie was certain he was out of earshot, she said, "The scent of money is everywhere."

Dean grinned. "I noticed."

She gazed at his mouth. Jodie discovered she had a little trouble breathing whenever he smiled at her. She couldn't forget the touch of his lips on hers.

"Sorry to keep you waiting," a newcomer said from behind her.

Dean stood and extended his hand. "Perfectly all right, Mr. Furukawa," he said.

"Please, call me Steve."

Steve wore a custom-made suit that showed off his trim figure and tanned face. His hair gleamed like polished pewter.

"Steve, I'd like you to meet Jodie Cameron, one of the employees with our firm."

Steve took her hand and bowed slightly. "It is a pleasure."

While they ordered and their meal was served, Jodie watched and listened as the men discussed several topics, none of which had anything to do with a possible security installation. She couldn't help but wonder why he'd brought her, unless the business meeting was to take place after their meal.

Dean included her in the conversation, and when Steve asked how she was enjoying Hawaii, she responded readily enough.

Once their plates were removed and they were left with fresh cups of coffee, Steve said, "I've been reading up on you, Dean."

"And?"

"You and your company have an excellent reputation in the security field. What kind of security do you offer?"

"We make certain that no unauthorized person can enter your place of business without a silent alarm going off, alerting the staff. We offer hidden surveillance cameras that record everyone who goes in or out. Security codes are installed and updated regularly. In addition, we install special software on each computer in your office that will also alert you should anyone attempt to gain illegal access to the company's computers."

"I see." Steve glanced at his watch. "I'd like you to see my setup and give me some idea of what your systems would cost to install and run."

Dean nodded. "Of course."

Steve signed for their meal and the three of them returned through the restaurant. Several people spoke to Steve while they made their way to the entrance.

By the time they reached the street, valet parking had his car waiting.

The men continued to chat during the drive. Jodie, in the backseat, made notes of the conversation that pertained to business, finally feeling as though she could be useful.

By the time they left Steve Furukawa that afternoon, he'd agreed to become one of the company's clients. On the way to the airport Dean called the office and left a voice-mail message for the legal department that he had a new client.

Once on the plane, Jodie—determined to ignore the butterflies in her stomach—said, "Your trip has been a success, hasn't it?"

Dean nodded. "Definitely. Thank you for taking such extensive notes. I'll fax them to the office so Lawrence Kendall will have the information he needs to prepare the contract." He studied her for a moment and then asked, "You doing okay?"

She nodded.

"Good. So shall we visit the volcano tomorrow?"

"I'd like that," she replied, hoping he didn't detect her lack of enthusiasm.

"Or we could stay at the condo and enjoy the beach area," he said casually.

"It's up to you."

"My only reason for suggesting the trip was to allow you to see more of the islands."

"Why don't we wait until the day before we leave then?"

"Whatever you say."

Once back at the condo, Dean said, "We have time to go for a swim before dark if you'd like."

"I'd like that." Jodie went into her room and closed the door. Somehow, some way, she would get through this week with the man she'd gotten to know here on the islands who only vaguely resembled her boss. The fact that she liked and enjoyed this new person unnerved her more than a little.

All she could hope was that once in the office again, he would assume his sardonic personality.

Seven

Saturday afternoon they left the condo for the last time and headed toward the airport.

They'd spent the carlier part of the day on the beach and swimming, chatting about their time there. Jodie hoped her manner hadn't betrayed how sad she was to be going home. Dean had made her laugh that morning. She so enjoyed his wry sense of humor.

She glanced at Dean driving the rental car. He'd already returned to his terse manner and stone face, which would help her adjust to the fact that the man she'd spent the week with was nothing like the man she worked with.

Once on the plane, Jodie picked up one of the magazines she'd bought and waited for takeoff.

Dean touched her hand and she looked at him. "Thank you for being here this week."

"I enjoyed it. I'm not looking forward to Chicago's winter, I can assure you."

She closed her eyes during takeoff and prayed that the pilot could get the large plane in the air without a problem since they were immediately over water.

Once they leveled off, the flight attendant brought their meals and drinks. After she ate, Jodie closed her eyes and willed herself to sleep, determinedly putting the islands and the memories there to the back of her mind.

They arrived in Chicago Sunday morning. Dean gathered their bags and said, "I'll take you home."

"Thank you."

"Wait here and I'll bring the car around."

While she waited, she looked out at the gray skies and the people huddled into their winter coats to get away from the wind. *Yes, Dorothy, you've returned to Kansas and Oz is only a memory.* There was nothing more tangible than the weather to remind her that her fantasy vacation had come to an end.

She saw a late-model sports car pull up to the curb, and Dean stepped out. She picked up her suitcase, and in a few strides he'd come inside and picked up the rest of their luggage. With customary efficiency Dean loaded the bags in the surprisingly roomy trunk and opened the passenger door for her.

Once they were both inside, he pulled away from the curb. "Where to?"

She gave him directions and settled into the comfortable seat. He drove with efficiency just as he did everything else. When he reached her apartment complex, she said, "You can let me out here. I can—"

"I'd like to see where you live," he said bluntly.

"Why?" she asked just as bluntly.

"No reason, really. Do you have a problem with my knowing where you live?"

"Of course not. Personnel has it on record."

"You've been really quiet this morning. Any particular reason?"

"I'm just tired. I had trouble sleeping on the plane."

"Well, now that you're home you can sleep the day away."

She directed him to the entrance of the underground parking and showed him her second parking space. He pulled in next to her red car.

"Yours?" he asked, getting out and going to the trunk.

"Yes."

He picked up her luggage, which included the ukulele case, locked his car with the remote and followed her to the elevator. Once inside, she pushed the button for her floor and they waited in silence.

When she opened her door and motioned for him to go ahead of her, he walked in. She'd hoped he would put the cases down in the hallway and leave. No such luck. He set them in the hallway and continued into the living room.

"Nice place," he said, glancing around.

"I like it."

He walked over to her and without a word took her in his arms and kissed her, taking his time. She didn't want to respond to him; she couldn't allow herself to respond to him and she was unnerved by how much she wanted to.

When he released her, his words were quietly prosaic. "I'll see you at work tomorrow," he said and let himself out.

Jodie stood there and stared at the door. With one kiss he had brought the fantasy home to Chicago. What was she going to do?

After she unpacked and began to wash clothes, she called Lynette. Kent answered.

"Hi, Aunt Jodie. Are you calling from Hawaii?"

"No, sweetheart. I'm back home. Is your mom there?"

"Uh-huh."

"May I speak to her?"

"Uh-huh."

She could still hear him breathing into the phone. She heard Lynette in the background say, "May I have the phone, please?"

Kent sounded fainter as he said, "Uh-huh."

Lynette took the phone and said, "Do you think I need to increase my son's vocabulary?"

Jodie replied, "Uh-huh."

They both laughed. "How was the trip? Did you throttle your boss? Toss him in the ocean? Drop him into one of the volcanoes? Tell me everything."

Her feelings toward Dean had changed so much in the week she'd been gone that for a moment she didn't understand why Lynette would say those things.

"Actually he was fun to be with. I enjoyed being there with him."

After a prolonged silence Lynette said, "Who is this? Hello? Was I cut off from my sister? Hello? Hello?"

Jodie chuckled. "Cut it out. And you needn't worry about my sanity. He was on vacation and I had an opportunity to see another side to him."

"Somehow I never expected to hear the words *fun* and *Dean Logan* in the same sentence coming from you. What in the world happened to turn Mr. Hyde into Dr. Jekyll?"

Jodie sighed. "Doesn't matter. Mr. Hyde was definitely present once we landed at the airport. By noon tomorrow I'll have forgotten completely the friendly, funny man I met on the island." The kiss didn't count.

"Speaking of meeting men, did you spot any good-looking hunks strolling the beaches?"

"Quite a few, actually," Jodie replied, grinning. "Of course, most of them were accompanied by professional swimsuit models. Or if they weren't, they should be."

"You can hold your own with the best of them, kiddo."

"I had at least ten pounds on the heaviest ones."

"And all in the right places. Did you have Dean drooling?"

Her throat tightened and for a moment she couldn't speak. Finally she said, "Not so you'd notice."

"Plan to come over tonight for dinner. I hope you took lots of photos so I can be envious and jealous and all that stuff."

Jodie laughed. "You are so full of it. You wouldn't be away that long from the kids."

"True. But I can dream. See you tonight."

Jodie turned off the handset and said, "Dreaming isn't real." She didn't need to tell Lynette that, of course. She needed to remind herself.

She took a nap before going over to Lynette and Chuck's. She carefully dressed and hoped that they couldn't read her face. Maybe they'd think the glow was all suntan. She could only hope.

Kent and Kyle greeted her at the door that evening with whoops and hollers that made her laugh.

"Boys!" Lynette said. "Hush or you'll wake Emily."

They immediately quieted. "Did you bring us something?" Kyle asked expectantly, eyeing the large shopping bag she carried.

"Kyle!" Lynette scolded. "You know better than that!" She hugged Jodie before she stepped back. "Don't you look great! The tan really emphasizes the color of your eyes."

Chuck joined them. "Looking good, little sis. Vacations obviously agree with you."

Jodie sat down on the sofa and immediately had two little boys eyeing the bag. She began to pull out various gifts, explaining where she'd found different ones. When she finished, she said to Lynette, "Dean bought me a ukulele."

"Did he know you play?"

"I made the mistake of telling him. Actually the chords came back to me fairly easily and I'm not too bad on the thing."

"Did you bring it with you?" Kent asked. "I didn't know you can play."

"No, I left it at the apartment. One of these days when you come to visit I'll get it out for you."

Eventually they sat down to eat. Everyone was full of questions and the time flew by. It was only when she got ready to leave that Lynette walked her to the door and quietly asked, "Something happened over there, didn't it?"

"What makes you think that?"

"Because I know you. There's a shadow in your eyes I've never seen before."

"I'm just tired. Traveling really wears me out."

"If you say so."

"It's probably the letdown of getting back home and picking up my routine again."

Lynette hugged her. "Okay. Then we'll see you Friday night, right?"

"Right."

Jodie let herself out of the warm house and into the cold. She hurried to her car and crawled inside. While she waited for the car to warm and the heater to kick on, Jodie thought about Lynette's comments.

Truly, nothing *had* happened except for a few shared kisses, and she had no intention of discussing her response to Dean with anyone. After all, the kisses had been an impulse of the moment…except for the one this morning. She hadn't needed the reminder that she was strongly attracted to Dean Logan, which wasn't very smart.

She turned on the car radio and listened to music during her drive home, determined to put him completely out of her mind.

Eight

"**W**ow! Look at you!" Betty said by way of greeting when Jodie walked into the office the next morning. "Quite a tan. You certainly stand out among all of us oatmeal-colored people. So where did you go?"

"Hawaii."

"Ooooh, well good for you. Does the boss know you took off the same week he did?"

"Yes. Is he in yet?"

"Haven't seen him, but that doesn't mean much. It's not unusual for him to get here before I do."

Jodie nodded and headed to her office.

Once there, she almost groaned at the sight of her desk covered in papers with notes attached, files stacked high and file drawers half-open. She glanced into his office and saw Dean at his desk, frowning at something he was reading.

She put her purse away and made coffee. While she waited for the coffee to brew, she sat and began to sort through the mess on her desk.

"Jodie? Is that you?"

She stood and walked over to his doorway. "Yes. How did you manage to go through so much work this morning?"

"Oh, that's from yesterday. I spent the day catching up on what's been happening. Is there coffee?"

She glanced over her shoulder. "Yes. I'll bring you some."

"Thanks," he said absently, leaning back in his chair, still reading.

There, you see? she told herself. He's already forgotten last week and has moved on with his life.

Or so she thought until she set his coffee on his desk and he looked up at her. The heat in his eyes made her tremble. He'd never looked at her like that in the office before.

"Was your family glad to have you back home?"

"My nephews were more interested in what I brought them," she answered. "Lynette and Chuck agreed that I looked tanned and rested, which, according to them, was just what I needed."

He nodded thoughtfully and straightened in his chair. "I'd like to meet them sometime."

"My family?" She had to be mistaken. That couldn't be what he meant.

"Yes."

"Oh."

"Have lunch with me today and we can discuss it."

"I, uh, generally eat lunch at my desk."

"Not today."

"Is this business-related?"

His frown deepened. "Of course not."

"Then don't issue orders about my personal time." She turned and went back to her desk. She started filing papers and folders, her back to his door.

After several minutes she heard Dean clear his throat. She looked over her shoulder and saw him standing beside her desk.

"What do you need?" she asked pleasantly.

"Some manners. Obviously. I apologize for ordering you around."

"Apology accepted."

"I, uh, I'd like to take you to lunch. Please?"

She shut the file drawer and walked over to him. "I don't think that's a good idea. I enjoyed the trip and appreciate your giving me the opportunity to get away from the cold weather for a few days. Now that we're back at work, I believe it would be better if we return to our regular routine."

"I don't see what's wrong with having lunch together."

"At the moment the office staff is under the impression I decided to take off a week while you were gone. Once they see us together and notice our tans, they'll figure out we were together."

"Do you care?"

"Yes."

"Why?"

"I don't want to become the stereotypical secretary who's seeing her boss socially."

"I'm not suggesting we date. It's no big deal to have lunch at the same time, is it?"

"You're being deliberately obtuse."

"No, I'm not. I prefer to think of myself as unconsciously obtuse."

"I'd rather not go out today," she said politely. "I plan to study over my lunch hour. I brought a sandwich."

He nodded slowly. "You're probably right," he said.

She picked up some papers and turned away to the filing cabinet.

Jodie waited until he'd returned to his desk and then rested her forehead against the filing cabinet. She hoped he hadn't noticed that she was trembling. His attitude had caught her off guard.

If she consistently turned him down, he would soon give up and get on with his life, which was just the way she wanted things. She knew his dating patterns. The last thing she needed or wanted was to become involved with him.

And…if she repeated that often enough, she might be able to convince herself.

Dean sat down at his desk and looked at the work awaiting him. Most of it was to approve what had been done in his absence and to sign off on it. He leaned back in his chair and swung around to face the windows.

Jodie was right. Of course she was. Just because he'd enjoyed her company this past week didn't give him the right to expect their relationship to continue in the same way here in Chicago.

She was his secretary. That's all. The thought reminded him that he needed to call Frank. He'd leave her alone. They'd probably get back to their routine all right if he could forget how much he'd enjoyed kissing her and seeing her in a swimsuit. How much he'd enjoyed their conversations.

He shook his head to clear it. Getting emotional about the trip was ridiculous. Dean turned back to his desk and reached for his private address book. Now that he was no longer seeing Rachel, he knew of several women he could call. He only had to pick one.

He reached for the phone.

That night Dean's home phone rang close to eleven o'clock. He glanced at the caller ID and shook his head.

"Hello, Rachel," he said when he picked up the phone.

"Oh! There you are. I've been looking for you all week. Your office said you were out of town, and when I asked to speak to Jodie, I was told she'd taken a week off, so there was no way I could think of to reach you."

"Well, now you've found me. Did you find something else of mine that I left at your place?"

"Oh, honey, I am so sorry for the way I treated you. I don't blame you for not returning my calls. I don't usually behave so atrociously. It was just a really bad day for me."

"I noticed."

"Please forgive me. I miss you so much." She lowered her voice. "I've missed making love to you."

He thought about the relationship he'd had with Rachel and realized that he'd put her completely out of his mind. That told him what he needed to know where she was concerned. Whatever they'd had, it was over.

"Did you remember that this is the weekend we were going up to Wisconsin to visit Winnie and Fred?"

"Rachel, I figured that when you broke up with me, we wouldn't be seeing each other again, much less Winnie and Fred."

"I was awful and I know I was. But I didn't mean any of it. I was just angry and I took it out on you."

"As I recall, I was the reason you were angry."

"Well...but that doesn't matter in the larger scheme of things. Let's face it, all couples quarrel. That's the first one we've had in the three months we've been seeing each other."

He didn't say anything.

"Dean?"

"I'm sorry, Rachel, but I've already made plans for the weekend."

"What sort of plans?" she asked suspiciously.

"Nothing you'd be interested in."

"Try me," she said flatly.

"I have a date Saturday evening with someone I've known for a long while. You don't know her."

"You're seeing someone else!" Her voice lost its rounded tones.

"You made it quite clear you never wanted to see me again. I took you at your word."

"I said I was sorry," she wailed. "Please don't do this to me!"

"Rachel, listen to me. There's no reason to continue seeing each other. The points you made were valid. If it took your getting angry to tell me, then so be it. I'm not going to change, you know. You were right. I am married to my work. I forget social events. I'm bad about escorting you to everything you want to attend. Why bother to continue to see me? There are lots of men who would be eager to spend time with you."

She didn't reply right away. When she did, she sounded

as if she might be crying. "I screwed up. I know that. I know your work is important to you. I was way out of line that night and I know it. I just want to see you once in a while."

"I'll call you when I can, but I picked up a new client last week and I'll be putting in long hours coming up with the right combination of security devices to protect his company." He thought about their situation for a moment. "I'll give you a call in the next week or two. Have fun with Fred and Winnie."

He hung up the phone and wandered over to the windows. His condo had a great view of Lake Michigan. As a rule he found the sight relaxing. Tonight he felt lonely, which was most unusual.

He went into his bedroom, undressed and stretched out on the bed.

He was doing what needed to be done. He'd see Susan Saturday night and catch up on her news. They'd lost touch after he'd moved his mother into the nursing home. Susan had been her live-in caregiver and a sweet woman. He'd been surprised that she hadn't remarried by this time. She'd been a widow for six years or more.

As for Rachel...he'd have to think about whether he wanted to spend much time with her. He discovered that although he was lonely, Rachel wasn't the answer. He refused to consider who might be.

Jodie's phone was ringing when she walked into her office the next morning. She dropped her purse on the desk and reached for the phone.

"This is Jodie."

"Hi, Jodie. It's me…Rachel."

"Oh. Good morning. I'm not sure if Dean's here yet. Do you want me to have him call you?"

"Oh, no! No. I, uh, I called to talk to you."

"Really?"

"Yes. You know, Jodie, I admire you a great deal and I know that Dean couldn't get along without you."

When Rachel paused, Jodie didn't know what to say. What was this phone call about?

Finally Rachel said, "I mean, I know you're discreet and I'd rather you not tell Dean that I called."

"All right."

"The thing is that Dean and I had a spat a week or so ago and I think he's still a little angry with me. He didn't return my calls last week, and when I spoke to him last night, he said he was seeing someone else."

Well, of course he was. Dean Logan didn't waste time. He must have found someone who would have lunch with him or was available for whatever else he wanted. Good.

"I see."

"He's just trying to make me jealous and he wouldn't tell me who he was seeing. Do you know?"

"I have no idea."

"Oh." Rachel sounded disappointed. "He said he'd known her for a long time. I thought you'd probably know her."

Jodie chuckled. "He knows so many people that I wouldn't be able to guess. After all, he's lived in Chicago for years."

"Oh, he'll probably tell me," Rachel finally said with a laugh. "Once he's over his anger. We were supposed to visit some friends in northern Wisconsin this weekend, but I guess he's planning to see her instead."

"I'm sorry, Rachel. I know this must be painful for you."

Rachel sighed. "It's my fault. I must have been going through PMS or something and took it out on him."

"I hope the two of you can work it out," Jodie said. She was sincere. It would be easier for her to have him completely unavailable.

"Thanks for listening, Jodie. I appreciate it."

Jodie hung up, dropped her purse in the drawer and peeked around the corner into Dean's office. It was empty. Thank goodness. She doubted that he'd appreciate her discussing him with Rachel, although in the past she and Rachel had talked to each other regularly.

The next time the phone rang, it was Dean.

"Hi, sorry I didn't let you know I wouldn't be in this morning. Something came up that I needed to take care of."

"No problem. Believe it or not, your phone has been quiet. Maybe everybody thinks you're still on vacation."

"Good. I should be in around two o'clock."

"Okay."

As soon as she hung up the phone, the intercom buzzed. It was Betty.

"Your secret admirer has left something for you at my desk."

"I'm sure. I don't have a secret admirer."

"Well, someone just sent you a beautiful bouquet of tropical flowers. They look and smell heavenly. He must be in looove." She drawled the last word.

What was Lynette up to now?

When Jodie walked into the reception area, she found a truly awesome vase filled with lush flowers. "Was there a card?" she asked.

"Don't know," Betty replied.

Jodie looked through the long stems and saw a small white card. She opened the envelope and stared at the message.

Thought you'd enjoy the scent of the islands in your office. D

"Well?" Betty asked brightly.

"Oh! A friend from school."

"No kidding. Have you been seeing him long?"

She looked at the flowers before answering Betty. "I've known him for years."

Jodie carried the large vase back to her office and placed it on top of the filing cabinet. The flowers smelled enchanting, and she wished she knew what Dean Logan was up to.

Nine

When Jodie arrived at Lynette's on Friday, she realized they had company. She stopped in the hallway to hang up her coat. As soon as she walked into the living room, Chuck said, "Look who's in town," motioning to Carl Grantham, who was sitting across from him.

"Carl! What a surprise. What brings you to Chicago at this time of year?"

Carl got up and hugged her. He'd been Chuck's best man at their wedding, and as the maid of honor, Jodie had spent time with him. He was a great guy. He was also gay, which she considered to be a loss to the female population.

"The company sent me. I tried to convince them that Florida would have been better, but they wouldn't listen to me."

Carl could have been a model had he wanted, but he preferred being an engineer.

"How long are you going to be here?" she asked.

"Until Tuesday. Chuck and Lynette insisted I stay here with them. I told them I could get a hotel since it was a business expense, but..." He shrugged his shoulders.

"I know. I've never been able to win an argument with Chuck either, and you've known him longer than I have!"

Chuck chimed in. "We've got a lot to catch up on. The guest bedroom is far enough away from the kids that he won't be disturbed by them."

Lynette came in from the kitchen. "Hi, sweetie," she said to Jodie, giving her a hug. "You're just in time to help me get the food on the table."

"Where are the boys?"

"They're spending the night with Chuck's folks, and Emily is asleep. I won't guarantee for how long, though, so let's eat."

Over dinner Carl told them what was going on in New York and discussed some of the plays he'd seen. His partner was an actor who was presently in one of the popular musicals on Broadway.

"I would love to see him onstage sometime," Jodie said. "His voice alone sends chills through me."

"And when did you hear his voice?" Lynette asked with a smile.

"While you guys were on your honeymoon and I called Carl to tell him he'd left his jacket in my car. Carl wasn't there, so Chris and I had a nice long chat."

"Telling tales about me is what they were doing," Carl said with a mock frown.

"As I recall," Chuck said, "he was touring when we got married and couldn't come to the wedding."

Carl nodded. "He'd just gotten in when Jodie called."

"I didn't see the coat in the backseat for several days. It had fallen to the floor."

"I was wondering if the three of you would like to see the musical showing at the McCormick. I saw it on Broadway and it's really good."

Lynette shook her head. "As much as I'd like to, I can't ask Chuck's folks to keep the boys two nights in a row."

"Which is an excuse," Chuck said. "She doesn't want to leave Emily with anyone."

"Well, that's true."

Carl looked at Jodie. "How about you?"

"I'd love to! I haven't gone to the theatre in much too long a time."

"Great. I'll see about tickets for tomorrow night. If they're sold out, we can catch the Sunday matinee—that is, if you're available."

"I think I can safely say that my social calendar is quite bare either day."

Carl shook his head. "Then the men around here are blind. You look sensational. Where did you get the tan? The contrast with your blond hair and blue eyes is stunning."

"I was in Hawaii last week."

"Alone?" he asked with a lifted brow.

She glanced at Lynette and Chuck. "Well, not exactly."

"Aha."

"No, no, nothing like that. I was with my boss who had business there."

"He must be eighty years old not to have been aware of you."

Jodie laughed and knew she was blushing. "He's a businessman, completely wrapped up in his company." She refused to look at Lynette. Instead she kept her eyes trained on Carl.

After dinner the men went into the other room while Jodie and Lynette cleaned up the kitchen. Jodie was putting dishes in the dishwasher when Lynette said, "I have a question. You don't have to answer it, but did Dean make a pass at you while you were there?"

Jodie took her time straightening and turning to face Lynette. "A pass?" she repeated, stalling for time.

"You know...did he try to kiss you or suggest you could be more than a secretary to him? I couldn't help but notice that you blush every time he's mentioned, which has never been your reaction to him before." She studied Jodie's face. "You're right. It's none of my business. You're a grown woman and I don't need to hover." She touched Jodie's cheek. "I just don't want to see you hurt."

"There's nothing going on between us," Jodie answered truthfully. "He's all business at the office. Nothing's changed. He's already dating someone else."

"Doesn't take him long, does it?"

"I'm sure they're lined up waiting for him to notice them."

They walked into the living room and Jodie turned to Carl. "I need to get home. Call me when you have the tickets."

"Even if we don't get the tickets for tomorrow night, I'd like to take you to dinner."

"I'd like that."

"Good."

"I'll draw you a map to her place," Chuck said. "She's moved since you were here last."

"Great," Jodie said. "I'll wait to hear from you."

Jodie drove home thinking about the evening. She thought the world of Carl. He was drop-dead handsome with a wry sense of humor, graduated at the top of his class at MIT, but most important, he was a warm, gracious person.

Nothing like Dean, who had returned to being a bear this past week, growling at whoever was closest, which was usually her.

The oddest thing, though. He'd sent her a dozen roses today. When she'd thanked him, he'd nodded without looking up and said, "I noticed the others were fading. It's nice to have fresh flowers in the office."

So the flowers weren't really for her. They were for the office.

Once home, Jodie went to bed. While waiting for sleep, she wondered what Dean was doing tonight.

Dean sat at his desk at home and read contracts that had been prepared for new clients. With all the security breaches in the corporate world these days, more and more companies were looking for high-tech solutions, causing his business to flourish. So why wasn't he more excited about the increase?

Was it possible he was bored?

Of course not. That would never happen.

It was almost midnight before he went to bed. Despite the hour, he had trouble falling asleep.

Carl had managed to get tickets for the Saturday-night performance. He picked Jodie up early enough for them to have dinner before the show.

As soon as she opened the door, he said, "You look fabulous, Ms. Cameron."

"Come in, Carl. You look stunning yourself."

"Stunning?" He quirked his eyebrow.

"You look like you should be modeling. Custom-made suit?"

He nodded. "So. Are we ready to go?"

"Absolutely." She put on her coat, picked up her purse and joined him at the door.

By the time they reached the theater, Jodie had laughed so much her tears had wiped off the little makeup she wore. Not that she cared. She couldn't remember the last time she'd so enjoyed herself.

With Dean perhaps?

Don't go there.

Once they were seated, she said, "I can't believe you got such good seats."

"Actually they were a last-minute cancellation. Looks as if we lucked out."

As the lights began to dim, Jodie noticed a couple being seated a few rows in front of them. She recognized the man immediately—it was Dean with his new girlfriend.

She couldn't believe that they had chosen the same night to see the musical. She gave her head a quick shake of dismissal.

"Something wrong?" Carl leaned toward her to ask.

"Not really. I just saw the man I work for. He doesn't seem to be the musical-theater kind, so I was a little surprised." She nodded toward the couple.

"How long have you worked for him?"

"Close to five years. It's a great company to work for.

They've paid for me to take college courses at night. I'll actually get my degree this spring."

"Great benefits."

She watched as Dean leaned over and said something to the woman he was with. She looked to be about his age, and from what Jodie could see, she appeared to be very attractive.

The overture finished and the curtains opened. After that, Jodie forgot everything else but the magical experience of musical theater.

Dean and Susan went into the lobby during intermission. He told her to wait there and he'd get them something to drink from the bar. While going through the crowd, he almost literally ran into Jodie.

"Well, hi," he said with a slight smile. "Fancy meeting you here."

"Hello, Dean," she said. "I'd like you to meet Carl Grantham."

Dean hadn't realized that she was with someone. He held out his hand. "Dean Logan." The man was everything he wasn't. Good-looking—all right, great-looking—debonair and appeared charming.

"Dean is the man I work for," she said to Carl.

"I'm glad to meet you. Jodie was singing your praises a little earlier."

Dean looked at Jodie and she turned a fiery red. He looked back at Carl. "That's always good to hear. If you'll excuse me, I was headed to the bar to get drinks for Susan and me. Good meeting you, Carl. I'll see you at the office, Jodie."

Dean turned his back and walked away before he did or said something outrageous. He wanted to flatten Carl and grab Jodie, proclaiming that she belonged to him and only to him. He'd never experienced such a surge of jealousy and possessiveness. What was wrong with him anyway? He'd never dated Jodie, so why should a few shared kisses last week make him feel so possessive of her, of all people? He wasn't jealous of women he dated.

Dean glanced back at the couple, who appeared to be enjoying each other's company. He frowned. Damn it, he didn't want her seeing other men. When he rejoined Susan, she thanked him and said, "What a striking couple you stopped and talked to. They look perfect for each other. Are they married?"

"No. She's my secretary."

"I see. Jodie, isn't it?"

"You've got a great memory. Yes, that's Jodie Cameron."

"I remember when you hired her. After a few months you couldn't say enough good things about her."

"Well, she's taking another position in the company in a week or so and I'm going to need another secretary. Don't suppose you'd be interested?"

Susan laughed. "I'm afraid not. I'm more comfortable doing private care work."

"How do you like your present assignment?"

"I like it. In fact, the son of the man I'm caring for has shown an interest in me."

"That's not surprising. The question is, are you encouraging him?"

"I believe I am," she admitted with a smile. "He's a single parent with two children. I have no idea where their mother is. She's never mentioned. The girls and I get along famously. They were upset that I was going out tonight with someone other than their dad."

"A ready-made family. Is that what you want?"

Tears filled her eyes. "That's the only way I'll have children. I think this could turn into something serious." She blinked away the tears. "I don't think he was particularly enamored of my seeing you either."

"It will do him good. We won't tell him that you're the sister I never had—"

"And the brother I never had," she finished.

He touched her cheek. "You know I'll always be there for you. Would you like me to meet him and make intimidating noises about his treating you right or he'll answer to me?"

Susan laughed out loud and gave him a hug. "I really don't think that will be necessary, but I'll keep it in mind."

Jodie watched the attractive woman with Dean hug him and turned away. The lights flickered, signaling that it was time to return for the next act. Once seated, Jodie did her best not to watch for Dean.

She also decided that she didn't need to see him with other women either. Next time she'd make certain not to go anywhere where she might run into him.

Ten

There was another bouquet of flowers on her desk when Jodie arrived at work on Monday. This time she didn't bother to thank him since the flowers were for the office. However, she did comment on how beautiful they were.

He looked up from his work. "Did you enjoy the musical?" he asked.

"Very much. I haven't seen a stage production in much too long a time. How about you?"

He shrugged. "It was okay, I guess. If you like that sort of thing. I've never been able to figure out why, when they become romantic, they sing to each other instead of kissing."

She smiled. "So why did you go?"

"Susan mentioned wanting to see it."

"She seems very nice."

He leaned back in his chair and studied her. "I spoke to

Frank earlier. He said he could put you to work in three weeks if that's okay with you."

She nodded. "That's fine with me. I'll call the employment agency and find someone to replace me."

He cleared his throat. "Jodie, there's no one who can replace you. I'd like to keep you here, but I know I'm being selfish. You deserve a chance to put your education to good use and I don't want to hold you back."

She blinked back the tears that suddenly appeared. "Thank you for giving me the chance. I promise I'll find someone who is every bit as good as I am. Within a week you won't notice there's been a change."

He shook his head. "That will never happen." He picked up a letter lying on his desk, a clear dismissal of her, which was just as well.

Jodie returned to her desk. She was going to miss seeing him every day, but it was better this way. The infatuation she seemed to have acquired while on Maui would die a natural death once she wasn't around him so often.

The days went by and Jodie slowly settled into a routine of doing her work and interviewing prospective employees.

Rachel seemed to be back in Dean's life. She called him every day or so, and Jodie happened to hear him making plans with her for a weekend next month.

Jodie spent her evenings working on school projects and studying for finals. She'd be glad when she moved to her new position. Being around the old Dean who never laughed and rarely smiled made her heart ache for him. He'd returned to his hard-crusted shell, and it was as though the man she'd gotten to know in Hawaii no longer existed.

She had hoped that, for his sake, he would look around him and enjoy his life more fully. It was his choice, of course, to revert back to the all-business-all-the-time man he'd been.

Why should she care?

She didn't want to think about the answer.

Sunday turned out to be almost springlike, which wasn't surprising considering that spring would be there in another few weeks. Jodie decided to go jogging. She hadn't been out much these past several weeks. She drove to one of the nearby parks, parked, stretched and started out in a slow jog.

She recognized some of the other joggers because they'd been coming there for years. The sunshine and blue sky must have encouraged them to get out, just as it had her.

Afterward, she stopped into a deli and bought a large sandwich and headed home.

She decided to shower before eating. She'd barely gotten wet when she heard the doorbell. Since Lynette always called first, she didn't have a clue who could be there.

Jodie hurriedly stepped out of the shower and grabbed a bath towel, then hurried to the door.

"Who is it?"

"Dean."

"Dean?" She panicked. "Hold on a sec." She rushed into the bedroom and found a robe to put on and hurried back to open the door. "I'm sorry to keep you waiting. I was in the shower when I heard the bell. Please. Come in."

He walked in and said, "I hope you don't mind my stopping by without calling first."

"I'll forgive you this once," she replied with a smile, "especially since I just got home and you wouldn't have reached me anyway. Would you like some coffee while I get dressed?"

He shook his head. "Had too much already, but thanks."

She waved at the grouping of sofa and chairs and said, "Have a seat. I'll be right back."

Jodie hurried into her bedroom and closed the door. What was he doing there? And why was she letting his presence rattle her so? She didn't have any answers. She dug out an old pair of jeans and a faded sweatshirt, stuck her feet in house slippers and went back to the living room.

He stood as soon as he saw her. "You look comfortably casual," he said with a lopsided grin.

"I am." She stood there for a moment, waiting, and when he didn't say anything, she said, "Let's sit down. I'm sure you have a reason for coming by."

He settled back on the sofa while she sat on the edge of one of her chairs.

"I've been thinking."

That sounded a little ominous. "About what?"

"Us."

She frowned. "There isn't an us."

"Actually there is, whether we do anything about it or not. We became friends while we were in Maui. I'd like to give the relationship a chance and see where it takes us."

Oh, dear. His reason for being there was worse than she'd thought.

After a moment she replied, "I don't think so."

"Why not?"

She rolled her eyes. "Oh, let me count the ways. One, I

work for you, which we've already discussed. Nothing has changed in that regard. Two, I'm not into flings. Besides, you're still involved with Rachel and I don't want to get in the middle of that."

He looked uncomfortable. "We've agreed that the relationship isn't working for either of us. I won't be seeing her anymore."

"I can't imagine her breaking up with you unless she found out you're seeing someone else, and I don't believe that's the case. I always know when you're seeing someone. You send them flowers, you get them tickets..." Her voice trailed off and she stared at him in dismay. "You sent *me* flowers."

"So I did."

She stared at him, feeling confused. "Well...but...you didn't mean them in that way," she said.

"I meant them exactly that way," he murmured.

"Oh, my gosh."

"You didn't guess?"

"Are you kidding? Of course I didn't think that's what they meant." She couldn't believe she was having this conversation with Dean.

He leaned forward, resting his elbows on his knees. "The thing is, Jodie, I'd like to start seeing you socially. I discovered that I enjoy your company. When I'm with you, I see everything through your eyes and I like the new perspective." He kept his gaze focused on her. "Teach me how to relax and enjoy life a little more, like we did in Hawaii."

"You're asking me to tutor you?" she asked, frowning slightly.

"If you want to call it that."

"For how long?"

"I don't understand the question."

"Well, let me put it this way. How long do you generally date one person before moving on?"

"What kind of question is that? I have no idea."

"Well, I do. It averages about two to two and a half months. How long do you expect to see me?"

He threw up his hands. "This isn't the conversation I thought I'd be having."

She crossed her arms. "Really? Did you think I'd rush into your arms when you decided you want to spend time with me away from the office?"

"If I did, that idea got blown out of the water."

"Dean?"

"What?"

"What's this all about?"

He leaned back on the sofa, rested his head against the back and sighed.

"I miss you more than I could have dreamed I would. We were good together. We had fun together. Or I did, at least. What's wrong with extending that?"

"We could try it, I suppose," she said thoughtfully.

"Your enthusiasm is underwhelming."

"I could be your transition person until you find someone else."

He closed his eyes. "Transition person," he repeated without inflection.

"Maybe we could do that. Still nothing serious."

He straightened. "So you'll do it?"

"Within reason. I'm busy with school, as you know, but maybe once a week or so we could spend some time together." She brightened. "We could meet for coffee after my classes. Have dinner on weekends. Is that what you want?"

"Never mind what I want. I'll take what I can get."

"All right then." She stood up. "I brought home a sandwich from the deli. I'm willing to share it if you're hungry."

"As a matter of fact, my appetite is definitely returning." He stood, putting him a step or two away from her. "Shall we seal our agreement with a kiss?"

She looked wary. "We were talking about food."

"Of course. Why don't I take you out for lunch? It's a beautiful day for this early in the year. We might take a drive after we eat." He lifted her chin with his forefinger. "Just know that food isn't the only cause of my hunger," he said and kissed her.

Not fair, not fair at all. He knew how his kisses affected her. There had been too many occasions when he'd felt her reaction.

This kiss was no exception, even though she stiffened at first, determined not to be swayed. It was his gentleness that destroyed her resolve, because she'd never considered him a gentle person until they'd spent the week together.

Now all the emotions he evoked within her poured out and she knew they were more powerful than her determination not to succumb.

The problem was that all her valid reasons still stood.

The problem was that she found him too compelling to resist spending a little more time with him.

The problem was that she was going to be hurt badly when the relationship ended. All she could do at this point was deal with the pain at that time.

Eleven

The following Wednesday Jodie reached for her purse as she prepared to leave the office when Dean called to her. She went into his office.

Without looking up from the schematic drawing covering most of his desk he asked, "What time are your classes over tonight?"

His question was the first personal remark he'd made to her since he'd left her on Sunday. Jodie had begun to wonder if she'd dreamed that her boss had come over to plead his case for seeing her socially or whether it was some fantasy she'd concocted to relieve an otherwise boring weekend.

"Nine."

"Tell me where to meet you," he said, marking something on the drawing.

"Uh, well, there's a coffeehouse a couple of blocks from—"

"No. I'll pick you up at school. Where are your classes being held?" When she didn't answer, he straightened away from the desk and looked at her. He was still in his boss mode, snapping out orders.

After a moment she gave him the address, turned around and walked out.

Dean watched her leave with a frown. He hadn't handled that right. He wasn't sure what he'd done wrong, but he could tell from the stiffness in her shoulders as she walked away that she wasn't pleased with him.

He rolled his head, trying to loosen the muscles in his neck and shoulders. Women were a mystery he'd never been able to solve. Until now he'd never particularly cared.

Ever since they had returned from Hawaii he'd had a tough time concentrating whenever she was around. He'd been disgusted at himself for not being able to clamp down on his emotions. All she had to do was walk into the room and he immediately wanted to make love to her. He'd been forced to stay behind his desk so that she didn't see his physical response to her.

So he didn't look at her any more than was absolutely necessary.

Not that his idea was much help, since he had a similar reaction whenever he heard her voice.

She was driving him crazy.

The problem was that it was too late to do anything about it. When they'd first returned from Hawaii and she'd refused to have lunch with him, he'd tried to force himself to forget about his attraction to her. He'd only been kidding himself.

Now that he'd finally gotten her to agree to see him, he'd managed to offend her in some way.

Great going, Logan.

When Jodie walked out of the classroom that evening, she saw Dean leaning against the opposite wall, his arms crossed. She did a double take. He looked too much like the man she'd gotten to know in Hawaii, not the man she worked for.

She started toward him at the same time he straightened.

"Hi," she said.

He smiled at her. "Hi, yourself. Ready for some coffee?"

"Sure."

"The weather is nasty. Would you like to go to my place?"

She lifted her brow. "For coffee?"

He looked innocent. "Of course."

"All right."

When they reached the doors of the building, she could see that rain and touches of sleet poured from the sky. He opened an umbrella she hadn't noticed and, pulling her close to his side, hurried her to the car.

"Wow," she said, a little breathless, once they were inside the car.

"Where's your car?"

"At home. I took the bus."

"Good thinking."

She watched the windshield wipers ferociously battle the rain and sleet. "I decided before all of this hit."

"You knew I'd get you home."

"There is that."

She'd never been to his home, although she knew where it was: in one of the high-rise buildings overlooking Lake Michigan. He entered the underground parking area and parked by the elevators in a space with his name and the word *Reserved*.

The elevator silently whisked them to his floor, and by the time he opened the door to his home, all Jodie could think was that she was way out of her league.

He helped her off with her coat and said, "Have a seat. I'll go make coffee."

Jodie wandered over to the windows and looked out at the shimmering lights muted by the rain. If ever she'd needed a reality check, his place did that for her. She remembered how she'd gone on and on about the luxury condo while they were in Hawaii. His home was more luxurious.

She closed her eyes. She would be an idiot to think that he could have more than a passing interest in her.

"Here you go," he said from behind her. Jodie turned and watched him put a tray on the coffee table in front of the long sectional furniture arranged to take in the view.

"What am I doing here?" she asked, walking toward him.

He straightened and looked at her. "Having coffee?"

She gave her head a quick shake. "That isn't what I mean," she replied and sat down on the edge of the sofa. "This isn't going to work."

He sat a couple of feet away from her. "I noticed you seemed to be upset with me when you left the office."

She reached for the coffee. "That was something different," she replied and sipped on the drink. She realized she was shaking, as much from nerves as from the weather. She held the cup with both hands, warming them.

"So what happened to cause you to change your mind in three days?"

She didn't answer him. Instead she continued to carefully drink her coffee.

When she didn't answer, he asked briskly, "Am I supposed to guess?" Now he sounded like the man she worked for.

Jodie set her coffee cup back on the tray and turned to him. The problem was that he didn't look like her boss at the moment. With his hair mussed and in his cable-knit sweater, he reminded her of the man she'd spent time with in Hawaii.

She bit her lip. "I know I said that I'd start seeing you, but the truth is that we come from two different worlds and nothing is going to change that. I live a simple life and have simple tastes. I'm not at all your type."

"What exactly is my type?" he asked, his jaw stiff.

She waved her hand vaguely at the room. "Women who are used to all this luxury, who expect it, women who go to operas and symphonies and are photographed whenever they attend some function. That's not me."

He studied her, looking quizzical. "I don't recall inviting you to an opera or the symphony."

"You know what I mean," she snapped.

"I wish to hell I did. What is going on in that busy brain of yours?"

"I've come to my senses. I can't do this. I'm sorry." She stood. "I need to get home. I'll call a cab."

"Not on your life. You're not going to run away from this discussion."

"Please date someone else instead of me. The woman

you took to the musical, for instance. Or...I don't care. Just someone else."

"I believe your prejudices are showing."

"What are you talking about?"

"You can't go out with me because I attend various functions around town? Or are we back to the fact that you work for me?"

"Actually I do dislike you giving me orders when it's not job-related."

"Care to give me an example?"

"This afternoon. You took charge once I agreed to see you tonight. Told me what you were going to do and where we'd meet."

"You could have said no."

"I could have, yes. I should have."

"I get the sense that we're talking in circles without getting to the crux of what's bothering you."

"All right. Then here it is. Hawaii was wonderful. I couldn't have imagined a more perfect vacation. But the vacation is over. Yes, there's a definite attraction between us. You want to encourage it. I want to ignore it, which is why I'm relieved to be moving into another department next week. Let's forget about Hawaii and get on with our lives."

"I believe we tried that, but I, for one, have found it impossible after getting to know you better."

She closed her eyes. "I can't do this," she said quietly.

The silent room seemed weighted with emotion.

He studied his coffee in silence. When he looked up, his face revealed nothing of what he was thinking or feeling. "I'll drive you home," he said quietly.

Jodie waited until she was alone in her apartment before she broke down and cried.

Jodie moved into the engineering department the next week. Dean had hired one of the women Jodie recommended. Her name was Candace Rudin and she appeared to be quite competent. Jodie had expected to spend several days with her, but Candace had quickly grasped the routine, the filing system and the way Dean liked to work.

Once in Engineering, Jodie was determined to learn everything she could as quickly as possible. Several weeks went by, and Frank praised her repeatedly, patiently answering her questions when she couldn't figure something out.

She had been there two months when Frank dropped an envelope on her desk one morning. She looked up. "It isn't payday, is it?"

He shook his head. "No. It's time you learned firsthand about installing our equipment. That's your plane ticket."

A plane trip. Great. "I don't suppose we could do this somewhere that we could drive to, by any chance?"

"Sorry. Besides, I won't be going. Logan said that since you'd already been to this particular office, it made sense for you to see the next step. He'll be going with you to show you the ropes."

There was only one office she'd visited and it was in Honolulu. She peeked into the envelope and saw the ticket, confirming her suspicions. She looked at Frank. "I haven't finished what I'm working on," she pointed out.

"Doesn't matter since there's no rush on that one. Besides, you'll only be in Hawaii a few days—four at the most."

"Oh." She forced herself to smile. "Well. That's good.

I mean, I'll enjoy being part of the installation process. I'm just surprised that Dean would be the one to do it."

Frank shrugged. "I'll admit he hasn't done an installation in a long while. Probably wants to keep his hand in. Don't worry, though. You already know how he can be and won't be caught off guard when he starts snapping at you for not working fast enough. Just ignore his moods."

"I'll do my best."

Twelve

Dean greeted her briskly when she arrived at the airport the next morning. She had a moment of déjà vu when she saw him, except that today he wore a business suit.

She had also dressed for a business trip, in a light-colored suit and matching heels.

"Good morning," she said, walking up to him.

He turned around. "It's nice to see you again," he replied politely. "Have you checked your bag?"

She nodded.

"Have you had breakfast? If you haven't, there's a restaurant along the concourse where we could get something."

"Fine."

He strode along the corridor, a man on the move, and Jodie had to skip a time or two in order to keep up with him.

Once they found the restaurant, sat down and ordered,

Jodie caught her breath. Her shortness of breath was in no way connected to seeing Dean again. He looked like a modern-day pirate in his dark suit. All he needed was a knife between his teeth.

"How is Candace working out?" she asked during their meal.

"She's all right."

She couldn't think of anything more to say to him. She wanted to ask him why he'd decided to do the installation himself rather than send someone else.

But she didn't.

She wanted to ask him why he'd decided to have her accompany him, given their situation.

But she didn't.

Was it because he wanted to prove to her that he'd moved on after she'd turned him down? Perhaps. No doubt he was already involved with someone else by now.

Which was just as well. She wished that she'd been seeing someone these past few weeks, someone who would have helped her forget about her attraction to him. This trip would be much easier for her if that were the case.

"How do you like working for Frank?" he asked after several minutes of silence.

"He's great. I'm fascinated by all that we're doing."

"You'll be able to see how we implement the work your department does in Furukawa's offices." He paused for a moment. "I thought you might enjoy seeing the islands again."

"Are we going to stay in the condo?"

"No. Candace made reservations for us to stay in one of the hotels in Honolulu."

"Oh."

"Are you ready to go to our gate?"

She nodded.

Once on the concourse, he continued his fast pace until Jodie finally said, "Dean, I can't keep up with you in these heels. Would you please slow down?"

He immediately stopped and waited for her to catch up with him. "Sorry. My mind was on other things."

They continued walking for what seemed forever to Jodie before they reached their gate.

They found seats although the departure lounge was rapidly filling up with passengers waiting to board.

Dean spotted their plane, which they could see through the glass wall. "Looks like they're finishing loading luggage and food." He glanced at his watch. "We should be boarding shortly." When she didn't comment, he asked, "Do you have something to read on the plane?"

"In my purse."

Dean was not usually so talkative. Making idle chitchat wasn't part of his personality.

"Dean?"

"Yes?"

"Look, I know this is awkward for both of us. I appreciate your taking me on this assignment. I know you didn't have to be the one to go."

"Actually I felt that Furukawa needed to know that his security was important to me. We've stayed in touch these past few weeks ironing out the contract and determining exactly what should be installed. The fact that I'll be installing the systems is personally important."

"Will we start this afternoon?"

"Not with the actual work, no. However, we'll go to his office, pay our respects and invite him to dinner if he doesn't have other plans. We'll get started on the installation first thing tomorrow morning. It won't take more than a couple of days if everything goes according to plan."

The flight attendant announced that it was time to board and they stood. Jodie had noticed that once again they were flying first-class.

As soon as she'd found out she'd be making this trip, she'd visited her doctor and asked for something to help her deal with her anxiety about flying. He'd given her a prescription for a mild anti-anxiety drug and told her to take it a half hour before flying. She'd taken it with breakfast and was already feeling calmer.

Dean escorted her to their seats. "Would you prefer to sit on the aisle?" he asked.

"Yes, please."

She reached for the airline magazine in the pocket in front of her and began to read.

"Are you okay about flying?" he asked.

"I think so. Yes."

She could tell that he didn't believe her. It didn't matter. She needed to get used to flying now that she was a representative of the company.

By the time they took off, she was getting sleepy. She'd had a restless night, dreading spending time with Dean again. Lack of sleep, together with the prescription drug, had her yawning by the time they leveled off.

Jodie leaned her seat back and went to sleep.

Dean took the opportunity to study her—the way her mouth was shaped, her thick lashes, the slight tilt of her nose. He'd missed seeing her each day. When he found himself going to her department in hopes of seeing her, he knew he had it bad.

His dreams were filled with her...talking with her, making love to her, riding in the car with her. He was never alone in his dreams now, which was tough when he woke up each morning to discover he *was* alone and none of it was real.

Dean couldn't figure out what was going on with him. Was it because he hadn't been with a woman since the first trip to Hawaii? He hadn't been interested enough in Rachel to respond to her sexual overtures, which was the major reason she knew their relationship had come to an end.

They'd spent a weekend together, a last-ditch effort on her part to prove something to him—or herself. Despite all her attempts at seducing him—provocative night wear, a full-body massage—nothing had worked.

He figured he'd been too tired that weekend. His dreams of Jodie were more satisfying than the reality of being with Rachel.

This trip was to prove something to himself—to prove that his fantasies of Jodie were absurd. Candace had booked a suite so that each of them had a bedroom. They wouldn't be spending much time there.

This was strictly a business trip.

He was not lusting after her.

What he needed to do was find someone nice to date—someone with blond hair and blue eyes, someone who looked trim and fit, someone who was fun to talk to, to be with, someone who could make him laugh.

Someone like Jodie.

* * *

Dean had awakened her as they'd approached Los Angeles. There had been little time for them to find their gate for the next leg of the journey and neither one of them had said very much.

Once they'd been back on the plane, Jodie had read a little but fallen asleep within the first hour. Consequently she felt rested and ready to go to work when they landed in Honolulu.

They checked in to their hotel and she discovered that they had a gorgeous view from the balcony off the main room. Their bedrooms were located on opposite sides of this room.

They met Steve Furukawa at his office and showed him the schematics for the job. Dean answered his questions at length, and when Steve was fully satisfied, they set up a time to begin the next morning.

Steve agreed to have dinner with them, but Jodie begged off. Once Dean left their hotel room, she changed into more casual clothes and took a long, contemplative walk along the beach.

She had to face a difficult fact: she was in love with Dean Logan. She wasn't certain when it had happened, but there was no doubt about it. Being with him again had taught her that she'd been kidding herself when she'd decided she was over her infatuation with him. Of course, she had no intention of acting on her desire for him. She wasn't that stupid or self-destructive.

She wondered if there was a group somewhere she could attend to learn how to get over him. If so, she would definitely join.

By the time she returned to the hotel, the exercise had worked its charm. She was pleasantly tired, tired enough—she hoped—to be able to sleep, since tomorrow would be a long day.

When Jodie opened the door to the suite, she was surprised to see that Dean was there. He was on the balcony, sitting on one chair, his feet propped on another, sipping a drink.

"How was dinner?" she asked, walking over to him.

He moved his feet and motioned for her to sit down. "The food was good and I enjoyed getting to know Steve a little better. He gave me a brief family history. He told me how his family came to Hawaii from Japan many years ago. He's an interesting man."

She sat down and propped her bare feet on the railing. "There's something about this place that seems almost magical. The scent of flowers, the soft breeze. It's easy to forget there's another world out there."

"I watched you walk along the edge of the water. I was relieved to spot you. I was worried when I discovered you weren't here when I got back."

"I had no idea you would return so soon."

"Steve wanted to get home to his family. I enjoyed listening to his stories about his sons and daughters. He's very proud of them."

"You constantly surprise me," she replied.

"In what way?"

"Somehow I can't picture you listening to stories about children."

"Why not?"

She shrugged. "I can't see you as a family man." When he didn't reply, she added, "I didn't mean to offend you."

"I'm not offended. I never thought of myself in that light, so I suppose you're right."

They stayed on the balcony enjoying the night air for a while. Then Dean said, "I'm going to bed. See you in the morning." He stood and stretched, and Jodie straightened and got up, as well.

Once inside, Dean switched off the lamp, leaving the room bathed in moonlight.

"Thank you for giving me this opportunity, Dean."

"No problem. I seem to get some masochistic pleasure whenever I'm around you."

"What do you mean?"

"Don't pretend you don't know, Jodie. I want to make love to you so badly I constantly ache with it. And that's when you're not around."

She hoped the darkness hid her flushed face and the trembling of her body. "I didn't know," she said faintly.

"Do you want a demonstration?" he asked. He walked over to her and drew her into his arms. His kiss was gentle at first. If he'd grabbed her, she could have easily pushed away from him. It was his gentleness that undid her.

The kiss quickly heated up and Jodie felt him pressed against her, his arousal very evident.

Alarms went off in her head...or were they bells? She couldn't tell and at the moment did not care. She slipped her arms around his neck and kissed him back with all the pent-up love and passion she had for him.

Dean was the one who broke away. "I'm sorry. That was inexcusable." He turned and strode toward his bedroom. "Good night."

Good night?

He had kissed the living daylights out of her and all he could say was good night?

Every nerve in her body tingled with anticipation. She took deep, steadying breaths, shaking so hard she could barely stand there. How dare he start something he didn't intend to finish.

She should be grateful.

She should be thankful for his restraint.

She turned away and started to her bedroom and then wheeled around and marched across the room to his closed door. Without knocking, she shoved the door open. She didn't see him but she knew he was there.

"That was a rotten trick, Dean Logan! How dare you start something and then walk away as though nothing had happened!"

She slammed the door and marched back to her room, slamming that door for good measure.

The nerve of the man. Just because she refused to date him. Just because she knew that making love to him would be the worst possible thing she could do to herself didn't mean that she could just walk away after the passionate kiss they'd just shared.

So maybe she did want a fling after all! That was all that Dean would ever have with her.

She went into the bathroom and took off her clothes. She'd take a shower until she was calmer.

She turned on the shower and, without waiting for it to warm up, stepped inside, needing the shock of cold water on her heated body. She stood with the spray hitting her face, forcing herself to let go of her frustration and get a hold on her emotions.

Which was why she didn't hear Dean enter the room until the shower door opened behind her and Dean stepped inside wearing nothing but a smile.

Thirteen

Too bad he didn't have a camera to catch the expression on Jodie's face when she saw him.

"You're right, as usual," he said smoothly. "A gentleman should never, ever start something he doesn't intend to finish." He took the washcloth out of her nerveless fingers and said, "Turn around and I'll scrub your back for you."

She looked down at him and blinked. If she thought he hadn't been affected by that kiss—which he felt certain was quite apparent at the time—she could have no doubt about his condition now.

"Dean?" Her voice sounded strangled as he gently turned her away from him. He traced her spine with his finger from the nape of her neck down to her luscious derriere.

"Yes?"

"What are you doing?"

"Isn't it obvious? Scrubbing your back." He took his time sliding the cloth up and down her spine, pausing at her hips to place his hands on either side.

"That isn't what I—" She stopped and dropped her chin to her chest.

"I never want to leave a woman angry at me for not finishing what I started."

She slowly turned and looked at him.

He smiled at her.

"We're really going to do this, aren't we?" she whispered, her breath catching.

He dropped the cloth and cupped his hands around her face. She really was adorable. "Yes, we really are," he replied…and touched her lips with his tongue. Her mouth was lush and smooth to his touch. He settled his mouth over hers, fighting to control his passion until she was as ready as he was.

If he could.

She placed her hands tentatively on his chest and leaned closer, her mouth opening to him like a rosebud blossoming.

He dropped his hands and stepped back, breathing hard. "I think our shower is over, don't you?"

She looked at him and nodded. Dean reached around her and turned off the water. He led her out of the shower, picked up a towel and quickly dried her off. He swiped the towel over himself, dropped it and picked her up.

She leaned her head against his shoulder, closed her eyes and sighed.

He placed her on his bed, slid the covers from beneath her and yanked them off the bed before he lay down beside her.

"I brought protection," he whispered and nodded toward the bedside table. Her eyes widened at the number he'd brought with him. He grinned. "Just in case," he said.

He kissed her again while he explored the curves and hollows of her body with his hands. He wanted to memorize every inch of her. She shifted and reached for him.

Dean quickly caught her hand. "No fair. This is for you, not me." He trailed kisses along her jaw, down her neck, and touched her nipple with his tongue.

She groaned and he glanced up to see her face. Her eyes were closed and her face was flushed, but it was the soft smile of pleasure that encouraged him. He pulled her gently into his mouth while he played with the other tip, then eventually shifted his mouth to her other one, his hand gliding over her stomach and abdomen until it rested in her nest of blond curls.

Jodie pushed against his hand in invitation and he moved downward, feeling her moist heat. Dean shifted and knelt between her legs. She reached for him, and he took her hands in his before he lowered his head and kissed her curls.

She jumped as though she'd been electrocuted, and he murmured soothing words to her while he explored. She quickly climaxed, crying out, and Dean moved over her, sliding deep inside.

Jodie hugged him to her and fell into the slow rhythm that was costing him a great deal. His body hummed with urgency and he finally gave up all pretense of control. They moved together, uttering soft sounds and breathing heavily.

When she tightened around him in a spasmodic rhythm,

he quickly climaxed with her and, in one final lunge, buried himself deeply inside.

He collapsed on his elbows, careful not to put much weight on her, before he rolled onto the pillow next to hers.

They lay there on the bed without speaking, catching their breaths.

Finally Jodie murmured a soft, "Wow."

He turned his head and gazed at her. "At the very least," he replied.

She turned onto her side and stared at him, which made him a little nervous.

"What are you thinking?" he finally asked as the silence went on.

"My brain shut off much earlier this evening," she replied.

He got up and went into the bathroom, wondering if she was already regretting their intimacy.

Jodie watched the bathroom door close behind Dean, forcing herself to face what had happened just now, what she had triggered by her earlier remarks.

If she'd given the matter much thought, she would have known that Dean would be wonderful in bed. When it came right down to it, she realized now, she'd expected sex. What she'd experienced with him was making love.

A little later he opened the door and peered out. "Want to try that shower again?"

She smiled. "All right."

Despite the fact that he'd seen all there was, she felt shy. She slipped her robe around her.

When she reached him, he immediately removed the robe before cupping her breasts in his hands. He kissed each one and looked at her quizzically. "This isn't what I expected."

"What is that?"

"I want you just as badly now as I did before."

She glanced down at him. "So I see."

He moved reluctantly away and turned on the shower. "However, I don't want you to think I'm some kind of animal." He held out his hand and guided her into the shower.

She took the washcloth and carefully soaped him, enjoying his reaction as she slid her hand along his hardened length. Eventually she soaped his back, as well, discovering the view was equally enticing on that side.

When he rinsed off, he quickly covered her with suds and as quickly rinsed her off before he slid his arms beneath her hips and lifted her, guiding her legs around his waist.

The position left her open to him, and he slipped inside her, leaning her back against the wall.

She closed her eyes, her arms around his neck, and gave herself up to the experience.

"Jodie?"

"Hmm?"

"We need to get up. It's almost six."

Her eyelids flew open. "Already? How did that happen? I feel as though I just fell asleep."

"Probably because you did. I'm afraid I kept you awake most of the night." He rolled out of bed and walked to the door. "If we hurry, we can get something to eat before we go to work."

Jodie wasted no time getting out of bed once he closed the door behind him. She quickly dressed, dismayed that her hair stood out everywhere. That's what she got for going to bed with wet hair. She shook her head at herself. Her hair was the last thing she'd been thinking of last night.

She did what she could with it, forcing it back into a tidy bun, and prayed that her hair would not give her trouble today, of all days.

Dean was waiting in the sitting area when she walked out of the bedroom. He wore a sports jacket and slacks, his shirt collar open.

They decided to eat at the coffee shop in the hotel. Once they'd ordered, Jodie sipped on her coffee and stared out the window. When she glanced at Dean, he was watching her intently, making her feel more self-conscious than she had before.

Finally she asked, "What are you thinking?"

"I'm concerned that you're already regretting what happened last night."

"It's too late for regrets," she finally replied.

"But you're sorry that it happened."

"It complicates matters."

"In what way?"

She raised her eyebrows. "You know better than I do that this relationship isn't going anywhere."

"I don't know that at all." He sipped his coffee. "Where do you want it to go?"

He'd given her the perfect opening to tell him that she wanted marriage, a home, family and a husband who loved their life. Dean Logan would not want to be that man.

When she didn't answer, he said, "I would never hurt you, you know. What's wrong with us spending our leisure time together? We're both consenting adults. Neither of us has any obligations to someone else."

Thankfully their breakfasts arrived, interrupting the conversation. While they ate, Jodie asked him about the job they'd be doing and what they would do first.

By the time they finished eating, caught a cab and arrived at Steve's office, each of them was concentrating on getting the job done as quickly as possible.

Jodie couldn't help but notice how well they worked together, speaking to each other in a shorthand that they'd developed when she was his secretary. By the end of the day Dean appeared to be pleased with their progress.

"If tomorrow goes as well as today has gone, we'll be ready to fly back to the States day after tomorrow."

"Sounds good," she said. The day had taken its toll on her energy, particularly since she had not gotten much sleep last night. They took a cab back to the hotel. Once there, Jodie said, "I think I'll order in tonight and go to bed as soon as I eat. I'm beat."

"I really worked you today. You did a fine job, by the way."

She clasped her hands in front of her. "If you'll excuse me, I'd like to take a bath before I eat."

He frowned. "Of course. Did I overwork you today?"

"Not really. I guess I used a lot of nervous energy trying to learn so much so quickly."

"You should have said something."

She smiled. "I am."

"I mean sooner."

"I'm fine, Dean. Just very tired."

"I don't feel like eating out either. Tell me what you want to eat and I'll order for us while you take your bath."

She didn't care. She wasn't hungry. She just wanted to have some time alone. "A chef's salad."

When he walked to the phone, she went to her room and closed the door, leaning against it and looking at her bed with longing. It had taken all of her concentration to stay focused on Dean's instructions today instead of thinking about what had happened last night.

She was well and truly hooked on him. The problem was that he had no intention of reeling her in. If she did continue to see him once they returned home, how long would it be before he tossed her back into the water?

Once in the tub, she was soothed by the warm water. She rested her head against the tub and closed her eyes.

Dean glanced at his watch when their meal was delivered. He hadn't heard anything from Jodie in more than half an hour. He tapped on her door. "Jodie? Your salad is here. Are you ready to eat?"

There was no response.

He opened the door and peered inside. The only light was in the bathroom. "Jodie?" He felt a twinge of alarm.

Dean stepped inside and went to the door of her bathroom. When he looked inside, he found her asleep in the tub. A feeling of tenderness washed over him, although he had no idea what the emotion was since he'd rarely felt it.

"Jodie," he said in a firm voice.

Her eyes flew open and she scrambled to sit up.

"Sorry to come in on you but I wanted you to know supper is here." He turned and walked out of the room.

Jodie stared at his retreating back in dismay. He sounded irritable. And then she chuckled. Dean usually sounded irritable, so what was different?

The difference had occurred in his lovemaking last

night, in his murmured endearments, in his eagerness to make love to her as the night passed.

She had definitely provoked him the evening before, therefore she had no one but herself to blame.

Jodie quickly dressed in pajamas and a robe and went into the other room. She found Dean staring out the window, his hands in his pockets. She could see his reflection and he looked grim.

"I'm so sorry for taking so long. As you saw, I fell asleep in the tub."

He turned and walked over to the table that held their food. "I owe you an apology for working you so hard today. I'm used to pushing myself until I get the job done."

"I didn't mind." She sat down at the table. "You should have gone ahead and eaten. Your food must be cold by now."

"Doesn't matter."

They ate in strained silence. Once they were finished, Dean rolled the table into the hall and returned to the sitting room. "I'd like to discuss something with you, if you don't mind."

Her nap had done wonders for her. "Of course," she said and sat on the sofa.

He pulled a chair closer so that he was facing her. "I need to apologize for last night. I had no business coming into your room and getting into the shower with you. Could I plead temporary insanity?"

So that was what had him looking so grim. She smiled. "After what I said to you, how could any red-blooded male have ignored the challenge?"

His shoulders relaxed and he smiled ruefully. "Well, there is that. However, my conscience has gotten the better of me and I need to confess. I brought you along on this trip hoping that something might happen between us."

"I suspected that. You're very aggressive when you set a goal for yourself, and I must have been on your list. Just remember that I was a willing participant last night."

"But you don't like flings."

"That's right. And I don't think we should continue to see each other once we're home. It would be too awkward for both of us. I admire and respect you—" *and love the living daylights out of you* "—but I can't be what you want."

"Exactly what is it I want?"

"A short-term companion who's there when you have time to see her, who can accept what you want without strings attached. Someone like Rachel."

"I thought I made it clear I'm not seeing Rachel—or anyone else, for that matter," he said, sounding frustrated. Dean got up and started pacing. "You make me sound very shallow."

"I don't mean to. Your commitment to the company is total. You have no room for anything but a casual relationship with someone."

"And you're not the casual type, I take it."

"Unfortunately no. However, you never seem to have trouble finding others who will accept the kind of relationship you want."

He stopped pacing and looked at her. "What do you want from me? Am I supposed to declare that my intentions are honorable? That I want to get married and move to the suburbs, have a family and settle into domestic bliss?"

She gazed at him for a long time before she finally said, "I would never suggest such a thing."

"Good. Because I'm definitely not that kind of guy."

"I know," she murmured.

"So last night was an aberration and won't happen again."

"Yes."

He crossed his arms over his chest. "Fine. I can live with that. Is this where I ask if it was as good for you as it was for me?"

She smiled. "It was sensational."

He suddenly sat down again. "Yeah, it was," he said, sounding a little bewildered.

They sat in silence for several minutes before he said, "We'd better get some sleep. Tomorrow's going to be another long day."

Jodie stood and said, "Good night, Dean," and went to her bedroom.

He sat there for a long time, staring blankly out the window. With sudden decision, he left the suite, went downstairs and walked out onto the beach.

He walked the beach until dawn.

Fourteen

Six weeks later

"Mr. Logan, Mr. Greenfeld is here to see you."

Candace Rudin had taken to her job with alarming ease. She was punctual, efficient, unobtrusive. In all, a well-trained secretary.

Damn, he missed Jodie more and more as each day passed...as a secretary, of course.

"Have Betty send him back, please."

She nodded briskly and went back to her desk.

Candace had quickly learned that he disliked the intercom and cheerfully came to his office door to give him messages.

Candace was a very nice woman. A little formal, perhaps; she'd told him she wasn't comfortable calling him by his first name. She lived alone except for two cats since her husband died two years ago. Her three children were grown. She didn't mind overtime and put up with his moods.

What more could he want?

While he waited for Greenfeld, Dean stood and walked over to one of his windows.

He hadn't seen Jodie since they'd returned from Hawaii. He'd stopped finding excuses to go to her department to see her. She'd made her position quite clear and he would respect that.

He'd taken dates out to dinner, to see a play or movie and once to a Cubs game. At the end of each evening, though, he'd kissed them good-night at the door and gone home.

None of them stirred him at all, despite their intelligence, their looks and their behavior toward him. The dating scene was really becoming a bore.

He heard Greenfeld greet Candace and turned. "Good to see you, Jacob," he said, walking to the man with his arm outstretched.

"You, too, Dean," Jacob replied with a smile as they shook hands. "Thank you for seeing me."

Dean grinned. "Are you kidding? I was glad to hear from you after all this time. You disappeared after we graduated from college. How've you been?"

Once again Dean immersed himself in business and put all thought of Jodie away...until later that night when he fell asleep hugging his pillow and dreamed he was with her.

What was wrong with him anyway? he asked himself, staring out at the lake the next morning. When had he ever taken no for an answer when he really wanted something?

The truth was, Jodie taking another job in the office had left a big hole in his life—and it wasn't about sex, although that had been great.

He missed seeing her. He missed the sound of her voice. He missed the delicate scent of her perfume. Even if he never made love to her again, he knew he would remember everything about the pleasure of bringing her to a climax, of holding her in his arms afterward.

She'd graduated from college and had not sent him an announcement. He'd sent her a gift anyway and received a polite thank-you note that could have been written to his great-aunt Harriet. If he had a great-aunt Harriet.

He'd hoped that over time she might change her mind and be willing to see him again, but he realized that he'd be tripping over his gray beard before that happened.

It was time for drastic action. As his plan began to appear in his head, he nodded. He was a man of action, after all. Hadn't she mentioned that he was aggressive when he wanted something?

Well, he was ready to admit that he wanted her and no one else.

He would wait no longer to get her back in his life, on whatever terms she set.

"Isn't this a beautiful day," Lynette said, stretched out on a blanket in one of Chicago's parks. "I'm so glad we planned this."

Jodie nodded. She had Emily in her lap and was playing with her while Chuck played catch with the boys.

"Me, too."

"How's it feel to finally be through with school?"

"A little lost, actually. I don't know what to do with all my spare time."

"Well, it's been a boon for me. Chuck and I have certainly enjoyed your staying with the kiddos and giving us some alone time." She grinned. "I feel definitely decadent sleeping until late in the morning once a week."

"You deserve it."

Suddenly Lynette shouted, "Way to go, Kyle, good one." When she turned back to Jodie, she said, "You don't talk about work much anymore. Why is that?"

Jodie shrugged. "Nothing to talk about. I'm learning so much stuff that my head spins at times, but I'm enjoying it."

"And we're still not going to discuss Dean, are we?"

"There's nothing to discuss. I haven't seen…" Her voice trailed off.

"What's wrong?"

"If I'm not mistaken, that's Dean Logan coming toward us now."

Lynette sat up. "Really? Where?"

Jodie nodded toward the man drawing closer.

"You're kidding me," Lynette said in awe. "He's gorgeous. And you always said he looked like he should be on Mount Rushmore with his great stone face."

"He could."

"The grin he's wearing could melt rock, honey. And I believe it's directed at you!"

"Hi," he said when he reached them. "I thought that was you." He glanced at Lynette and back at Jodie. "Mind if I join you?"

Before Jodie could find her tongue, Lynette scooted over

and patted the blanket. "We'd be delighted. Wouldn't we, Jodie?" she asked, her eyes wide in mocking innocence.

He didn't wait for her answer but sat on the blanket.

"What are you doing—" Jodie began to ask when the boys interrupted her.

"Hi!" Kyle said. "Do you know our aunt Jodie? We have sleepovers at her house and she's—"

"Hush!" Lynette said, gaining Jodie's eternal gratitude for stopping him. Kyle wasn't known for his tact or diplomacy.

"Dean, I'd like you to meet my sister, Lynette, and her children." She nodded to the boys. "Kent and Kyle." Then she looked down to the infant in her arms and said, "This is Emily."

Chuck joined them. "Hi. Chuck Patterson," he said, his hand out.

Dean shook hands. "Dean Logan."

"Ah," was all Chuck said.

"I don't care what rumors Jodie has brought home to you, it isn't true that I eat young children for breakfast."

"Ooooh, gross!" Kent said with a grin.

Chuck sat down. "Why don't you let me rest for a few minutes, guys? Go toss the ball between you."

When the two of them moved away, he turned and looked at Lynette in disbelief. "Did you see that? They actually minded me. And without argument." He looked at Jodie. "Boy, if you ever decide to hire yourself out as a nanny, I can give you a glowing recommendation."

"If you haven't already guessed, Chuck is my brother-in-law."

Chuck reached for the ice chest. "Would you like something to drink? We have colas, lemonade and water."

"Water sounds great," Dean said.

Chuck pulled out two bottles of water. He gave one to Dean and rolled the other across his forehead. "I'm getting too old for this," he said, grinning.

Jodie cleared her throat. "What a coincidence that you should be at the same park we chose."

Dean smiled blandly. "Isn't it?" He turned and asked Chuck about his police work, giving her no chance to probe any further.

When they were packing things to go home, Lynette suddenly said, "Dean, why don't you come have supper with us tonight? You and Chuck seem to have a lot to discuss."

"Oh, I'm sure he's—" Jodie leaped in to the conversation just as Dean replied.

"That sounds great, Lynette. Thanks."

"—too busy," Jodie ended lamely.

"Don't expect anything fancy. It will probably be leftovers."

"My favorite meal."

Chuck and Lynette laughed.

Jodie glanced away for a moment before she said, "Look, you guys, why don't you go on and I'll get home. I have a dozen things to do and—"

Lynette gave her the famous big-sister stare for a moment before she replied, "Nonsense. We'll meet you over there."

Jodie watched them head to their car in silence.

"If you don't want me to go, I can make my excuses," Dean said quietly.

She shook her head, unable to say anything.

"What's wrong with my getting to know your family?"

"Nothing at all. Why do you want to?"

"Because I've missed you. I thought we were friends. We worked amicably together for several years. Now I feel like a leper where you're concerned."

She took a deep breath. "It's called self-preservation, Dean. I thought we'd come to an understanding. I don't want to get hurt."

"I would never hurt you."

"Not intentionally, I'm sure."

"Let's make a deal. Let's spend the next three months seeing each other as friends. Strictly platonic. I'd like to spend time with you, that's all."

"Friends. You think we can do that?"

He grinned. "I can if you can."

She sighed and then held out her hand. "Well, friend, we'd better get over to Lynette's before she sends Chuck out to find us. I wouldn't put it past him to put out an all points bulletin over the police scanner if we don't get a move on."

Fifteen

"Lighten up, sis, would you, please? I've never seen you so quiet!"

Jodie picked up a large salad and a platter of spaghetti and headed to the dining area. "I thought you'd appreciate the fact that I'm not talking your ear off!"

Lynette followed her with a large bowl of sauce that'd she'd removed from the freezer and heated, together with a basket of French bread drenched in garlic butter.

Jodie could hear Dean and Chuck chatting away in the living room like old buddies.

The sisters paused and looked at the table to be sure everything was ready. Lynette glanced at Jodie. "You've been keeping secrets, haven't you, sis?"

Jodie's heart lurched. "What do you mean?"

"That man is more than a boss to you. The way he looks at you is a dead giveaway."

"Oh, please. We've known each other for several years. We had a comfortable relationship when I worked for him. I rarely see him now."

"Whatever you say, dear," Lynette replied. She walked into the living room and said, "Sorry to interrupt your bonding, guys, but dinner, such as it is, is served."

"Lynette!" Jodie snapped from behind her.

Lynette turned and said, "I repeat. Lighten up."

Within five minutes Dean had charmed the Patterson family. His behavior contradicted everything she'd ever told them about him. Great. Now she looked like a liar.

Dean interrupted her glum thoughts by saying, "Jodie, why don't we catch a movie tomorrow and maybe have dinner afterward?"

Before she could respond, Kent piped up with, "She's your girlfriend, isn't she, Mr. Logan?"

Okay. That was it. Jodie saw no hope for her except to silently slide out of her chair and under the table.

"Well, Kent," Dean replied, winning points for remembering his name, "we are definitely friends—very good friends."

Kyle went into action. "Are you going to marry her?"

Jodie knew her face flushed a fiery red while Chuck scolded the boys. "It's not polite to ask personal questions, boys," Chuck said sternly. "Now eat your dinner."

When Jodie glanced at Dean, he winked at her, causing her to shake her head and shrug.

Thankfully Chuck introduced an innocuous subject that lasted through the rest of the meal.

Once dinner was over, Jodie helped Lynette clear the

table and load the dishwasher. She'd wiped down the counters when Emily cried out.

Lynette looked at her watch. "Right on time. I'd better go feed her."

"And I need to get home. Thanks for dinner again. Two nights in a row seems a little excessive."

"Don't worry about it. You know you're welcome anytime."

Lynette went upstairs and Jodie returned to the living room. "I'm going home now. Thanks for everything," she said to Chuck.

Dean immediately stood. "I need to go, as well." He turned to Chuck. "Enjoyed getting to know you. We'll have to find the time to go to a Cubs game soon."

Chuck also stood. "Sounds like a plan, Dean." He hugged Jodie. "Take care, sweetheart."

Jodie and Dean went outside to where they had parked their cars. She turned to say something when she realized he was right behind her.

"You never answered my question," he said, his hand massaging the nape of her neck.

She took a deep breath before saying, "Thank you for asking, and yes, I'd enjoy going to the movie with you." There. She'd just dived into the deep end.

He grinned. "See how easy that was?" He leaned closer and kissed her, his hand still caressing her neck and shoulders. As usual, the casual kiss turned into much more, and when they stepped away from each other, her heart was pounding so hard she wondered if she was having a heart attack or a stroke.

"That was a little more than a friendly kiss," she managed to say, catching her breath.

He shrugged. "What can I say? All's fair in love and war."

"Which one are we talking about?" she asked.

He gave her a brief hug and turned. "You'll have to figure that one out on your own," he said over his shoulder as he strode to his car.

When Jodie got home that night, she faced her fears. Of course, he hadn't been serious about being in love with her. He'd been up-front about what he wanted from her. Friendship. There was no reason in the world to run away from a friendship. The only way she could get hurt was to hope for some kind of commitment from Dean, which she knew she'd never get. One of the reasons his relationships ended was because the women wanted to marry him. She knew because she'd listened to a few who'd hoped she would put in a good word with him.

Lynette was absolutely right. She needed to lighten up. It wouldn't be the end of her world when he moved on to someone else. She wouldn't let it be.

She spent the next hour trying to figure out what to wear tomorrow.

Once home, Dean wondered why he'd mentioned love or war. Seeing Jodie was neither love nor war. He missed her, that's all. He'd always enjoyed being around her. What was wrong with that?

She'd made it clear she would not go to bed with him. He'd accept that. He didn't particularly like it, but he'd accept it in exchange for having her in his life again.

Dean looked at the stack of papers he'd brought home earlier today. When was he going to have time to go over them? Not tonight, anyway. He'd review them in the morning before he left to pick up Jodie. He'd never let his social life interfere with business before, but what he didn't get done, he'd do at the office on Monday.

He'd enjoyed seeing her again and meeting some of her family. He and Chuck had clicked. Chuck had been friendly without being overbearing, and Jodie's name had never been mentioned between them.

Once in bed, he thought about Jodie until he fell asleep.

"I can't remember laughing so hard in a long time," Jodie told Dean once they left the movie theater the next evening. "My sides hurt."

"I can relate," he replied with a smile. "I'm glad you enjoyed it."

She had, and not just the movie. They'd watched the comedy with fingers entwined like a couple of teenagers. Dean had laughed out loud on a few occasions, and the sound had cheered her. Maybe she did have an influence on him, since she couldn't imagine his going alone to see a movie.

Once seated in a Greek restaurant, they ordered. Over their salads Jodie asked, "Everything still working out with Mrs. Rudin?"

"She's very efficient. What I hadn't realized was how often you and I discussed business matters. You were my sounding board for most of my decisions. I hadn't realized it until after you were gone."

"If I can help, you know I'd be happy to."

"Thank you. I also have a request to make…more like a plea, actually." He looked grim. "There's a dinner and dance I'm expected to attend on Saturday night. I'd skip attending it since I've already made my donation, except that I'm one of the speakers. It's a benefit to raise money for Alzheimer's." He paused a moment. "My mother was diagnosed with the disease a while ago, so if they need me to make a speech, I will. I just hate like hell to go by myself and I'm not seeing anyone these days."

"Of course I'll go with you, Dean. I'd like to hear you speak."

"No, you wouldn't, believe me. The regularly scheduled speaker was forced to cancel at the last minute, so I'm filling in for him."

Dean still wasn't seeing anyone? How strange. Dean was never one to wait to find someone else when one of his relationships faltered. Of course, they'd never had a relationship—except for work…and when they'd visited Hawaii. But other than that, she hadn't seen or heard from him. He was a virile male who never lacked having a woman in his bed.

However, it was none of her business and she didn't comment on that part of his remarks.

They discussed several business matters during their meal, falling into a familiar routine. Jodie felt comfortable with Dean for the first time since she'd gone to Hawaii with him—that is, until they reached her front door.

She turned to him and said a little stiffly, "Thank you for this evening."

He lifted an eyebrow. "Aren't you going to invite me inside?"

"No."

"Even if I beg?"

She chuckled. "Dean, if I invite you inside, we both know that we'll probably end up in bed together."

"And your point is?"

"That's a little too friendly for me, I'm afraid."

"Okay."

She looked at him quizzically. "Okay?"

He shrugged. "You're right, that's all. Our relationship is strictly platonic, I swear." He held up his right hand. After a moment he asked, "Is it all right if I kiss you good night?"

She glanced down the deserted hallway and felt that her self-restraint would be helped by being there. "Okay."

He took his time pulling her closer to him. He started by nibbling on her earlobe before he planted small kisses along her jawline. Just as she knew it would, Jodie felt her control slipping. She moved her hands from his chest to around his neck, and when he finally found her mouth she was more than ready for him.

The kiss went on and on until the sound of the elevator brought her back to reality. She released him, gasping a little. Her body quivered with passion, which he knew darned well.

His smile was slow and intimate.

A couple got off the elevator and turned the other way without seeing them.

"Good night," Dean said gently. "Pleasant dreams." He turned and walked to the elevator, which conveniently opened when he pushed the button. She stepped in quickly, watching Dean until the door closed.

Jodie closed and locked the door and made it to her bedroom on wobbly knees before collapsing on the bed.

Who had she been kidding? Whether she saw Dean or not, her emotions were in a tangle where he was concerned.

Of course she wanted to experience again what they'd shared in that Honolulu hotel. He aroused a passion in her she'd never known existed. Now he was using that knowledge to remind her what they could have if she wanted an intimate relationship with him.

However, she was determined not to give in to her baser instincts. She would not. She could not.

Which meant that another restless night awaited her.

Sixteen

Jodie opened her door on Saturday evening to find Dean Logan looking drop-dead gorgeous in a tuxedo that was obviously custom made. His shoulders looked broader than ever, and since she vividly recalled how they felt beneath her fingers, she found it difficult to speak.

She finally said, "Come in," sounding hoarse. She cleared her throat.

He paused in the doorway for a moment before stepping inside. "I'm early. I apologize."

"No apology needed." She picked up her evening bag and tried not to notice the way he looked at her. During another shopping trip she'd found what she considered to be the perfect little black dress to wear. The style was deceptively simple and she knew she looked good wearing it.

Dean's look made clear that he approved and it made clear that he wanted her.

Some friendship this is going to be. Who was she kidding anyway?

So why are you willing to see him?
Because I have a masochistic streak in me, that's why.
Oh.

She picked up a lacy stole and slipped it around her shoulders.

They were silent in the elevator. Once in the car, Dean turned to her and said, "Is it overstepping the boundaries of friendship to say you are a knockout in that dress?"

She smiled demurely. "Thank you." He started the car after a quick shake of his head, as though clearing his brain. "Have you decided what you plan to say tonight?" she asked.

Once on the street, he replied, "I suppose. I never say what I've written anyway. All I know is that it will be short."

They pulled into one of the large conference centers and turned the car over to the valet. Other people in formal dress converged on the entrance to the hotel, and Dean guided her along in the same direction.

Several people spoke to him while eyeing her surreptitiously. He introduced her briefly to those who stopped to speak to him.

They'd almost reached the ballroom when Jodie heard a familiar voice behind them.

"Dean! I thought that was you. I never expected to see you at one of these things."

They stopped and Dean turned. "Hello, Rachel." He

recognized her escort. "Good to see you, Bailey," Dean said and shook his hand.

In a bright voice Rachel began to say, "So aren't you going to introduce us to—"

At that point, Jodie reluctantly turned to face them.

"Jodie? Is that really you? You look— I mean, uh, it's good to see you again." The look she gave both of them belied the comment. "So," she said to Dean, "I'm surprised to see you with your secretary." Her implication that he'd resorted to attending the gathering with the hired help wasn't lost on either of them.

"Actually," Dean said, looking amused, "she no longer works for me. She's working in Engineering now."

Jodie looked down at her toes. She could imagine Rachel's guess at how she got the promotion. She mentally squared her shoulders and looked Rachel in the eye. "That's true. I graduated from school at long last. Dean told me a few years ago that when I got my degree he'd move me into one of the other departments."

Rachel looked at Dean. "I bet you're lost without her...being your secretary."

"Somehow I've managed to survive," he replied wryly.

Once the two couples entered the ballroom, Rachel looked around and said to Bailey, "Do you recall our table number?" and they drifted away from Dean and Jodie.

Jodie looked up at him. "Rachel's looking good, don't you think?"

He frowned slightly. "I guess she looked okay. I didn't notice." He started toward the front of the room where the dais was set up. "We're at table one."

When they drew closer, Jodie saw that their table was

filled except for the two seats reserved for them. She recognized a couple of the men but only because she'd seen their photographs in the paper.

The movers and shakers of Chicago were there tonight. Dean hadn't told her that the affair would be so well attended. She wondered if the size of the crowd would bother Dean. She'd never thought of him being a public speaker.

Dean introduced her to the table at large. Everyone was gracious and she found herself relaxing—until one of the wives asked, "What branch of the Cameron family are you, my dear?"

"The Wisconsin branch."

"Oh." The woman sounded disappointed. "You're not related to any of the Camerons here in Chicago?"

Jodie smiled politely, wishing for the evening to end. Right now. "Not that I'm aware of."

"Pity. I suppose you've traced your roots back to Scotland."

"Not yet."

"Genealogy is fascinating work. You'll enjoy it once you get started."

Jodie was relieved when the waiters came out with their salads and the conversation became more general.

She hated feeling so inadequate in situations such as this. She thought about telling the woman that her mother was a waitress in Phoenix just to see her reaction.

As the meal progressed, Jodie was surprised to discover that the food was delicious. No telling how much the meal had cost, but it was a vast improvement on the rubber chicken usually served at the events she'd attended.

After dinner the emcee of the event spoke to the gathering, thanking them for coming and introducing Dean as the speaker.

Why she should feel so nervous for him she had no idea, because he appeared composed enough as he strode to the dais.

Within minutes after he started speaking he had the room mesmerized. He drew from his personal experience and the pain involved watching a loved one slip away from reality.

As promised, he kept his speech short and very much to the point and when he finished, he received a standing ovation. Jodie stood with the rest, tears in her eyes. She'd never been more proud of him.

The emcee thanked him and told everyone to enjoy the music and dancing. The dance floor filled quickly with the first song. Everyone at their table was on the dance floor when Dean turned to her. "Shall we dance?"

Jodie nodded and they walked out onto the floor. Once they were dancing, she said, "I was impressed with your speech. Your calm discussion of such a personal and painful situation touched us all."

"I felt it was the best way to explain the need for more money for research."

"You are a man of many talents, Mr. Logan."

He pulled her closer to him and she put her head on his chest. She was surprised to discover his heart racing and lifted her head.

"Sorry. I react this way when I'm around you."

Only then did she realize that he was aroused. She couldn't help blushing.

"Would you prefer not to dance?" he finally asked.

"Oh, Dean, you're making things very difficult for me."

"And you have a way of making things hard for me."

"It's not that I'm playing hard to get…."

"I know. It's not your fault that I can't stop myself from reacting to you." He continued to dance but held her a few inches away from him. "This friendship thing isn't working."

She shook her head, unable to speak. That's when she knew what she had to do. "All right then."

"All right what?"

"I'll sleep with you tonight."

He stopped dead in his tracks, causing another couple to run into them. "Sorry," he said and slipped his arm around Jodie's waist. "Please tell me that you're serious," he said roughly.

She nodded, her gaze direct. "I'm serious."

"We need to go," he said. He took her hand and started off the dance floor before the song finished.

Jodie remained silent while they waited for his car to be brought around, and neither of them spoke on the way to her apartment. She realized that she quivered with need, a need she'd tried to ignore for weeks. She wanted him. She wanted him now.

The door barely closed behind them when he lifted her, pulling her legs around his waist, leaned her against the door, fumbled with his zipper and shoved inside her as he ripped her panties.

Their lovemaking was hot, strong and very passionate, both of them climaxing within minutes. Dean gathered her closer and walked—as much as he was able to with his pants around his ankles—into her bedroom, where he carefully placed her on the bed.

She watched him remove his tuxedo and allowed him to slip her dress and underthings off her. Still without speaking, he joined her on the bed and made slow, sensuous love to her. They responded to each other as they had in Hawaii. Jodie knew that she would never, ever, forget this night.

He left at dawn.

The following Monday morning Jodie handed Frank her resignation. By that afternoon, she was on the road heading south.

Seventeen

Dean called Jodie's apartment several times on Sunday but got no answer. He figured she'd gone to her sister's and he fought the temptation to call her there just to hear her voice.

He owed her an apology for his Neanderthal behavior Saturday night. The problem was, he couldn't promise that he wouldn't behave the same way the next time they were alone.

What kind of spell was he under that she was on his mind most of the time? All right, all of the time. He'd be in meetings with clients and his mind would wander.

This was not the way he'd ever conducted himself and he didn't like it. The problem was that he didn't know what to do about it.

On Monday he had back-to-back meetings, most of them out of the office, and he didn't return until after four.

He decided to check with Jodie to see if she'd like to have dinner with him that night. Nothing wrong with that. He'd make certain they weren't alone, either during their meal or when he took her home. He would show her that he could, in fact, restrain himself around her, but being alone with her would be too much for him.

For that matter, he could bring her back to the office to get her car.

Feeling pleased with his plan, Dean went to the department where she worked. When he didn't see her, he strolled into Frank's office.

Frank looked up. "How did the meeting with Flynn go today?"

"He liked the presentation you made last week and he's ready to sign on."

"Good to hear."

"I, uh, was looking for Jodie. Did she go home early?"

Frank frowned. "Didn't she tell you?"

"Tell me what?"

"She resigned this morning—used her vacation time in lieu of notice and left."

Dean sank into the nearest chair. He felt as though Frank had punched him in the diaphragm, knocking the breath out of him. When he didn't say anything, Frank said, "I figured you knew about it."

"No. No, I didn't." He was quiet for a moment and then asked, "Did she say why. I thought she was happy here. Did she mention another job?"

"Sorry. Actually she said very little, just cleaned out her desk. I'll admit, I hated to see her go. She's good. Sharp. Creative. In the time she's worked for me, I've been very impressed with her work. She was one of the people who worked on the presentation I made."

Dean nodded, although he didn't hear what Frank had said. His mind was racing with questions. Why had she quit so abruptly? And without telling him?

What the hell was going on?

"You all right?" Frank asked after a lengthy silence.

"I'm fine. Just surprised. The news caught me off guard, that's all." He stood up and said, "I'll talk to you later."

Dean didn't go to his office to check messages or mail. He went directly to the parking garage, got into his car and drove to Jodie's apartment.

There was no answer after repeated knocks.

His next stop was the Pattersons' home. As soon as he knocked, the door opened wide. It was Kent.

"Hi," Kent said with a big smile.

Dean returned his smile. "Hello, Kent. Is your mom home?"

"Uh-huh." He turned away and yelled, "Mom, it's Aunt Jodie's boyfriend."

"Have him come in and have a seat. I'll be there shortly."

Dean stepped inside. A tornado had recently come through the living room, judging from the scattered toys, shoes and jackets.

"Can I get you something to drink?" Kent asked politely.

"No, thank you."

"Oh." Kent sat across from Dean and looked at a loss as to what to do next.

"Don't let me interrupt whatever you were doing," Dean said, equally polite.

Kent grinned. "Okay," he replied and immediately slid

to the floor, where he'd been playing with small racing cars on a track that wound around the couch.

Lynette came hurrying in a few minutes later. "I'm so sorry to keep you waiting. I just got home from picking up the boys at school and it was time to feed Emily."

"No problem."

Lynette immediately began picking up toys, coats and shoes. "I'd apologize for the way the house looks except it would be a waste of time, since this is the way it looks more often than not."

"I won't keep you. I dropped by to see if you've talked to Jodie in the last day or two."

Lynette straightened and looked at him, obviously puzzled. She sat down in the chair recently vacated by her son. "She was here Friday night."

"Did you talk to her yesterday or today?"

"No. What's wrong? Has something happened to her?" she asked, making no effort to hide her alarm.

"That's what I'm trying to find out. She quit her job today, used accrued vacation time as her notice and left."

Lynette placed her hand on the side of her neck. "Good heavens. I had no idea she was considering such a thing."

"Neither did I. We went out Saturday night and she seemed to be fine when I left. I thought you might have some idea why she quit and where she might be."

She shook her head. "I'm sorry, but I don't. Have you tried her apartment?"

He nodded. "And I've left several messages on her machine."

"I'll call Chuck and have him check out her apartment. I hope nothing's happened to her."

She picked up the phone and made the call. When Chuck answered his cell phone, she told him what she'd just learned. After she hung up, she said, "He'll go check. Do you want to wait here for him to call back?"

He stood. "That won't be necessary. I'd appreciate your calling me when you find out anything." He gave her his cell phone number and left.

His phone rang as he parked his car at his condominium. "Logan."

"Hi, Dean, this is Lynette. Things are getting more and more curious. Chuck said her apartment looks okay but most of her clothes and personal things are gone."

Numbly he replied, "Thanks for letting me know."

"No problem. I'm sure I'll hear from her soon. She isn't one to want people to worry about her, which is why all this is such a surprise. This isn't like Jodie at all. Anyway, I'll have her call you when I hear from her."

"Thank you."

He pocketed the phone and walked to the elevator.

Was it something he'd said Saturday night? Or done? Or did her disappearance have nothing to do with him?

He had no way of knowing.

Friday morning Lynette's phone rang. When she answered, Jodie said, "Hi, sis. Thought I'd let you know I won't be there for dinner tonight."

"Joanna Louise Cameron, where in the world are you? I've been frantic since Monday when Dean told me you'd quit your job."

"Dean told you?"

"Yes. When he couldn't reach you at home, he came

over here to see if I knew anything. Chuck went to your apartment to see if you had been hurt or worse. Why didn't you let anyone know where you were going?"

"Because I wasn't sure where I intended to go when I left Chicago."

"Where are you?"

"I showed up here at Mom's late last night. I plan to stay a while and will probably look for a job down here."

"Have you lost your ever lovin' mind? What's wrong with the job you had here? You loved it. You were excited about it."

Lynette heard Jodie sigh. Finally she said, "It's a long story."

"I've got time to hear a long story. The boys are in school and Emily just went down for her nap. Tell me."

Jodie wasn't ready to talk about Dean to anyone, but she knew she owed Lynette an explanation. Finally she said, "I had to get away from Dean."

Silence greeted her admission. Finally in a horrified voice Lynette asked, "What did he do? It must have been serious for you to run like this. Did you call the police?"

"It's nothing like that, Lynette. I did a really stupid thing and it's so trite I'm embarrassed to admit it. I fell in love with my boss."

"So? He appears deeply enamored of you, as well."

"Not really. He decided he wanted for us to date and I agreed. I truly thought I could handle my response to him, but I can't. Whenever he's nearby, all he has to do is look at me and I go up in flames."

"Oh, honey. There's absolutely nothing wrong with that. Is that what scared you away?"

"Partly. The thing about Dean—and he's the first to admit it—is he isn't interested in a long-term commitment. And that's the only kind I want. I've been careful not to tell him how I feel, but now he's going to guess that I'm crazy about him. Once a woman tells him she's in love with him, he practically leaves skid marks getting away from her.

"So I decided that it would be better for me to leave before I had to go through that. I've tried to make a clean break with him, but somehow I end up going out with him again. I have no willpower where he's concerned. None. So I realized that I would have to go someplace where there was no chance of running into him. So I resigned."

"Maybe you're different. Maybe he'd be willing—"

"No. It's our ego that tells us that we can cause a person to change if we just love them enough. That's our fantasy, but the reality is that Dean knows what he wants and has no reason to change."

"Maybe so," Lynette replied. "But he was very concerned about you. I told him I'd have you call him. I guess that's not going to happen."

Jodie rubbed her forehead where a headache loomed. "I'll admit, I didn't expect him to contact you. If you should hear from him again—which I very much doubt—tell him whatever you want, but don't tell him that I'm in love with him. I want that to be our little secret, Lynette, okay?"

"I don't keep secrets from Chuck."

"All right. Tell Chuck. That's all."

"Well, honey, you have to do what you have to do, I suppose. I can't bear the idea of you living so far away. How's Mom taking all this?"

"I haven't told her. She had to leave early to go to work at the diner. She'll be home a little after two."

"Maybe you can convince her she doesn't have to work. Each of us is contributing to her support. It's not as though she has to work."

"She knows that, but she said she'd miss visiting with the locals who stop in every day. You know Mom. She loves people. I'm sure she's in her element there."

"Try to get some rest. That's a long trip from here."

"Tell me about it. I'm going back to bed. I'll talk to you later."

Lynette hung up the phone and immediately called Chuck. As soon as he answered, she told him about the call.

"So she ran away," Chuck summed up.

"Yes."

"That's too bad."

"I promised her that I wouldn't tell anyone but you about her feelings for Dean."

"Okay."

"However…you didn't make her any promises. So if you wanted to let Dean know…"

"No way am I going to get involved in any matchmaking. I don't need both of them cursing me. Come on, sweetheart; let her live her life the way she wants."

"Even if she's miserable?"

"Yes."

"Oh, Chuck, why do you have to be such a guy!"

"What? What, may I ask, is wrong with being a guy?"

"You just don't understand women."

"Probably. Especially at the moment. I haven't a clue what you're upset about."

"I'm upset because you have the opportunity to get two people who love each other together. That's not matchmaking. They've made the connection. They're obviously involved with each other. At least give Dean the information, okay? Then whatever he does about it will be up to him."

After a moment of silence Chuck grudgingly replied, "I'll think about it."

"You do that and I'll be eternally grateful—and I will express my gratitude in a number of creative ways."

Eighteen

Candace stepped to Dean's door a few days later and said, "There's a Mr. Chuck Patterson on line two. Shall I get his number and have you call him back?"

Without answering her question, Dean grabbed the phone. "Chuck! Good to hear from you. Hold on a minute, will you?" He raised his voice slightly and said, "Candace, please close the door and hold my calls."

He uncovered the mouthpiece of the phone and asked, "Have you heard from her?"

There was a pause and then Dean heard Chuck's laugh. "You've got it bad, my friend. I called to see if you wanted to go to the Cubs game tomorrow afternoon. My treat."

"Oh. Let me check my schedule." He looked at his calendar. He had two appointments that morning but none in the afternoon. "Sounds good. Where should I meet you?"

"I'll pick you up in front of your building," Chuck replied and named a time.

"Okay. Is she all right?" Dean asked.

"She's fine, Dean. She's visiting her mother. We can talk more tomorrow."

"See you then," Dean said and hung up the phone.

She was in Phoenix? Just like that, she quits her job, walks out on him without a word and goes to see her mother?

It would seem so.

Dean and Chuck arrived at the game early. They'd talked about everything under the sun on the ride to the stadium... everything but Jodie's sudden departure.

At any other time Dean would have enjoyed Chuck's company, but knowing that he was withholding information about Jodie made Dean want to throttle him.

At long last Chuck brought up the subject by throwing Dean a curveball. "So what's going on between you and Jodie anyway?"

"Uh, well, I mean, we've known each other quite a while. She was my secretary for several years."

"I understand that and that's not what I'm talking about. Most men don't respond to a former secretary leaving as you have."

Dean nodded. Chuck wasn't going to accept any vague remarks. If he wanted to know what was going on with Jodie, he'd have to bare his soul. Since he was a very private man, he found the idea excruciatingly painful...almost as painful as missing Jodie.

"I finally faced the fact that I'm in love with her, that

I've probably been in love with her for years and was too dumb to recognize it. I've done some really stupid things in my life, but letting her slip away from me like this has to be the biggest mistake I've ever made."

The sentence hung in the air and seemed to expand on the breeze. There. He'd said it. Too bad he hadn't realized that what he felt for her was love until after she was gone.

"That right?" Chuck asked with a smile.

"Yeah."

"So her leaving like that has been tough on you."

"You could say that." What an understatement that was.

"What did she say when you told her?"

"What? That I love her?"

"I believe that's the topic of this conversation, yes."

"I never told her," Dean mumbled.

"Sorry, I didn't catch that."

Dean cleared his throat. "I said that I never told her, fool that I am, because I didn't realize it until very recently."

"I see."

"So how is she? Have you talked with her? Do you know when she plans to come back?"

"I haven't talked with her, but Lynette said she seems to be doing okay. Jodie told her that she might look for a job in Phoenix."

"What! You're kidding, right?"

"Nope. That's what Lynette reported to me."

The crowd roared its approval about something. Chuck and Dean hadn't been paying attention when the game started, and the Cubs were up to bat.

"Looks like a single," Chuck commented.

"Yeah."

"I don't know if you want to hear any suggestions from me," Chuck said briskly, "but here's one anyway—go to Arizona and tell her how you feel. I'm sure the news would have more impact with her if you're there in person."

"I could do that."

"Good. Now, then. Let's watch the game, okay?"

Jodie had been at her mother's for two weeks and was getting restless. She missed work. She'd been tempted to call Frank to see how things were going until she remembered that she no longer had a job.

She'd set up a couple of job interviews for the following week, but in the meantime there was nothing much for her to do. The house was spotless and her mom's garden had already been weeded within an inch of its life.

This morning she decided to enjoy the early-morning coolness outdoors before the sun got too hot.

She loved her mom's backyard. It was very private, with a six-foot wall surrounding it. Inside the wall her mom had planted all kinds of colorful flowering plants, which reminded Jodie of the lush foliage in Hawaii.

Jodie put on a two-piece bathing suit and, once outside, stretched out on one of the lounge chairs and removed the top to her swimsuit. A small hand towel covered her breasts, leaving her shoulders bare. Next she picked up the book she had started the night before and began to read.

Sometime later the doorbell startled her awake, and she realized that she'd dozed off. She considered getting up and answering the door, but she was too relaxed to move. Besides, all of her mom's friends knew that she worked mornings. It was probably some kind of salesman.

She decided to ignore the door and let her eyes close, basking in the quiet and serenity. She'd had trouble sleeping since she'd been there, and from her reflection in the mirror each morning she knew the lack of sleep had taken its toll on her.

"Ah, there you are."

Jodie's immediate reaction to the sound of a very familiar voice was to scream involuntarily and jerk upright.

"Sorry. Didn't mean to startle you," Dean said. "When no one answered the door, I decided to check back here." He looked around. "The garden is beautiful by the way."

When she could speak, she said, "What are you doing here!" Without waiting for an answer, she grabbed a large towel and wrapped it around her.

"Mind if I sit down?" he asked, his voice bland.

She stared at him as though he were an apparition. Finally she nodded.

Once he sat down, he took his time looking her over, from her ponytail to her freshly painted toenails.

"You're looking rested," he said, which she knew to be a lie. He wore a golf shirt and slacks, the shirt clinging to his wide chest and his pants outlining his massive thighs.

"Did you ever play football?" she blurted out. How did that manage to pop out of her mouth? She was losing it.

The look on his face was indescribable. He finally answered, "Yes, in high school and college. Why do you ask?"

"Just curious," she replied faintly. "If you'll excuse me, I'll, uh, go get us something to drink." She didn't give him time to respond before she fled the patio, ignoring the kitchen and racing down the hallway to her room.

She quickly put on some clothes.

Dean Logan was there? In Phoenix? This couldn't be happening. What was she going to have to do, find some deserted island somewhere to make certain she didn't see him?

She hurried into the kitchen, removed a pitcher of lemonade from the fridge and set it on a tray. She added two glasses filled with ice and returned outside.

Dean watched her walk toward him without expression. She placed the tray on the table between them and poured the juice. Once seated, she glanced quickly at him, then away.

She took a swallow of lemonade to aid her dry mouth. "You haven't answered my question. What are you doing here?"

He leaned back in his chair and looked around the garden. "The same thing you are. Enjoying the sun."

"How did you know where I was?"

He lifted his brow. "Was it supposed to be a secret?"

She shrugged. Lynette probably told him. Jodie hadn't told her not to mention her whereabouts to him for the simple reason that she hadn't expected him to come looking for her.

When she didn't comment, he said, "I decided that I work much too hard. I work ridiculously long hours and have a slave driver for a boss." He paused and drank some lemonade. "I decided to follow your example. I quit my job and came to Arizona."

"What do you mean you quit your job? That's impossible."

"Actually it isn't, because I did it. Others can manage the place as well as I can. I've trained them well."

"You could barely get through a week away from the office when we were in Hawaii the first time. The only way you managed was to call the office several times a day."

"Once I realized that I am, in fact, a workaholic, I decided it was time to change my lifestyle."

"So you came to Phoenix? This isn't the best time of year to visit, unless you're looking for sunstroke. I never stay out later than ten o'clock for that reason."

What was the matter with her? She was babbling. The last thing she would have expected was for him to come there.

He sipped from his glass, looking totally relaxed. "Actually Chuck happened to mention that you were visiting your mother while we were at a Cubs game together." He gave her a steady look. "You left without telling me you were leaving, and I thought I'd find out what I had done to offend you."

This was exactly why she'd left Chicago—to avoid explaining why she couldn't deal with their relationship. "You didn't do a thing, Dean," she finally said.

As though she hadn't spoken, he said, "I've been thinking about our last night together. You gave no hint that you intended to walk away from your career and leave town. May I ask why?"

"It was a personal decision I made. I didn't tell anyone."

"I got quite a shock learning that you'd resigned. You seemed to be enjoying your new position."

"Dean, I really don't want to discuss this."

"The thing is, I feel like a fool," he went on to say. "I've been pretending that it didn't matter to me whether I saw you or not, when the truth is I want to be with you all the time." He paused and scrubbed his hand over his face. "I'm not saying this right. What I'm trying to say is that what we have together is too precious to let go of. I want to share my future with you. I thought if I came here and told you that I finally figured out that I'm crazy in love with you—and have been for who knows how long—that you might consider marrying me."

All right. Now she knew she was hallucinating. Dean Logan proposing marriage? It was almost laughable…if she felt in the least like laughing. Which she didn't.

"How quickly we forget," she said. "It was only a couple of months ago when you told me that a commitment and marriage were the very last things you were interested in." She glared at him. "Remember? No house in the suburbs for you. No tiny people to make claims on your time."

She was proud of her little speech. Too bad her teeth were chattering with nerves during the whole thing.

"That was a dying man going under for the third time, unaware that it was way too late for him to be spouting such nonsense."

"Nonsense?"

He leaned toward her and took her hand, which lay limply on her thigh. "It must already be in the nineties out here and you're chilled." He stood and started toward the sliding glass doors into the house. "I'll find something to wrap around you."

She jumped to her feet and followed him into the house. He didn't pause but continued down the hallway looking into rooms. He saw a crocheted afghan lying on the foot of her mother's bed, swept it up and returned to the hall, where he wrapped it around her. Then he pulled her close, holding her tightly against him.

"I know I've given you every reason to believe that I'm a confirmed bachelor. My only excuse is that I'd convinced myself, as well. My feelings for you have always been there, but it wasn't until we went to Hawaii the first time that they shot to the surface. I just didn't recognize them for what they were at the time."

She pulled away from him and walked to the living room, where she sank into her mom's cushy chair. "I'm sorry, but I'm having a little trouble taking all of this in," she said, feeling light-headed. She must have gotten too much sun.

He knelt beside her chair. "I want what Chuck and Lynette have—a lovely home, three great kids and, yes, a place in the suburbs where we can raise our own."

She covered her cheeks with her hands. "This can't be happening."

"Would you at least consider the idea of marrying me? I don't want to sound maudlin and say that I don't know how I'd get along without you in my life, but there it is. I know I'm not much of a catch. I'm impatient and irritable, I work too much, I don't know how to sit back and enjoy life. But you've shown me a whole new world out there, away from the office, and I'd like to learn more…with you as my teacher."

Dean watched her closely, wondering if he'd made a colossal mistake by coming to Phoenix to see her. She'd left everything she'd worked for in Chicago. Was it just to get away from him?

"Why did you leave?"

Some color had come back in her cheeks. Funny, but he'd never thought that his proposing marriage would cause a woman to almost faint.

"Because we can't seem to be together without ending up in bed."

"I'm afraid that's true. I have very little self-control where you're concerned." He took her hand once again. "I suppose that I've gone about all of this backward. Since it's the first time I've ever proposed, I'm not very good at it. The real question here is, do you love me?"

Her eyes filled with tears. He was such an idiot. The last thing he wanted was to make her cry.

She laced her fingers with his. "Yes, Dean, I'm in love with you despite everything I can do not to be."

"Is loving me so bad?"

"It is when you made it clear that you weren't interested in love."

"I was wrong. I can't think of a greater gift than you loving me."

The tears trickled down her face.

He cleared his throat. "As long as I'm already on my knees, I'd like to formally ask. Jodie Cameron, will you do me the great honor of marrying me, of loving me, of saving me from the horrible state of bachelorhood?"

She laughed through her tears. "Oh, Dean." She cupped his face in her hands. "If I'm dreaming, please don't wake me up."

"You can't be dreaming because my knees are killing me." He stood and held out his hand. "Well?"

She answered by throwing herself into his arms, covering his face with kisses.

After a lengthy and very passionate kiss, he pulled away long enough to say, "Is that a yes, by any chance?"

"Yes, Mr. Dean Logan, I will be most happy to marry you."

"And have a few children?"

"If that's what you want."

"That's very much what I want. Speaking of which—" he looked around the room "—where's your mother?"

"At work. She'll be home early this afternoon."

"I have an idea how we could spend our time waiting for her."

Yes, there was passion in his eyes, but Jodie saw something more, something she'd never expected to see—his eyes shining with love and tenderness. He had well and truly convinced her that he loved her. What more could she possibly want?

"Perhaps you'd like to show me what you have in mind," she replied.

With a shout of laughter he picked her up and carried her back down the hall to her bedroom.

He was right. He'd found the perfect way to spend the rest of the morning.

Epilogue

Six months later

"**Y**ou look like a princess in a fairy tale," her mother said to Jodie. She'd carefully placed the tiara and veil on Jodie's head while they stood before the large oval mirror in a room set aside for the bride.

Lynette added, "And who would have believed that Dean Logan would turn out to be a prince after all? If you'd told me a year or two ago that you would end up marrying Dean, I would have been convinced you were truly marrying an ogre."

"Lynette! Shame on you," her mother said. "Dean is a lovely man…polite, considerate and a joy to be around."

Jodie and Lynette shared a glance in the mirror and smiled at each other. Dean had done a great job of selling himself to their mom. Once Dean and Jodie had returned to Chicago, Jodie and Lynette had convulsed into laughter when Jodie had told Lynette about his visit to Phoenix.

"I've never attended a wedding this large, much less been in the wedding party," Mom said. "As you know, George and I eloped. And Chuck and Lynette had a small ceremony."

"Believe me, the idea of eloping ran through my mind many times these past few months," Jodie said. "I turned everything over to the wedding planner and went back to work."

"Dean said that since this would be his one and only wedding, he wanted a large celebration," Lynette explained. "He didn't care how much it cost. Everyone who's anyone in the business world was invited."

Jodie closed her eyes. She didn't need the reminder. She could see herself tripping down the aisle—literally tripping down the aisle—and skidding to a stop at Dean's feet.

There was a tap on the door. "Come in," she said.

Her three brothers, who were ushers, stepped inside. "Everyone's seated," Dave, the oldest, said.

Randy spoke up. "Wow, sis. You clean up pretty good."

"Gee, thanks, Randy. I'm glad you approve."

Rick, the impatient one, looked at his watch and said, "C'mon. Let's get this show on the road."

The three women followed the men out into the foyer. To save argument, both Kent and Kyle were ring bearers. Of course, that created an argument between them because each of them wanted to carry Jodie's ring. Lynette finally got that straightened out by threatening not to let them be a part of the wedding.

The music started and the young boys started down the aisle, looking sharp in their new suits. They were growing up so fast. Jodie blinked the moisture from her eyes. Get real. These are the same angelic beings who kept her constantly embarrassed with their frank questions to Dean every time they saw him.

Jodie had asked two of her coworkers to be bridesmaids. Lynette was her matron of honor and her mother would walk her down the aisle.

After Lynette reached the front of the church, the music switched to the well-known wedding march and the guests stood. Jodie's throat closed up. She was not going to cry, she was not going to cry, she was not—

Then she saw Dean waiting at the altar and that did it. Tears slid down her face as she started toward him. She couldn't stop smiling.

Jodie didn't remember much about the actual ceremony. She heard the rumble of Dean's voice and had responded when it was her turn, but all she could think about was the fact that she was actually marrying Dean Logan after all these months of answering the wedding planner's incessant questions.

"You may kiss the bride."

The pastor's words jolted her out of her reverie. Jodie turned to Dean, who was watching her with amusement. What? What did he find so amusing?

When he leaned toward her, he whispered, "I thought you were going to fall asleep there for a minute," and he kissed her.

He really kissed her. It wasn't a brushing of lips or a ritual peck on the mouth but a leisurely kiss. When he finally raised his head, her face was flaming and the guests were laughing and applauding.

Music filled the sanctuary as they started up the aisle. Once in the foyer, Dean turned to her. "Hello, Mrs. Logan. I hope you're having a good day."

"I wasn't going to fall asleep! I was just distracted a little."

"You must have been, since the pastor had to ask a couple of his questions to you twice."

"Oh, no." She covered her face with her hands. "And I didn't want to do anything to embarrass you. At least I didn't trip over the gown and fall down coming down the aisle!"

"You could never embarrass me, Jodie. I find you delightful, besides being the love of my life."

By now they were surrounded by well-wishers. After greeting several people, Dean and Jodie hurried outside and got into the limo waiting to take them to the large hotel where the reception would be held.

They settled into their seats, and Dean reached inside his coat pocket and pulled out a small, long and narrow box. "I want to give you your bride's gift before we get to the reception."

A necklace. He'd bought her a necklace. "Oh, Dean, what a thoughtful gift."

He lifted one eyebrow. "Aren't you going to open it?" he asked.

"Oh! I'm sure I'll love it," she said and lifted the lid.

There was no necklace. Only a folded envelope and a key. Bewildered, Jodie looked at him. He smiled.

She opened the envelope and found a note and two airline tickets to Hawaii. "Oh, we're going back to Hawaii!"

"Why not? That's where I really got to know you. This time we'll stay as long as you like."

She unfolded the note and read. "No, this isn't the key to my heart because you already have it in your safekeeping. This is a key to your new home."

"My home? What have you done?"

"Conspired behind your back. I got Lynette to go house hunting with me to find a home she thought you might like. Of course, if you don't like it, I can always—"

She threw herself into his arms and kissed him all over his face, his ears, his jaw and his mouth. "You are the most high-handed man I've ever known," she finally said, laughing with delight. "You bought me a house without consulting me?" She looked at him with mock disapproval, his face cupped in her hands.

"Actually I haven't bought it yet. I waited to sign the contract until you have a chance to see it. The Realtor gave me the key, and I thought we could go over there after we leave the reception. If you approve of it, I'll sign the papers before we leave."

So maybe a man could change a little. She was touched that he was trying. "I can hardly wait to see what you've picked out for us."

She knew that she would love the house because Lynette knew her so well. She would love it even more because Dean had chosen to surprise her with it.

One thing she knew for certain: there would never be a dull moment being married to Dean Logan.

* * * * *

DEVLIN AND THE DEEP BLUE SEA

by
Merline Lovelace

MERLINE LOVELACE

spent twenty-three years in the Air Force, pulling tours in Vietnam, at the Pentagon and at bases all over the world. When she hung up her uniform, she decided to try her hand at writing. She's since had more than fifty novels published, with over seven million copies of her work in print.

For the Old Farts gang
—thanks for a fun day of war stories and
tall tales about life on the patch!

Prologue

"You sleazy bucket of slime!"

Fury seared Elizabeth Moore's veins as she glared at the e-mail she'd printed out less than a half hour ago. In the light of the fat, round Baja moon she could just make out the message her fiancé had zinged her.

Correction.

Ex-fiancé.

Fuming, Liz ripped the e-mail into halves, then quarters, then jagged eighths. Waves, tinted to liquid gold by the moon, lapped at her bare ankles. With May slipping fast toward June, the heat of the Mexican night wrapped around her like a spongy blanket.

Digging her toes into the wet sand, Liz tore the eighths into sixteenths and threw them into the sea.

A receding wave carried off the scraps. The soggy bits floated for a few seconds before slowly sinking, drowning Liz's shattered dreams down with them.

"I can't believe I fell for such a jerk!"

The truth was only now beginning to register. The man she thought she'd share her life with, the fiancé who'd convinced her to take this job in Mexico while he racked up hours flying as a civilian contract pilot in Singapore had just zapped her an e-mail informing her he'd fallen for another woman. A Malay correspondent for NBC news by the name of Bambang Chawdar.

Bambang, for God's sake!

As if that wasn't bad enough, the bastard had also cleaned out their joint bank account.

Liz couldn't decide which infuriated her more—the fact that she'd convinced herself she was really in love with Donny Carter or that she'd remained faithful to him during their long separation.

"Seven months," she ground out. "Seven months I've lived like a damned nun."

She'd certainly had plenty of opportunities for sin. The oil crews she choppered to the offshore rig some forty miles off the Baja peninsula generally consisted of prime specimens. And when they came off their month-long rotations, they were hungry for female companionship. In the past seven months Liz had become an expert at dodging propositions from horny roughnecks and roustabouts. Most had required only a breezy smile or a firm "no, thanks." One or two had required a little more forceful response.

Liz certainly didn't feel like smiling now. She felt like hitting something. Or releasing her fury in a way that would soothe her battered pride *and* her pent-up frustration.

"I swear to God I'm going to jump the next halfway-sober male I meet!"

Her fierce vow carried clearly over the murmur of the Pacific. So did the amused drawl that came out of the darkness behind her.

"I'm sober, darlin'. And if you're looking for someone to jump, I'd be happy to oblige."

Liz's heart leapfrogged into her throat. She spun around, searching the dunes, until a dim shadow materialized. The moon was behind him. She couldn't make out his features, but the rest of him telegraphed a clear message. With each step he took toward her, a marquee inside her head flashed the words tall, rangy and buff.

What the heck was he doing out here on this isolated stretch of beach so late at night?

What was *she* doing here, alone and weaponless?

Cursing the anger that had made her leave both her cell phone and her collapsible baton in the Jeep parked up by the road, Liz stood her ground. She'd spent four years as an air force pilot. Her survival, evasion, resistance and escape trainers had taught her some pretty brutal moves. She could take this guy down if she needed to, despite his height and the impressive set of muscles she could just make out under his black T-shirt and jeans.

"I appreciate the offer," she replied with a lift of her chin, "but you might want to rethink it. The mood I'm in, a midnight tussle in the sand might not be a particularly enjoyable experience for you."

She saw his head angle, felt the prickly heat of his gaze as it traveled from her face to her stretchy white T-shirt to her cutoffs and the bare legs below. His face was a blur in the darkness, but she couldn't miss the wolfish grin that appeared as he stepped closer.

"I'll take my chances."

The slow drawl pegged him as an American. The laughter lacing it stirred an unexpected response from Liz. For an insane moment she was actually tempted to follow through with her rash vow. God knew she could use a little stud service, and this six-foot-plus hunk of hard muscle certainly looked like he could provide it.

Maybe it was the moon, she thought wildly. It had to be the moon exerting some weird gravitational pull, like the riptides so prevalent along the Baja coast. Whatever is was, Liz felt the surge of something dangerous. Powerful.

Caution shouted at her to step back, put a safe distance between her and this broad-shouldered stranger. Anger, singed pride and an uncharacteristic recklessness kept her in place as he moved closer.

She could see his features more clearly now. With the precision of an aviator verifying her course headings, she cataloged each one. Strong, square chin.

Nose with a slightly flattened bridge, as if it had taken a punch or two. White squint lines at the corners of his eyes. A grin that was pure sex.

"How about we...?"

A sharp crack split the night. Another followed a heartbeat later. The stranger spit out a curse, lunged forward, and slammed into Liz. She went down hard and landed on her butt in the shallow surf.

He went down with her, but rolled to his feet a second later and sprinted in the direction of the shots.

"Stay here!"

Like she could move? She was sprawled like a beached porpoise, wheezing from the impact of what had felt like 180 pounds of solid male.

It took Liz several seconds of painful effort to suck air back into her lungs before she, too, was up and running.

One

In the silent hours before dawn, only the occasional set of headlights stabbed through D.C.'s embassy district. The brick town houses lining a side street just off Massachusetts Avenue were shuttered and dark. From the outside, the elegant, three-story town house halfway down the block appeared as somnolent as its neighbors.

Light from a nearby streetlamp glowed dully on the discreet brass plaque mounted beside the front door. The plaque identified the building as housing the offices of the president's special envoy. Old-time Washingtonians knew the title was meaningless, one of dozens doled out after every election to wealthy campaign contributors itching to be part of the hustle and bustle of the capital. Only a handful of insiders knew the special envoy also doubled as the director of OMEGA, a secret agency that reported directly to the president and was activated as a last resort, when all other measures failed.

One of OMEGA's operatives was in the field now, and behind the darkened windows of the town house's third floor a high-tech operations center vibrated with rigidly restrained tension. The agent's controller sat at an elaborate console, his face tight with concentration.

"I didn't copy that last transmission, Rigger. Come again, please."

Joe Devlin, code name Rigger, responded with a heavy dose of disgust. "I said this part of the op just blew all to hell. I've got a corpse floating in the surf and I'm following a set of tracks fast getting washed away."

"Is the corpse our informant?"

"Negative. The contact said to look for someone in a Mazatland *Tigres* football jersey. The dead guy's in a Tommy Hilfiger T-shirt. My guess is he followed our pigeon, spooked him and got drilled in the process."

Everyone in the control center shared the frustration in Devlin's terse reply. Their first real lead—their *only* lead so far—to the ring suspected of murdering U.S. citizens and selling their identities to dangerous undesirables was now on the run.

Devlin's controller flicked a glance at the man listening to the exchange from a few yards away. Nick Jensen, code name Lightning, stood with the jacket of his Armani tux shoved back and his hands buried in the pockets of the hand-tailored trousers. He'd swung by the control center on his way home from one of the endless ceremonial dinners he regularly attended, and stayed for Rigger's anticipated report.

His wife, Mackenzie, sat perched on the edge of the console, sleek and elegant in a sheath of black silk and matching spike heels. With or without those three-inch stilettos, Mackenzie Blair Jensen was a force to be reckoned with. Formerly OMEGA's chief of communications, she now directed a team that supplied several agencies, including OMEGA, with equipment that would give any techie wet dreams. She remained as quiet as the others in the control center until Devlin came back on, huffing a little.

"Dammit! The shooter just jumped into a vehicle and took off. He's heading south on the coast road. Get some surveillance in the air ASAP."

"Will do. And I'll—" The controller broke off, eyeing a blinking red light. "Stand by, Rigger. I'm getting a flash override."

He switched frequencies, listened for a few seconds and switched back.

"We just intercepted a phone call to the Piedras Rojas police. There's a female on the line, reporting a shooting at approximately your location. Our listener says she sounds like an American."

"Well, hell! The blonde!"

"Come again?"

"There was a woman on the beach. I was just about to get rid of her when the bullets started flying."

Frowning, Lightning stepped forward. "What was

she doing at the rendezvous point so late at night? Acting as a lookout? A decoy?"

Three thousand miles away, Joe Devlin scrubbed a hand across the back of his neck. He'd spent almost six years as an OMEGA operative and had learned long ago never to take anyone at face value. He'd also learned to trust his instincts. The little he'd overheard suggested the blonde had come out to the beach to conduct a personal exorcism.

"I don't think she's part of this op. Sounded like she just got a 'Dear Jane' letter and was working off steam."

Judging by her crack about living like a nun, it also sounded as though she'd built up a bad case of the hungries. Wishing like hell he'd had time to satisfy them, Devlin got back to business.

"We need to run her through the system and see what pops."

"Did you get a name?" Lightning asked.

"No, but I did tag her Jeep when she drove up."

Luckily, he'd arrived at the rendezvous site early. He'd seen the woman drive up and had tracked her from her Jeep to the water's edge. He'd planned to call in her tag and have OMEGA check her out, but matters had moved too fast. Drawing the numbers from his memory bank, Devlin relayed them along with a brief physical description.

"I'd say she's about twenty-eight or -nine. Five-six or so. Maybe 120 pounds. It was too dark to be sure, but I'm guessing her eyes were brown."

"We'll run her," Lightning advised. "How about the corpse? Did you find anything on him that gave you a clue as to his identity or why he showed up at your rendezvous?"

"I didn't have time to check. I'll go back now and do a search."

"Better do it quick. The locals will arrive on the scene shortly."

Devlin flipped the lid on what looked like an ordinary cell phone. Despite its innocuous appearance, the device contained enough ultrasonic signals, secure satellite frequencies and encryption capabilities to orchestrate an intergalactic expedition. Mackenzie Blair, bless her state-of-the-art soul, believed an operative couldn't carry too much in the way of communications into the field.

Keeping an eye out for the blonde, Devlin jogged back to the dark hump in the surf-washed sand. Damn! Whoever this guy was, his untimely demise sure put a kink in the mission.

Dropping to one knee, Devlin dragged out the tail of his T-shirt to use as a glove. A quick search turned up a fat wad of pesos wrapped with a rubber band, the kind of switchblade you could buy in any Mexican market and a container of dental floss.

Flipping the cell phone up again, Devlin punched a single key. "Robbery obviously wasn't the motive. The guy's still carrying his stash."

"Any ID?"

"Negative."

Lightning greeted that news with a grunt. "What about the woman? Can she ID you to the police?"

"Not by name, but she can give them a general description."

"Then I suggest you disappear. We'll track the locals' investigation. In the meantime you need to maintain your cover."

Devlin acknowledged the order but threw a regretful glance along the shoreline. He hated to leave with so many unanswered questions. Not to mention a very curvy, very delectable female who sounded as though she was in dire need of male companionship.

So long, Blondie. Sorry to leave you with this mess.

An hour later Liz wished fervently she'd hightailed it back to town instead of calling the local gendarmes. They were hardly CSI types.

The first officer on the scene had poked at the body with the toe of his boot, tugged on plastic gloves and shooed away the crabs. After feeling around in the victim's pockets, he extracted some objects and entered a sort of inventory in a notebook before ambling over to Liz.

She told him what happened. He made a few more notes and asked her if she knew the deceased. She didn't.

About that time, Subcommandante Carlos Rivera and the crime scene unit arrived. Liz waited while the inspector studied the corpse and conferred with the uniformed officer. Finally he turned his attention to her. Slowly and methodically, he went over every word of her statement. Such as it was.

"You say you do not know the identity of the man who has been shot?"

"No, I don't."

"What about this Americano? The one you say appeared out of the darkness?"

"I don't know his identity, either."

"Yet you spoke with him."

Liz had done more than speak with the guy. She'd responded to the laughter in his voice and that damned grin and let the man get close enough to touch her. Worse, she'd *wanted* him to touch her. Okay, more than touch her. She'd actually entertained notions of rolling around in the surf with him. How stupid was that?

Too stupid to admit to Subcommandante Rivera.

"We only exchanged a few words," she muttered.

The inspector nodded, his face grave beneath the visor of his cap. "Perhaps you will be so kind as to explain again what brought you to such an isolated spot at this late hour."

Liz dragged a hand through her cropped hair. She'd gone through this with the first officer on the scene. It didn't sound any better the second time around.

"I received news that upset me. I needed to vent."

"And you could not do this in Piedras Rojas, where you live?"

After receiving Donny's e-mail, Liz had thought about stopping by her favorite cantina in town and drinking herself into a stupor. But she had a flight tomorrow morning. Her training and professionalism went too deep to climb into a cockpit hung over. Since the small, sleepy village of Piedras Rojas offered no other outlet for her anger, she'd headed for the beach some miles south of town.

Piedras rojas. Red stones. When the sun sank toward the sea and set the cliffs along this stretch of coast aflame, there wasn't a more awesome sight anywhere in the world. The other twenty-three and a half hours of the day, dust swirled, trees drooped, and the locals baked in the unrelenting heat.

For all these months Liz had ignored the dust and the heat and the flies and socked away every peso she earned ferrying crews out to and back from the offshore drill site. She and Donny had talked about purchasing a fleet of helos and starting their own charter service. Anxious to make the dream a reality, Liz had used her savings as collateral and taken out a loan for deposit on their first bird. The sleek little Sikorsky single-pilot craft had a Rolls Royce turbine engine, a 2,000-pound load capacity and the best auto-rotational characteristics of any helicopter flying today.

Now her savings were gone, she'd have to forfeit the nonrefundable deposit and she still had to make good on the damned loan. Pissed all over again, Liz shoved her fists into the pockets of her cutoffs.

"No, I couldn't work off steam in town. Look,

Subcommandante, I've told you everything I know. Are we done here?"

"We are done. For now."

"Fine. I'll head back to town."

With a curt nod, she turned and plowed through the dunes. Talk about your all-around crappy nights! This one ranked right up there with the night she'd said goodbye to Donny. Liz had dreaded another long separation. He'd seemed eager to return to Malaysia and finish out his contract. Too eager, she now knew. He wanted to get back to Bambang.

Bambang. God!

Liz shoved her Jeep into gear, slinging mental arrows at her former fiancé. To her surprise, she had trouble putting a face on the target. The tall, lanky American who'd appeared out of the night seemed to have crowded Donny out of her head. No wonder! The man had shaved a good five years off her life popping up like that.

If and when she met up with him again, Mr. No-Name would have to answer a few pointed questions. Like why he'd been out here at the beach so late at night. And why he'd disappeared. And whether he knew who had put a bullet into the dead man's skull.

As Liz navigated the narrow road that led up from the beach and along the rocky cliffs, the questions buzzed around inside her head like pesky flies.

They were still buzzing the next morning when she pulled into the small regional airport that serviced the resorts springing up along this stretch of the Mexican Riviera.

The temperature was already climbing toward the predicted high of one hundred plus. Liz threw a glance at the wind sock drooping in the heat above the building that served as both terminal and tower and knew she'd be swimming inside her flight suit by the time she returned from her run. Sighing, she retrieved her flyaway bag from the passenger seat.

The corrugated tin Quonset hut that constituted Aero Baja's hangar and operations center occupied a patch of rock- and cactus-studded red dirt to the left of the terminal. Liz was one of three Aero Baja helicopter pilots under contract to the American-Mexican Petroleum Company to ferry crews and supplies to the giant rig forty miles off the coast. All of the pilots were qualified in a variety of craft, but their platform here at Piedras Rojas was the Bell Ranger 412.

The Ranger sat on the red dirt pad, being prepped by Aero Baja's chief mechanic. This particular model had been configured for over-water operations by a single pilot, could carry up to fourteen passengers and cruised at 120 knots. The aircraft was almost as old as Liz. Thankfully, it had been updated with two GPS receivers, a new altimeter and a marine band radio in addition to the usual UHF, VHF and HF radios. It looked and handled like a mosquito on a leash after the heavily armed, superpowered choppers Liz had flown in the air force, but she'd gotten used to its aerodynamics and thoroughly enjoyed taking it up.

The mechanic prepping the Ranger had seen as much service as the aircraft itself. Retired after thirty-plus years with the Mexican air force, Jorge Garcia could take the Ranger apart and put it back together in his sleep.

Liz had formed a close friendship with the affable, mustachioed mechanic during her months in Mexico. She couldn't count the number of beers they'd shared after work or the meals his wife, Maria, had fed her. Hefting her flight bag, Liz joined him on the pad.

"*Buenos días,* Jorge."

"*Buenos días,* Lizetta."

His pet name for her usually produced a smile. Liz had to work to dredge one up this morning. She was gritty-eyed after the late-night session on the beach and still steaming over Donny's betrayal.

"Is the Ranger ready to fly?"

Grinning, Jorge patted the helicopter's fuselage with a callused palm. "She is."

Stowing her bag in the cockpit, Liz did a careful walk-around. The American-Mexican Petroleum Company was paying her serious bucks to ferry its cargo and crews. She took her responsibilities to AmMex and to her passengers seriously. Before transporting anything or anyone out to the patch, as they referred to the monster rising up out of the sea, she made sure her craft was airworthy.

Jorge followed, marking off the checklist items as

Liz completed them. They had worked their way from the rear rotor to the main-engine driveshaft before Liz dropped a casual question.

"Did you hear any rumors about some trouble last night?"

There hadn't been any mention of a shooting in Piedras Rojas' morning newspaper. Probably because Piedras Rojas didn't have a newspaper, morning or otherwise.

"What kind of trouble?"

"Gunshots down at the beach just after midnight. A dead body, maybe."

The mechanic's eyes rounded above his bushy black mustache. "Are you saying you go to the beach after midnight?

"Yes."

"Alone?"

"It started out that way."

"Ayyyy, Lizetta, that is not wise!"

She certainly couldn't argue the point. Last night's misadventure had driven home just how *un*wise.

Despite its slow pace and *mañana* approach to just about everything, Piedras Rojas was only a half-hour drive from La Paz, situated at the very tip of the Baja California peninsula. The city had become a major crime center since antidrug operations in the Caribbean had forced Colombian drug lords to shift their operations to the Pacific coast.

The cartels' vehicle of choice for their smuggling trade was the Mexican tuna fleet that operated out of ports all along the coast. The tuna boats were fast, long-range clippers that could spend months at sea. In a good year the fleet generated approximately a hundred million dollars in tuna revenue. A single boat could carry a load of cocaine worth twice that. As a result, drugs, corruption and violence had become a part of life in this corner of the world.

"Then why do you go to the beach so late?" Jorge wanted to know.

"Donny sent me an e-mail." The words tasted as sour as three-day-old frijoles. "He's dumped me. Seems he's fallen for a foreign news correspondent."

The mechanic fired off a string of highly colorful Spanish. Liz caught only a few of the more exotic phrases, but they were enough to produce a reluctant smile.

"That was pretty much my reaction, too."

Spitting out a final curse, Jorge squinted at her through the iridescent waves of heat rising from the dirt pad.

"Will you go back to the States now?"

"Maybe. I haven't decided."

"But the helo you have saved every peso to buy! The charter service you plan to start! You do not need this pig, this Donny. You can start your own company without him."

Liz didn't tell him about her now-empty bank account. No sense broadcasting her monumental stupidity in making Donny joint on her account when he'd somehow never got around to putting her on his.

Nor did she care to reveal that she didn't have enough cash left to cover her rent, due tomorrow. She'd have to swallow her pride and ask the smarmy AmMex on-site rep for an advance on next month's salary. Trying not to wince at the prospect, Liz repeated her often made promise.

"When I do open my own charter service, you will most definitely be my chief mechanic."

"Bueno! We make a good team, yes?"

"That we do."

Satisfied, Jorge returned his attention to the preflight checklist. While he inspected the main driveshaft forward coupling for grease leakage, Liz checked the engine inlet and plenum to make sure they were clear of obstructions. The rumble of an approaching vehicle announced the arrival of their passengers.

The bus pulled up at the terminal and a half-dozen men filed into the building. Liz went back to the preflight inspection, knowing it would take the sleepy-eyed terminal official a good half hour to search the crew members' bags for drugs and alcohol, weigh both men and luggage and show them a video explaining the safe boarding and ditching of a helicopter at sea. The video would play twice, once in English, once in Spanish. Hopefully, the non-English-, non-Spanish-speaking crewmen would get the idea from the video.

When the crew filed out of the terminal, Liz pasted on a smile and went to double-check their IDs against the manifest provided by AmMex. Like most of the men working the big rigs, these were a mixed bag of nationalities and skills.

A big, beefy Irish driller led the pack. A Filipino welder followed, then a Mexican radio operator and two Venezuelan cooks. When the last passenger stepped forward, Liz read off his name from the manifest.

"Devlin, Joe."

"Yes, ma'am."

The slow drawl brought her head whipping up. "It's you!"

He responded to that with the same wolfish grin he'd given her last night. "Yes, ma'am."

Two

Devlin waited while a variety of expressions flickered across the face of the woman OMEGA had ID'd as Elizabeth Moore. He'd spent most of what was left of the night after the fiasco on the beach assimilating the background data headquarters had assembled on her.

He had to admit the info was pretty impressive. After completing USAF flight school at the top of her class, Moore had opted to fly rotary wing aircraft because that's what her father had flown during his long and distinguished military career. Brigadier General Moore had died of a massive coronary less than a year after his daughter pinned on her wings, but she'd lived up to both his name and his reputation as a crack pilot. She'd spent four years inserting special-ops teams into particularly nasty spots all over the globe before leaving the military with the announced intention of opening her own charter service.

Unfortunately for her, Captain Moore's smarts didn't extend to her choice in men. According to OMEGA's hastily assembled dossier, she'd fallen for a jerk by the name of Donald Carter and let him talk her into taking this boring, if highly lucrative, job as a contract pilot in Mexico while he did his thing in Malaysia. In recent months said jerk had reportedly been getting his rocks off with a Malaysian newswoman.

It didn't take a NASA engineer to fit the pieces together. Obviously, Moore had just found out about her fiancé's affair. Just as obviously, she'd gone to the beach last night determined to flush the bastard out of her system.

Devlin wished to hell he'd been able to help with the flushing. The woman looked even better in the bright light of day than she had in the glow of the moon, and she'd looked damned good then! Her zippered flight suit didn't display her long, sexy legs the way her cutoffs had, but the tan fabric hugged her curves very nicely. Very nicely indeed. Devlin almost hated to depart for the oil rig.

Assuming he did depart. The issue looked doubtful at the moment, judging by the suspicion in Moore's brown eyes.

"Jorge!" Her face tight, she called to a mechanic

in grease-stained overalls. "Get our passengers briefed and strapped in. Devlin, you come with me."

She shoved the clipboard at the crew chief and stalked toward the corrugated tin hangar. Devlin followed, eyeing her trim behind with real appreciation.

"In here."

She led the way into an office with a beat-up metal desk, a single file cabinet and an ancient air conditioner rattling in the window. The walls were decorated with the usual clutter seen in operations shacks around the world. Weather updates. Flight schedules. Area NOTAMs. A fly-specked calendar depicting a luscious Miss May falling out of a blouse unbuttoned almost to her navel.

Devlin spared Miss May only a passing glance. Ms. Moore held his full attention. Her blunt-cut hair swirled in a silky arc as she slammed the door behind them and spun around.

The woman didn't waste time. Spearing him with a narrow-eyed stare, she launched a direct attack. "What were you doing on the beach last night?"

Devlin had anticipated this meeting since learning Moore's identity and had his cover ready. Luckily, it fit him like a second skin. Born and raised amid the oil fields of Oklahoma, he'd worked his way up from mud man to pipe handler to site supervisor. Along the way he'd accumulated undergraduate and graduate degrees in petroleum engineering and drilled holes in every ocean floor from the Gulf of Aden to the Bering Strait.

He'd also racked up a brief marriage and quick divorce. Candace had insisted his pay and benefits compensated for the long separations, but had soon gone looking for other distractions. Devlin didn't blame her. Divorce was an occupational hazard in his line of work.

His life had become even more erratic after he'd joined the OMEGA team. Nick Jensen, aka Lightning, had recruited him just months after terrorists blew up an American-operated rig in international waters off the coast of Kuwait. Devlin had lost friends in that explosion and had jumped at the chance to use his civilian cover as a means of bringing the murdering bastards to justice.

Now another friend had disappeared. A close friend. And a real badass who specialized in transporting underage aliens across the border to sell into sexual slavery had been picked up while using Harry Johnson's passport and ID. Law enforcement officials from a dozen different agencies had grilled the imposter but didn't get much. Turned out he'd never met the man who'd supplied the stolen documents. They'd been left at a designated drop site after the recipient had deposited a hefty sum in the same location.

Nor had Harry's body ever been recovered. All his fiancée knew, all anyone knew, was that Harry had disappeared after rotating off an AmMex oil rig, and someone using his passport had popped up on U.S. customs screens a few weeks later. What little intelligence OMEGA had been able to gather indicated the brains behind the ring supplying stolen passports operated out of this general vicinity. Devlin fully intended to nail the bastard. He wouldn't let anyone—Captain Moore included—jeopardize this mission.

Hitching a hip on the desk, he responded to her sharp question with a deliberate combination of fact and fiction. "I went to the beach last night to meet someone."

That part was true. What came next wasn't.

"He said he had a one-time good deal for me on personal gear for use on the rig."

"Why didn't he come to your hotel in to conduct this sale?"

"My guess is he lifted the equipment from a roustabout, either on the rig or after he came off."

That didn't happen often, but it did happen. Rig crews hailed from just about every country on the planet. That made communication a distinct challenge. Their staggered rotations also presented opportunities for high-dollar tools and unsecured personal items to disappear.

Still suspicious, Moore tapped a booted toe. "So who fired the shots? This light-fingered entrepreneur?"

"Maybe. Or maybe the man he stole from. The shooter had departed the scene when I reached his victim."

"This victim. Was he dead when you got to him?"

"He took a bullet between the eyes. You don't get much deader than that."

Her foot tapped the floor again. Once. Twice.

"You didn't kill him," she said, scowling. "I could have vouched for that. So why did you disappear?"

"I only arrived in Mexico with the replacement crew yesterday." Another lie, followed by another truth. "But I've been around enough to know you don't get mixed up in an incident like this unless you want to spend some not-so-quality time with the *federales*."

"So you left me to do the explaining?"

The disdain in her eyes stung. Devlin deflected it with a shrug. "I went back to look for you. You had departed the scene, too."

"Wrong! I ran up to my car to get my cell phone and call the police."

He hooked an incredulous brow. "And you hung around to wait for them?"

"Someone had to."

He let that pointed barb hang on the air for a moment before giving her a smile of genuine regret. "I have to admit, I had to think twice about leaving. If I'd stuck around, I might have gotten real lucky."

The ploy worked. The reminder of her rash vow brought her chin up and a flush to her cheeks.

"Not hardly, Devlin. You're not my type."

"Best I recall, you didn't specify a type last night."

The pink in her cheeks deepened to brick. "Yeah, well, that was last night."

He pushed off the desk and moved closer. She wasn't wearing a speck of makeup that he could see, but her gold-flecked brown eyes didn't need any goopy mascara to emphasize either their depth or their intelligence. And he had to admit the light dusting of freckles across her nose turned him on. That, and her unique scent. It drifted on an air-conditioned breeze, a tantalizing combination of soap and perspiration and aviation fuel.

He needed to keep her off balance, he reminded himself. Prevent her from probing too deeply. Throwing himself into the task, he gave her a wicked grin.

"How about this morning? Nothing says we can't take up where we left off."

"Oh, sure! With a rotation crew waiting outside in the heat?"

"I'm game if you are."

Liz shook her head, suspended between suspicion and disbelief. "You're something else, cowboy."

"Yes, ma'am. I do believe I've been told that once or twice."

She was damned if she could figure this guy out. He certainly looked like the roustabout he claimed to be. The sun had bleached his close-cut hair to golden brown. The white squint lines she'd noticed last night cut into skin tanned to dark oak by wind and sun. A couple days' stubble darkened his cheeks and chin, as if he was getting a head start on the bushy beard most of the crews sprouted while on the rig. Then there was the palm he slid under her hair to circle her nape. It was callused and leather tough.

Liz stiffened at the touch of his skin against hers.

Her eyes met his and telegraphed an unmistakable warning, which he ignored.

"If we can't finish what we started," he murmured, his gaze sliding downward to fix on her mouth, "how about we just settle for a kiss?"

Holding her in place with that thorny palm, he bent and brushed her lips with his.

Liz stood stiff, debating whether to whip up a knee or ream out his gut with her elbow. Devlin took full advantage of the hesitation, as brief as it was. Shifting his stance, he brought his mouth came down on hers with a hunger Liz hadn't tasted in seven months.

Or longer, she realized with a jolt as his lips molded hers. To her chagrin, she couldn't *remember* the last time a man had kissed her as if he meant it. Donny's affectionate pecks hadn't come close to packing this powerful a charge.

She savored the sizzle for a moment, maybe two, before breaking the contact. Feeling the loss of warmth immediately, she buried it in biting sarcasm.

"Finished flexing your masculinity, cowboy?"

"Guess so."

"Then I'll chalk this little interlude up to my stupid remark last night and let you walk out of here." She looked him square in the eye. "Touch me again without my permission, however, and you'll be drilling for something besides Mexican crude."

Spinning on her heel, she strode out into the smothering heat. Jorge was waiting beside the pad with a question in his eyes. Liz answered it with a small shake of her head and brisk order tossed over her shoulder to the man who'd followed her from the operations shack.

"Get aboard and buckle up."

Devlin joined his companions in the passenger compartment. Only after Liz had climbed into the cockpit and buckled her seat harness did she realize she'd bought his story about the supposed thief he'd gone to meet last night.

Frowning, she strapped on her kneeboard and forced herself to concentrate on the power-up sequence checklist. The engines whined. The forty-four feet of main rotor blades churned up dust, slowly at first, then in a reddish whirlwind. The aircraft began to shimmy as Liz radioed the tower.

Once she received clearance to taxi, her years of training and experience kicked in. Flying an aircraft that operated in both horizontal and vertical planes required a level of coordination not all pilots possessed. As always, getting her bird in the air and shifting smoothly from one plane to the other produced an adrenaline rush.

Her second in less than twenty minutes, Liz thought as she banked and aimed for the blue, sparkling Pacific. Her mouth still tingled from the kiss Devlin had laid on her.

Scowling behind her mirrored sunglasses, she set a course for floating the platform designated American-Mexican Petroleum Company Drill Site 237.

* * *

She must have made the run to AM-237 forty or fifty times in the past seven months. Every time, the sheer immensity of the ultradeepwater semisubmersible rig inspired awe. It was as big as a city block—a floating platform spiked by two giant cranes and a derrick that rose to impossible heights.

Anchored to the ocean floor by chains and 45,000-pound anchors, the superstructure sat on massive pontoons and four corner columns. Once the platform was positioned over a drill site, the columns were flooded with seawater. This caused the pontoons to sink to a predetermined depth and lessened the platform's surface movement, making it relatively stable.

Relative being the key word. To a pilot aiming for the helideck that jutted out over the rig's bow some seven stories above the water, even slight up and down movement had to be taken into consideration. The trick was to contact the helideck at its highest point and ride it down. Slamming into it on the way up stressed the landing gear and made the passengers just a tad nervous.

Liz chose a leeward approach and put the helo into a descending spiral a quarter of a mile out. The fat orange flanges for pumping the crude into tankers stood out like beacons on the east side. She lined up on the flanges to begin her final approach.

"AM-237, this is Aero Baja 214 on final."

"Roger, 214. We have you on the scope. We're putting out the welcome mat."

While the rig's two crane operators lowered the booms to clear the airspace, a support ship maneuvered into position at the pontoon closest to the helideck. The ship's mission was to pick up survivors if the incoming aircraft hit the drink instead of the deck.

"The LO is standing by."

The rig's landing officer climbed onto the pad, clearly visible in his bright yellow vest.

"I see him," Liz acknowledged.

Although this was only a secondary duty for him, she knew he'd been doing it a long time and trusted him to guide her in. Keeping one eye on his arm signals and another on the instrument panel, she put her aircraft into a hover above the deck and brought her down.

The skids touched, lifted and settled with a small thump. While the red-vested tie-down crew ducked under the blades to anchor the helicopter to the deck, Liz powered down. Once the blades had chugged to a halt, she keyed her mike.

"Welcome to AM-237, gentlemen."

Swinging a leg over the stick, she clambered into the cargo compartment.

"Claim your gear and pass it to the deckhands," she instructed the new arrivals. "Make sure you hang on to the lifelines when you climb out onto the pad."

The old-timers knew the drill, but there were questions in the eyes of a couple of obvious newcomers. Liz repeated the instructions in Spanish, then in elaborate pantomime. Looking both doubtful and nervous, the newbies poked their heads outside the hatch. Liz saw several Adam's apples bounce and knuckles turn white as the crewmen measured the distance from the pad to the ocean below.

"Don't piss yourself," the beefy Irishman advised one of the Venezuelans. "Just hang on to that strap. Out you go now, there's a good lad."

Since the brawny oilman supplemented his friendly words of encouragement with a solid thump between the shoulder blades, the cargo compartment soon emptied of everyone but Liz and Devlin. Passing his gear bag to a waiting deckhand, he turned back to her.

"How often do you make this run?"

"Five maybe six times a month. Depends on whether they need supplies or there's a crew rotating off."

"Maybe I'll see you on your next run."

"Maybe."

He took a step toward her, his sun-streaked hair ruffled by the wind whistling through the open hatch. "Do I have your permission?"

"My permission? For…? Oh! No, as a matter of fact, you don't. No touching, Devlin, and definitely no kissing."

"Sure you won't reconsider? It's going to be a long twenty-eight days out here."

"Just grin and bear it."

"I'll do my best."

Tipping her a two-fingered salute, he exited the aircraft and made his way to the stairs leading to the main deck.

Liz saw to the unloading of the replenishment supplies and accepted the sealed outgoing mail pouch, but instructed the landing officer to wait before bringing up the departing crew members.

"I need to talk to the company rep," she informed him, holding back her wind-whipped hair with one hand. "Do you know where he is?"

"Try the galley. Conrad is usually there this time of morning, swilling coffee and shooting off his... Er, shooting the breeze."

She gave the LO a wry smile. She'd dealt with AmMex Petroleum's on-site representative before. She had no doubt she would find him pontificating to anyone unfortunate enough to be stuck in his immediate vicinity.

She took the stairs, crossed the deck to the main superstructure and entered a world like none other. The ever-present reek of fresh paint and diesel fuel flavored the air. Machinery constantly in motion thumped out the rig's steady heartbeat. Metal creaked as the massive platform rode the waves.

The giant anchors and stabilizers minimized the motion until it was almost imperceptible, but Liz had to lay a palm against the bulkhead once or twice as she followed the scent of fried onions to the galley. Sure enough, the AmMex on-site rep was sprawled in a mess chair at the officers' table, holding forth.

Big and amiable and impervious to all attempts to shut him up, Conrad Wallace never seemed to tire of the sound of his own voice. Today's topic appeared to be a crew Ping-Pong tournament that evidently didn't come off to Wallace's satisfaction. The rig's Pakistani-born doctor sat across from him with a glazed expression on her face. When she spotted Liz, relief sprang into her eyes.

"Hello, Elizabeth. Did you bring the waterproof cast liners I ordered?"

"Sure did."

"What about the metronidazole tablets?"

"They're on back order, but marked priority. I'll fly them out as soon as they arrive."

"Thank you. I need them. Excuse me, Conrad. I must go inventory the new supplies."

She hurried out, leaving Liz to help herself to the coffee before joining Wallace at the gleaming teak table reserved for the rig's officers. The officers lived well out here on the patch, as did the hundred-plus crew members. Accommodations included hotel-class rooms, a galley that served international cuisine, a cinema showing satellite TV and movies and a gym that would get a gold stamp of approval from Arnold Schwarzenegger. Oil companies had to provide such facilities along with high-dollar salaries to induce men and women to live surrounded by miles of empty water for months at a time.

Cradling her coffee, Liz sank into a padded captain's chair. The company man shifted his bulk in her direction and picked up almost where he'd left off.

"We were talking about the fluke shot that won the

crew Ping-Pong tournament last night. Did anyone tell you about it?"

"No, I just got down."

"It was crazy. The ball ricocheted off a steam pipe, hit the forehead of one of the watchers and slammed back on the table. No way the referee should have allowed that shot, but you know how these foreigners are. They make up their own rules as they go."

Liz started to remind the man the rig sat in Mexican territorial waters and *he* was the foreigner here but didn't want to set him off on a new tangent. Instead, she cut straight to the point.

"I need an advance on next month's salary."

Wallace blinked at the abrupt change of topic and pursed his lips. Liz recognized his pinched expression. She categorized it as his company face.

"Payday was last week," he pontificated, as if she weren't well aware of that basic fact. "Don't tell me you've already run through the exorbitant flight pay AmMex shells out to you."

Her supposedly "exorbitant" flight pay was an old issue, one that came up every time Liz renewed her contract.

"What I did with my pay is my business, Conrad."

Frowning at the cool reply, Wallace shifted in his seat. He was a big man, but soft around the middle. Not lean and hard like the roughnecks who wrestled pipe or the roustabouts who performed general maintenance work.

Not like Joe Devlin.

Irritated at the way the man kept popping into her head, Liz laid out her requirement. "I need six hundred."

Living was considerably cheaper in Mexico than in the States, thank goodness. That amount would cover the payment due on the loan and get her though to the next payday with no problem.

"Six hundred?" Wallace echoed, looking as horrified as a man asked to sacrifice his firstborn child.

Liz should have known he'd balk. The man managed a multimillion-dollar operating budget, yet was so tight he squeaked when he walked.

"You know, Conrad, you're the perfect company man. You think every cent you dole out comes out of your own pocket."

"Well, it does! Anything that impacts the company's bottom line affects its profit margin, which in turn affects its stock value. Since I receive a large portion of my compensation and retirement in stock options, I'm obligated—"

"I know the spiel," Liz interrupted ruthlessly. It was the only way to get through to the man. "You're obligated to act as a responsible guardian of company funds. Are you going to give me the six hundred or not?"

"All right. All right. I will. But you'll have to sign a voucher. Let's go down to my office."

Liz lifted her bird off the patch a half hour later with a check for the six hundred zippered into her jumpsuit pocket and an exuberant crew strapped into the passenger compartment.

Ahead stretched forty minutes of open sea. Liz had flown the route so many times she could put her conscious mind on autopilot and switch her thoughts to the mess Donny had landed her in.

She thought briefly of hiring a lawyer and going after him. Pride and utter disgust at her own stupidity quashed that idea. She'd just have to tough it out down here in Mexico for a while longer. If she watched her pennies, she should be able to repay the loan she'd taken out for that blasted nonrefundable deposit and get back on her feet within a few months.

Which meant she'd probably ferry Devlin back to shore when he rotated off the patch.

Hell, there he was again! Bouncing around inside her head like a damned yo-yo. She couldn't seem to get him out. Or his outrageous offer of stud service.

What the heck. If Liz *did* ferry him back to shore a few weeks from now, maybe she should take him up on the offer. She didn't quite trust the man. And she wasn't sure she bought his story about last night's events. Yet she had to admit the kiss he'd laid on her this morning had curled her toes inside her boots.

Like a DVD played in digital high definition, she saw again the glint in Devlin's eyes as he bent toward her, felt the heat of his mouth on hers and cursed herself for being a fool.

Dumped less than ten hours ago by one man and

here she was, fantasizing about another! How many kinds of an idiot did that make her?

Thoroughly disgusted, Liz skimmed her bird toward the postcard-perfect shoreline.

The men poured out as soon as the skids touched down and Jorge set the chocks. Most clutched e-tickets and were eager to get through customs and onto the bus to La Paz. Once there, they'd board the jets that would carry them to homes scattered from the Azores to the Strait of Malacca. A few intended to head for town and the women who would soon relieve them of a healthy portion of their accumulated pay. First they had to be cleared by the Mexican official who routinely met Liz's incoming flight.

Today there were two officials. She recognized the bored-looking bureaucrat who usually rubber-stamped the crew's papers. The other she hadn't seen before.

"What's up?" she asked Jorge as she hefted the mail pouch from the empty copilot's seat. "Why the extra *funcionario?*"

"I do not know."

Interesting. Maybe Devlin's story had basis in fact. Maybe a deckhand *had* stolen some valuable equipment and authorities were now shaking down all crews coming off the rig. Funny Wallace didn't mention the theft to her, though. The company rep was such a motormouth about everything else.

"Perhaps it has something to do with this," Jorge said.

He dragged a folded piece of paper from the pocket

of his overalls. It was a flier with a Xerox photo of a man Liz didn't recognize. Her eyes widened as she translated the Spanish under the picture.

"Does this say what I think it does?"

"¡*Sí!* There is a reward. Fifty thousand pesos for information about whoever shot this man last night."

"Last night, huh?"

Liz licked suddenly dry lips. The image of a body floating in the surf jumped into her head.

"This is Martín Alvarez," Jorge said grimly.

The name didn't register. Her expression must have indicated as much, as Jorge clicked his tongue like a hyperactive cricket.

"Ayyyyy, Lizetta! You do not know him?"

"No."

"He is the nephew of Eduardo Alvarez. The one known as El Tiburón."

El Tiburón. The Shark. *That* registered.

Goose bumps prickled Liz's skin. Gulping, she stared at the grainy photo of the nephew of one of the biggest, baddest members of the Mexican mafia.

Three

El Tiburón. The nickname echoed in Liz's head all day. She'd heard about the man from various sources during her months in Mexico, and what she'd heard was *not* good.

She drove home after work to peel off her sweat-soaked flight suit and to shower. Cool and comfortable in flip-flops, jeans and sleeveless cotton blouse, she got back in the Jeep and navigated the narrow streets to her favorite cantina for dinner. A few tourists wandered through the shops, but most had retreated to the luxury resorts strung along the cliffs for cocktails by the pool.

El Poco Lobo was crowded with shop owners, street vendors and boatmen back from fishing charters and swim or snorkeling tours. The locals jammed elbow to elbow at the smoky bar. Empty Corona bottles filled with red pebbles formed a pyramid against the flyspecked mirror backing the bar. Liz usually ate at one of the rickety tables outside, but the cantina owner waved her inside.

"Hola, Elizabeth."

"Hola, Anita."

Avid interest filled the woman's black eyes. "Is it true what we hear? You were at the beach last night?"

"Yes. What's the special this evening?"

"Beans and roast pork. I will get you a dish and you will tell us what happens, yes?"

Hunching over her heaping plate of succulent *carne asada*, Liz did her best to play down her role in the night's events. Yes, she'd heard the shots, she said in a reprise of her conversation with Subcommandante Rivera. No, she didn't see who fired them. And no, she didn't know who'd been shot until Jorge told her this morning.

She managed to dodge most of the more persistent of her questioners. Unfortunately, she couldn't dodge the two men who were waiting for her when she parked her Jeep in its usual place under the droopy jacaranda tree that shaded the stairs to her apartment.

The two tough-looking strangers stepped from behind the massive, twisted trunk. One was short and squat and walked with a limp. The other wore a lavender shirt, pleated black slacks and black-and-white wingtip shoes. The wingtips were bad enough. The shoulder holster he didn't bother to conceal was worse.

"El Tiburón wishes to speak with you," the shorter of the two said in English.

"What if I don't wish to speak with El Tiburón?"

The men obviously considered the question rhetorical, as neither bothered to answer. Nor did they seem particularly worried about the hand she'd slipped into the side pocket of the driver's door. She discovered why when Wingtips produced the collapsible baton she usually kept there.

"Is this what you search for?"

With a small smile, he passed her the baton and folded himself into the Jeep's cramped backseat. Short Guy settled in the front passenger seat.

"Take the coast road south, toward Cabo San Lucas. We will tell you where to turn off."

Liz weighed her options. She could refuse to comply but suspected that might result in something unpleasant. Like a gun barrel whacked up alongside her head. She could try shouting for help while wielding the baton, which would no doubt result in similar consequences. Or she could go along for the ride.

Shrugging, she rekeyed the ignition and backed out from under the tree. As she negotiated the narrow space, she regretted swinging by her apartment to change after work. Flip-flops and jeans weren't exactly what she would have chosen to wear for a meeting with the local mafia king. Not that the flight suit would have provided much more protection against an Uzi. Wishing fervently for a bulletproof vest, Liz took the coast road toward Cabo.

The Pacific sparkled on her left. To her right, cactus speared out of the sunbaked Baja desert. As they neared the tip of the peninsula, the cliffs lining the shore grew more rugged and the resorts more opulent. Some kilometers past Todos Santos, Short Guy directed her to turn onto a gravel road. This led to a high-walled adobe fence. Broken glass shards in a variety of greens and browns provided a jagged barrier atop the adobe. Rolled concertina wire added another welcoming touch to the vicious glass.

Liz slowed before an elaborately carved iron gate. Her escort waved to the armed guards manning the thatch-roofed shack at the entrance. When they obligingly hit the switch, the gates swung open to reveal an avenue of tall, swaying palms. They shut behind the Jeep with a clank that resounded in Liz's ears like a clap of doom.

Wrapping her sweaty palms around the wheel, she followed the drive through the kind of tropical paradise usually seen only at five-star resorts. Lush green grass was manicured to within an inch of its life. Bushes exploded with red and pink and orange bougainvillea. Fountains splashed at regular intervals.

At the end of the drive sat a sprawling adobe structure constructed from the native ochre-colored mud. The wood trim at the windows and doors was painted almost the same shade of turquoise as the Sea of Cortez on a sunny day. Escorted by Short Guy and

Wingtips, Liz exited the Jeep and stepped out of the blazing sun into a blessedly cool foyer.

"This way."

Her flip-flops slapped against beautifully glazed marble tiles as she passed through a succession of open, airy rooms before being ushered into what could have passed for a Wall Street executive's office. Stock quotes flashed across the plasma TV screen hung on one wall. A state-of-the art pedestal computer with a twenty-three-inch monitor sat on the massive slab of glass that served as a desk. The only personal touch was what looked like a family photo in a silver frame.

The snapshot had been taken aboard a gleaming white yacht. A trim, athletic-looking man in swimming trunks lounged in a deck chair. He looked relaxed and happy, an arm hooked around the shoulders of the woman lounging next to him. She laughed up at him while two children—kids? grandkids?—stood behind them and mugged for the camera.

The woman was draped in enough jewelry to open her own branch of Tiffany's. A rock the size of Rhode Island sparkled on her ring finger. The diamond studs in her ears had to have weighed two carats each. Her gold Rolex was studded with sapphires.

The man beside her wore only a gold chain with some kind of charm hooked through it. The pale, triangular object nestled against his dark chest hair. It was a shark's tooth, Liz realized with a gulp. From what had to be one hell of a fish. Scenes from the movie *Jaws* were flashing through her head when a side door opened.

The man who entered was the same one in the photo. Tall and trim, with neatly cut salt-and-pepper hair, he wore tan slacks and a short-sleeved white shirt with an embroidered monogram on the breast pocket.

"Welcome to my home, Ms. Moore."

He held out his hand. Liz offered hers more slowly. He didn't *look* as though he intended to chop it off. Then again, The Shark had a reputation for devouring his enemies whole.

"Thank you for agreeing to speak with me."

"Did I have a choice?"

"One always has a choice. Please, be seated."

He waved her to one of the leather chairs grouped around a glass coffee table and took the other.

"Would you care for a drink after your long drive? We have Dos Equis on ice. I believe that is the brand you prefer."

Uh-oh. This guy knew her preference in beer. A shiver slithered down Liz's spine as she wondered what else he knew about her.

A bunch, she learned after she politely declined refreshment.

"So," he said, "we shall get right to business. A friend who works with the local constabulary tells me you reported a shooting on the beach near Piedras Rojas last night."

"Yes," Liz replied cautiously, "I did."

"According to this friend, you saw a man floating in the surf."

"That's correct."

His gaze locked with hers across the glass coffee table. "That man was my nephew."

Liz searched his eyes for some sign of pain or grief. If he was feeling either, it didn't show. Still, she offered her condolences.

"I'm sorry for your loss."

"It is my sister who weeps."

Another shiver danced along Liz's spine. If she remembered correctly, sharks were cold-blooded fish who often ate their young.

"You told the police you did not see who shot Martín?" Alvarez commented.

"That's right. I was some way down the beach. I heard the shots and ran to see what happened."

"You are very brave to run toward the sound of gunfire," he said slowly. "Or very foolish."

Liz had already decided B was the correct answer. Devlin had the right idea. She should have disappeared into the night.

"There was another man," Alvarez said, as if reading her mind. "An Americano. You did not tell the police his name."

"I didn't know it. We bumped into each other just a few seconds before we heard the shots and never got around to introductions."

It was the truth, as far as it went. She and Devlin hadn't gotten around to names *last night*. Resisting the urge to swipe her palms on her jeans-clad thighs, Liz waited for Alvarez to rephrase the question and ask if she had any idea as to the American's identity. Instead, he knocked her completely off balance with a cool remark.

"I understand you have taken a loan with Citibank for $20,000 to make a down payment on a helicopter. The fourth payment on that loan is due in three days."

Liz didn't bother to ask how the heck this guy knew her personal financial arrangements. She suspected he was supremely unconcerned about such things as confidentiality laws.

"Tell me exactly what you saw on the beach, Ms. Moore. If it helps me to locate my nephew's killer, I shall wipe out that debt for you."

"What?"

Liz sucked in a breath. An image of the Sikorsky streaked into her head. Six hundred and fifty horsepower of lift. Low noise factor, almost no vibration. Luxury leather seats for the passengers. Enough avionics to make even the most seasoned pilot drool.

The chopper would be hers. All hers. She could thumb her nose in Donny's and Bambang's faces. All she had to do was reiterate what she told the police, give this guy Devlin's name and let him squeeze what information he could out of the roustabout.

Liz had no idea what held her back. Maybe it was the thought of wading deeper into a swamp she might never slog out of. Or the utter lack of familial concern in Alvarez's black eyes.

"I told the police exactly what I saw."

"Tell me. I wish to hear it from you."

"There was a shot. No, two shots. The man, the Americano, shoved me down. Then he got up and ran in the direction of the gunfire. I followed and saw him standing over what looked like a body. Then I ran for my car to get my cell phone and call the police."

"The Americano was standing over the body?"

"That's right."

Alvarez touched fingertip to fingertip and rested his chin on the steeple. Seconds slid by, stretching Liz's nerves wire thin.

"My nephew was carrying something that belonged to me, Ms. Moore. Something that was not on his body, according to the police. I want it back."

Any inclination, however slight, to tell Alvarez about Joe Devlin evaporated at that point. The man didn't give a crap about his nephew. Just this piece of property, whatever it was.

"I didn't take anything off your nephew, if that's what you're suggesting. I waited up by my vehicle for the police to arrive. I never got close to the body."

The Shark said nothing for another second or two. Just studied her with those black predator's eyes.

"I want you to think very hard. Is there any detail you might have missed? Some bit of information that would enable me to locate this item?"

This guy was creeping her out. Somehow Liz managed a shrug. "I've told you everything I saw or heard."

He kept her pinned by that unblinking gaze for several more moments, then gave a curt nod.

"Very well. The offer stands, however. If you should think of some detail that enables me to find Martín's killer and this property I mentioned, I will pay off your loan. Juan, show Ms. Moore to her car, if you please."

Liz drove back to Piedras Rojas in a puddle of sweat, torn between relief that she'd survived her meeting with The Shark and the dead certainty that this mess wasn't over.

"Damn you, Devlin! I hope I don't live to regret covering your ass."

That worry was still hovering at the back of her mind two days later when a delivery van drove up to Aero Baja's operations center. Liz signed for the package and sought out AB's chief mechanic.

"Let's gas up the Ranger, Jorge. This is the back-ordered medicine Doc Metwani needs. It's marked priority, so I'm going to fly it out to the patch."

"Have you checked weather? There is a front forming."

"I saw it. They're forecasting thirty-knot winds with eight- to twelve-foot seas. I should be able to make it out and back before things get too bad."

Or at least make it out. If necessary, Liz could tie down and ride out the storm. It wouldn't be the first night she'd spent on the rig, or probably the last. And, she thought with a combination of anticipation and determination, an overnighter would give her a chance to have a nice long chat with a certain roughneck.

Ducking into the tiny cubicle laughingly referred to as the pilot's lounge, she spun the combination on her locker and traded her jeans and T-shirt for Aero Baja's mud-brown flight suit. The civilian clothes went into her gear bag, along with a plastic bag of toiletries.

She spent the first half of the flight thinking about the questions she wanted to ask Devlin, the second fighting the storm that blew up faster and fiercer than the forecasters had predicted. Rain lashed the windshield, the ceiling dropped to two hundred feet and the winds were a bitch by the time the LO waved Liz down and the skids touched.

The rig's tie-down crew was waiting in their bright red vests. While Liz completed the shut-down sequence, the crew secured the helo and extended the retractable hangar. Once her aircraft was protected from the elements, Liz ducked out of the rain and now howling wind.

"Looks like you'll have to ride out the storm with us tonight," the rig's quartermaster said as he signed for the medicine.

"Looks like."

"You know where the guest quarters are. Pick a bunk and make yourself comfortable."

Liz stowed her gear bag in the room set aside for transients and made a quick visit to the head before navigating the narrow corridors to the galley. It was just after shift change, so the first rotation was chowing down. The babble of conversations carried on in a half-dozen different languages rose above the thump, thump, thump of the rig's heartbeat.

Liz scanned the thirty or so men and handful of women present. She didn't spot the wide-shouldered American she sought, so she approached the big, brawny Irishman who'd rotated out to the patch with him. The driller looked up with a cheerful smile on his face as she approached.

"Back so soon, lass?"

"Had to deliver some medicines Doc Metwani needed. I'm looking for Joe Devlin. Have you seen him?"

"He was late coming off the deck. He's probably still in his cabin cleaning up."

She could wait. Or she could get some answers out of him in private. Liz chose option two.

Retracing her steps, she traversed the monstrous recreation/entertainment center that constituted the rig's social hub. Long hallways led off in both directions. Devlin's cabin was in the officers' wing and had only his name on the plate beside the door. Liz eyed the brass plate with its slip-in label thoughtfully.

Like the military and most other large organizations, offshore rigs operated under a strict hierarchical structure. Petroleum engineers planned and supervised overall operations. Drilling superintendents were in charge of the deck crews, which consisted of four or five drillers, derrick operators and the roughnecks who muscled the pipe into place. Less skilled roustabouts performed general maintenance tasks. Then there were the pumpers, acidizers, sample takers, welders, electricians and machinists, along with a support team that included the rig's officers, radio operators, cooks, barge operators and a medical contingent.

That Devlin rated private quarters meant he ranked fairly high in the organizational structure. Impressed despite herself, Liz rapped on the door and got a muffled shout in response.

"It's open!"

Once inside, she was greeted with the splash of running water and a gruff call from the head.

"Hang loose. I'll be right out."

She used the interval to take a quick look around. His cabin was like all the others on the rig, just a little more spacious. The built-in lockers, bunk, desk and chair were compliments of the American-Mexican Petroleum Company. So were standard-issue items that littered the cabin. A hard hat and safety goggles sat on the desk. Steel-toed boots were positioned beside the chair. A set of grease-stained overalls lay in a discarded heap, waiting to be stuffed into the laundry bag hanging from the locker handle.

Since the crews rotated every twenty-eight days and space was at a premium, they generally brought few personal items besides tools, photos and the occasional CD player, iPod, or laptop. Devlin's was a sleek, titanium-encased model that raised instant envy in Liz's breast.

Drawn by the brilliant screensaver images flashing across the liquid crystal display, she nudged a hip against the desk. But it was the Beanie bear propped next to the computer that snagged her attention. The poor guy looked as though he'd gone a few rounds with a real live grizzly and come out the loser. One ear had been torn and restitched by hand. His button eyes didn't match. The red ribbon around his neck must have once formed a neat bow, but the ends now hung limp and ragged and stained.

Interesting, Liz thought. She'd checked the next-of-kin information Devlin had provided before she'd flown him out to the patch. He'd listed a brother in Oklahoma. No wife or kids. And he certainly hadn't struck Liz as the type to tote along a childhood toy to keep him company for a month.

"So who did you belong to?" she asked, lifting the sad-eyed bear until they were nose to nose.

"The son of a friend."

The gruff reply spun Liz around. Devlin stood framed in the door to the bathroom, his chest bare. A flat, hard belly showed above the waist of his low-riding jeans. His hair was still wet and tobacco brown from his shower. His hazel eyes registered something that looked very close to suspicion.

"What are you doing here?"

It wasn't the greeting she'd expected. Particularly after the kiss this guy had laid on her back in Piedras Rojas.

"I want to talk to you."

Moving with the same, pantherlike grace that had struck her that night on the beach, he crossed the cabin, removed the bear from her hand and returned it to its comfortable slouch against the laptop. His expression wasn't particularly friendly when he faced her again.

"What about?"

Liz didn't understand *or* appreciate his attitude. Folding her arms, she gave him a saccharine smile.

"How about the fact that two thugs forced me to drive at gunpoint to the house of a seriously unnice guy? Turns out that floater you found was the nephew of El Tiburón."

His brows slashed into a quick frown. Obviously, he'd heard of The Shark.

"Are you okay?"

"I'm here, aren't I?"

Still frowning, he caught her chin and tipped her face from side to side. Checking for bruises, Liz assumed, and was immediately irritated by the heat his touch generated. So irritated she almost forgot the promise she'd made back in Piedras Rojas.

Almost.

"You don't listen very well, do you, cowboy?"

The sudden widening of his eyes told Liz he got the message a mere second or two before she brought her knee up. Devlin deflected the nut-cruncher just in time and took the jab on the tender inside of his thigh instead.

She saw his jaw lock, saw the muscle that jumped in one cheek and braced herself for some form of retaliation. It didn't come.

Liz had to admit the control he exerted over himself was impressive as hell. And just a little scary. His hazel eyes shot bullets, but he subdued the beast within and backed off with just a pained grunt.

"Damn, woman! You pack some punch with that knee."

"I warned you," Liz said coolly.

"Yeah, you did."

Eyeing her with a combination of wariness and respect, he took the conversation back to the precontact stage. "What did The Shark want with you?"

"Two things. His main concern was locating some object his nephew supposedly had with him when he died. It didn't show up among the possessions the police returned."

Devlin forgot about the spiking ache on the inside of his thigh. His botched rendezvous had suddenly taken on another twist.

OMEGA control had briefed him on the corpse's identity. Martín Alvarez had racked up a five-page rap sheet but had managed to beat every charge from drug trafficking to running prostitutes to shooting a farmer's entire litter of pigs just for the fun of hearing them squeal. Devlin was sorry he hadn't put that bullet between the goon's eyes himself.

He ran a quick mental inventory of the items he'd found during his search of the body. Martín had been carrying nothing of any significance besides that roll of pesos. Was that what The Shark wanted back? The money?

Devlin didn't think so. He'd received a thorough area brief before this op. He knew El Tiburón controlled the crime on this entire stretch of the coast. That wad of pesos wouldn't even constitute pocket change for the man.

Glancing up, Devlin caught Liz studying him with more than a trace of suspicion. "I didn't lift anything off the body," he said flatly.

"Someone did."

"Maybe it was the man who shot him. Or the police. Or someone in the coroner's office. Or you," he tacked on.

A shudder rippled through her. "Trust me on this. If I'd helped myself to a souvenir of that night, I would have returned it during my visit to Casa Alvarez."

Devlin's conscience did some serious pinging. He still regretted melting into the night and leaving this woman holding the bag. Looked like that bag was bigger and heavier and dirtier than either of them had anticipated.

"You said The Shark wanted two things. What was the second?"

"The name of the Americano who was with me that night."

Well, hell! Talk about your botched operations. This one had already gotten off to a shaky start. Devlin had a feeling it was about to completely blow apart. The Shark wouldn't swallow the story he'd fed Liz about going out to buy stolen tools.

"Did you give him my name?"

"No."

"Why not?"

"Damned if I know. But El Sharko offered me some serious bucks for information leading to the recovery of this object, whatever it is."

Her chin angled. Her brown eyes speared into him. Devlin was wondering how the hell the woman could look so belligerent and so kissable at the same time when she laid matters on the line.

"We're talking *very* big bucks here. I might just do some name dropping unless you tell me the truth about why you were on that beach."

So much for her swallowing the stolen-tool story! Devlin wouldn't make the mistake of underestimating this woman again. Going with his instincts, he told her as much of the truth as he could.

"I went to meet an informant."

Four

"Informant?"

Liz chewed on her lower lip and processed that for several seconds. A dozen possibilities kicked around inside her head. Some put Joe Devlin on the side of the good guys. Some left the issue in serious doubt.

"Was Martín Alvarez the informant you were going to meet?"

"No. As far as I know, Alvarez was an uninvited visitor to the scene. The theory is he spooked my guy, who proceeded to plug him between the eyes and disappear."

"The theory, huh?"

Liz was feeling goosier by the second. Red warning flares shot off like rockets. Her sensible, cautious inner self shouted at her to turn around and leave now, before she got in any deeper. Trouble was, she rarely listened to her sensible, cautious self. If she did, she wouldn't be saddled with an absent ex-fiancé, a bitch of a debt and the memory of El Sharko's flat, black eyes drilling into her.

"I think you'd better start at the beginning, Devlin. I want to know who you are and why you're on this rig."

"This could take a while. What time are you scheduled to make the return flight?"

"Guess you haven't stuck your head outside in the past hour or so. A good-size front has moved in. My aircraft and I are hangared in for the night."

Liz tossed the information off without thinking. Devlin's response was slower and almost as annoying as the speculation that leaped into his eyes.

"Is that so?"

Dammit! How could the man make her skin prickle with just a few drawled syllables?

"Yes, that's so." She tapped a foot. "Anytime you're ready, cowboy."

His gaze went past her. The speculation went out of his face, replaced by a hard edge. Liz looked to one side and saw he'd fixed his sights on the ragged Beanie bear.

"I told you that belongs to the son of a friend of mine," he said. "She was engaged to another friend. Harry Johnson."

"Was?"

"Harry rotated off an AmMex rig several months ago. He never made it home."

Liz scoured her mind. She ferried men back and forth every week. A few of the more gregarious—and more obnoxious—stood out in her memory. She didn't remember a Harry Johnson fitting into either category.

"Was he on this patch?"

"He was on AM-251, further south."

She knew the rig. Smaller than 237, it was serviced by one of Aero Baja's competitors.

"What happened to your friend?"

"No one knows. He disappeared."

Liz digested that information with an internal wince. "You said he was engaged. Men have been known to change their minds about little inconsequential matters like marriage. I speak from experience, you understand."

The hard edges of Devlin's face softened for a second or two. "Yeah, I got that impression the other night. Your fiancé must be a real jerk."

"Ex-fiancé, and you won't get any argument from me on that. Back to your friend. I still don't understand. If you're looking for information about him, why are you working here instead of 251?"

"Because agents from the San Diego FBI office busted a man using Harry's name and passport a few weeks ago. The bastard was running nine- and ten-year-olds across the border and selling them to brothels."

Liz zinged a glance at the Beanie bear. How awful

that a vicious child abuser would steal the identity of a man about to acquire a young son through marriage. His fiancée must have died when she heard about it.

"We now know at least two other AmMex crew members have disappeared under similar circumstances," Devlin said, his voice tight. "Both were single, with no close relatives to report them missing. Harry was pretty quiet about his personal life. Only a handful of his friends knew he was dating Evie, let alone that he'd asked her to marry him. We suspect he was targeted for that reason. We also suspect whoever fingered him operates off this rig."

"Why?"

He raked a hand through his hair and frowned at the water that dripped from his fingers. He must have forgotten he'd just stepped out of the shower. With half an acre of male chest staring her in the face, Liz was all too conscious of that minor detail.

"The informant I was meeting that night on the beach supposedly knew someone willing to supply U.S. passports for the right price. He hinted the seller was local. Our information suggests he or she also had direct access to AmMex personnel."

He didn't put any particular emphasis on the feminine pronoun, but it hit Liz like a marline spike.

"Whoa! You don't think *I* was out the on the beach to sell stolen passports, do you?"

"We considered the possibility," he admitted without a trace of apology. "The background investigation we ran on you suggested otherwise. That," he added, hooking one brow, "and the vow I overheard you make."

"You're not ever going to let me forget that, are you?"

His grin slipped out, quick and all male. "What do you think?"

"I think I'll choose a more private setting the next time I let rip," Liz muttered before latching onto his previous statement. "You keep saying 'our' and 'we.' Are you working this problem for AmMex or someone else?"

"Let's just say a few top officials at AmMex know why I was hired on for this rotation."

Lord, he was slippery! Liz wasn't sure she believed him even now. Before she could quiz him further, however, a heavy fist pounded on his cabin door. He opened it to a roustabout in a hard hat and soaked AmMex coveralls.

The deckhand's glance widened when he spotted Liz, but the apparent urgency of his mission shifted his attention right back to Devlin. "Castlemaine needs you on the drill deck. The heavy seas are torquing line number two."

"Hell!" Whirling, Devlin snagged a clean set of overalls from a locker. "This could take a while," he said to Liz. "You want to wait here?"

"I'll grab something to eat and hang with the guys for a while. If you're too late, you can find me in the transient quarters."

She left him dragging on the overalls and returned

to the galley for a late dinner. She had to fight to keep her coffee from sloshing into her plate of curried rice and chicken before staggering down the hall toward the crew lounge. At the far end she spotted a surprised Conrad Wallace.

"What are you doing here?" the AmMex rep asked, shouldering the walls as he navigated the narrow corridor.

"I delivered the medicine Doc Metwani had on back order."

Wallace's lips pinched. Liz had no doubt he was calculating the fuel costs of an unscheduled flight. Tough. She was in no mood for one of his long-winded lectures.

"I'm flying out in the morning," she said, squeezing past his bulk. "Let me know if you have any mail or reports to ferry back."

The front seemed to settle right over the rig. Rain pounded the deck and waves crashed against the four giant columns. The rig's ever-present creaking rose in both pitch and volume until it sounded an unceasing chorus.

Inured to the groaning and creaking, off-duty crew members were engrossed in a movie in the rec center and invited Liz to join them. She enjoyed the action sequences, but the sex was a little too over the top for her tastes. She left the men to their semiporn and retreated to the transient quarters to wait for Devlin.

After a quick shower, she slipped into her favorite T-shirt, tossed her jeans over a nearby chair and stretched out on her bunk. Like most pilots, she'd trained herself to sleep in odd places at irregular hours. She intended just a quick nap, the kind of light doze that usually satisfied her body's immediate needs. She didn't count on the swaying motion of the rig, however. Within moments she was rocked into total unconsciousness.

She had no idea how long she'd been out when someone rapped on the cabin door. "Whoizzit?"

"Devlin."

Still half-asleep, she fumbled for the door lock. Her semiconscious brain registered little more than the fact that he'd shed his coveralls and now wore the shirt he'd been missing when she'd surprised him in his cabin a while ago. The well-washed denim looked as soft as cotton.

"Did you get line two untorqued?"

He didn't answer for several moments. It took Liz that long to connect his silence with the fact that she'd forgotten to pull on her jeans. Her first hint was the slow trip his gaze made from the hem of her T-shirt to her bare feet. Her second, his husky drawl.

"Two's untorqued. Can't say the same for myself at the moment."

Fully awake now, Liz tried hard for irritation. With her skin tingling everywhere his glance touched, though, all she could manage was a half-hearted indignation.

"Oh, for pity's sake! Get a grip, cowboy. I'm covered from neck to midthigh."

"Not a problem." Closing the door behind him, he flicked the lock. "We can remedy that quick enough."

The glint in his eyes clogged Liz's breath. She crossed the room with the vague intention of putting some space between them. "Careful," she warned. "Remember what happened last time you didn't ask first?"

"I remember."

He strolled across the cabin and propped both hands on the upper bunk, caging Liz between them. None of their body parts made contact. They didn't need to. His heat seemed to arc across those few inches, searing her through the thin cotton of her T-shirt.

"Permission to come aboard, Captain?"

Liz pulled in another breath, this one flavored with the tang of the saltwater glistening on Devlin's skin. She could think of a hundred reasons to refuse his request. She didn't really know this man, wasn't sure she believed everything he'd told her. And she sure as hell didn't want to get dragged any deeper into this dangerous business he hinted at.

Yet she couldn't deny he acted on her like a spark plug. Every time he got close, he transmitted an electrical energy that fired Liz's internal engine. She could feel her skin warming. Her pulse was revving faster than a main rotor at full throttle. Still, she was pretty sure she would have denied his request if the rig had remained stable.

It didn't pitch much. Only a few degrees. Just

enough to send Liz staggering forward a step, smack into Devlin's denim-covered chest.

He kept one hand anchored on the upper bunk. His other arm whipped around her waist. A slow smile spread across his face, creasing the tanned skin, crinkling the white lines at the corners of his eyes.

"I'll take that as a yes," he said, the laughter in his voice edged with a husky note that had Liz's toes curling into the deck.

She could have ended it there. Knew he'd back off if she said the word. To her profound disgust, she couldn't push out a single syllable.

She wanted this. The feel of his arms around her. The sudden heat bubbling in her blood. Had wanted it since the night on the beach, when he'd appeared out of the darkness and tempered her anger and her hurt with his cocky grin and outrageous offer.

Liz had all of two seconds to wonder if she'd lost her mind before he tightened his arm, bent his head and covered her mouth with his. She'd question her sanity later, she decided, when she got back to dry land. Right now her world had narrowed to the deck rocking beneath her feet and the solid male overwhelming her senses.

She could feel him against every inch of her body. Hear the catch to his breath as his mouth moved over hers. See the hunger that stretched his skin taut across his cheeks when he worked her T-shirt up to bare her breasts.

"I've pictured you like this a dozen times since we met," he said, his voice rough.

Since they'd met only a few nights ago, the gruff admission stroked Liz's ego even as his hand stroked her eager flesh. His callused palm was rough against her skin, his thumb gentle and incredibly skilled as it teased her nipple. The sensations streaked straight from her breast to her belly. Her vaginal muscles tightened, producing another set of sensations.

Liz's breath was coming hard and fast when she decided it was time to level the playing field. With her blood pounding and her nerve endings snapping, she attacked the buttons of his shirt.

"You know this is crazy," she muttered as she traced the contours of his shoulders and biceps with her palms. He gave a little grunt when one palm slid south, inside the waistband of his jeans.

"Yeah, I know."

His hands were all over her. Liz's locked around the length of steel poking at her belly. Sliding her fingers to the base of his shaft, she toyed with his taut sac before retracing a path along his hot, smooth length to the tip.

She was thinking that he more than lived up to the oil rig crews' reputations for supersize derricks when he shed the rest of his clothes and rid her of hers. Locked together, they tumbled to the lower bunk. Unlike the bunks aboard navy vessels, these were long and wide enough to sleep the roughnecks who regularly muscled thousand-pound lengths of pipe into place.

Thank God!

Liz was no shrimp herself. Together, she and Devlin filled the confined space between the bunks. Which made for some *extremely* stimulating friction as they traded kiss for kiss and tongue for tongue. Then his hand cupped her mound and his fingers found her slick flesh. Parting the folds, he played with her hard, tight nub.

Within moments Liz was ready to fly. She hooked a leg over his, straining against him. He got the message.

"Okay," he panted, groping for the jeans lying on the floor next to the bunk. "All right. Just hang tight a sec."

As if Liz could do anything else! His shoulder squashed hers into the mattress. His knee was wedged between her thighs. Using an elbow for leverage, he propped himself up to wrestle a condom out of its package and onto his straining flesh.

Liz observed his contortions with a wry smile. "Planned ahead, did you?"

"Yes, ma'am." His grin was fast and unrepentant as he repositioned himself between her thighs. "I told you. I've been thinking about this since the night we met."

If she hadn't believed him before, she certainly did now. With his body poised above hers, and every inch of her skin pulsating with anticipation, she could hardly do otherwise. She was ready when he eased into her, wet and welcoming when he sank home.

Devlin took it slow. *Very* slow. His blood was pounding with the force of a rotary drill boring through solid rock and his body had pretty much taken over from his brain. If he didn't keep the pace deliberate, he'd blow like an uncapped West Texas gusher.

The small corner of his rational mind that still functioned kept insisting Liz was right. This was crazy. Downright stupid, in fact. With everything else coming down, he should have put this woman out of his head days ago.

But she was lodged like a burr inside his skull. Her and that ridiculous vow. Every time Devlin had thought about it, he regretted all over again not being able to take her up on that rash vow. He also got hard as hell imagining what would have happened if he had.

Now she was here, beneath him, smooth and sleek and responsive to his every move. Devlin intended to do his damnedest to make sure *she* had no cause for regrets.

Then she clenched her muscles and he forgot about taking it slow. Forgot how insane this was. Forgot everything but the need to drive into her wet heat.

The storm peaked just after midnight. Liz did, too, when Devlin nudged her awake for a second round. She was on her side, her back to his front. He used the position to best advantage, merely wedging her leg up with one of his and coming into her from behind.

They pistoned and plunged, back to belly, thigh slapping thigh. Liz felt the top of her head almost come off with the force of her orgasm, then fell asleep again spooned against his body, his arm draped over her waist like an anchor.

She wouldn't have believed she could zone out so completely, wedged into a single bunk with a male of Devlin's size, but when she woke once more and squinted at her watch, she let out a squawk.

"Good Lord! It's almost nine."

"So?" Devlin rumbled in her ear.

"You might be on a twelve-on, twelve-off shift, but I'm not. I need to check the weather, see if I have anything or anyone to ferry back to shore, and haul ass."

She slithered out from under his weight and into the T-shirt she scooped up from the floor. Morning-afters were always awkward, this one especially so. She and Devlin weren't just casual acquaintances. They were involved to differing degrees in some pretty nasty stuff.

Tugging the hem of the shirt down to midthigh, Liz rocked on the balls of her feet. "Look, about this business with El Tiburón…"

"I'll take care of The Shark. You stay clear of him."

Her brows shot up. Devlin lay naked under the tangled sheet, his head propped on his hands, his sun-bleached brown hair standing in short spikes. He looked lazy and relaxed. His tone was anything but.

"It wasn't my idea to get up close and personal with the man in the first place," she replied with a touch of acid. "I'm curious, though. How, exactly, do you plan to take care of him? You're stuck out here on the patch for at least another three weeks."

Tossing the sheet aside, he rolled out of the bunk. When he turned to shag his jeans, Liz got a great view of shoulders roped with hard muscle; a long, tapered back and world-class buns.

The view was just as good when he faced her. The bristles on his cheeks and chin were the same golden brown as the scattering of chest hair that arrowed toward his hard, flat belly. Battling the ridiculous urge to trail a fingernail down that tantalizing line, Liz folded her arms and waited for his response.

"The how isn't important," he told her. "Just trust me on this, okay?"

"Oh, that's good coming from the man who decamped and left me to explain a dead body to the police."

"Sorry 'bout that." He scraped a palm over his bristles, his smile rueful. "It won't happen again."

"What? Me explaining a dead body or you decamping?"

Devlin kept his smile in place, but her tart comment hit home. Like most rig men, he'd made a career of going wherever the job took him. He'd lost a wife to the long separations. He had no business making promises he might not be able to keep. But he *would* ensure Liz was safe before he departed the scene again.

Crossing the few feet separating them, he curled a knuckle under her chin. "Someone will contact you within the next eight to ten hours. They'll tell you Rigger sent them."

"And Rigger is?"

"That's me, darlin'."

He dropped a kiss on her nose and scooped up the rest of his clothes. The taste of her was still on his lips when he entered his cabin, flipped up his cell phone and activated the secure satellite link to OMEGA control.

Five

"I want someone on her, and fast."

The grim urgency in Rigger's voice bled through his controller's headset. Andrew MacDonald, code named Riever, after the fierce warriors who'd roved the borderlands between Scotland and England, acknowledged the request.

"I hear you."

"This El Tiburón is one bad piece of work. We don't have proof he's involved in this stolen passport ring, but he's sure to have his hands in it somehow. He's got them in everything else down here."

Drew shot a quick glance at the electronic status board that dominated one wall of OMEGA's control center. Four operatives including Rigger were already in the field. Another was undergoing an intensive course in Arctic survival. Yet another was sporting a full leg cast, compliments of the crowbar wielded by the slasher she'd recently taken down.

Drew had already coordinated with the CIA and U.S. customs for undercover operatives to conduct additional screening of crews coming off the various AmMex rigs scattered along the Baja peninsula. He'd have to scramble to get someone down to Piedras Rojas to cover Elizabeth Moore.

"Okay, Rigger, I'll work it and get back to you."

Twenty minutes later Drew took the elevator to the first floor. He made a quick scan of the closed-circuit surveillance screen before exiting the elevator. The chief's executive assistant had already cleared him for access, but someone might have just walked in off the street. Every agent exercised great caution when leaving OMEGA's secure facilities and entering the domain of the president's special envoy.

The grandmotherly figure seated behind an ornate Louis XV reception desk greeted him with a smile. Nothing in Elizabeth Wells's neat appearance or guileless blue eyes gave any hint that she regularly qualified at the expert level with the 9 mm SIG-Sauer secreted in a special compartment in her desk.

"Go right in, Riever. Lightning is waiting for you."

"Thanks."

When she buzzed Drew into the inner sanctum, he saw that Nick Jensen wore his business uniform this morning. Drew had no doubt the tie was silk, the shoes Italian and the gray pinstriped suit made by the hand of a master tailor. He knew Lightning's cover required a patina of sophistication. He also knew the chief was as deadly with a switchblade and garrote as he was with a Beretta, which made him an all-round ace in the estimation of OMEGA's stable of operatives.

"I've been working Rigger's request for cover for Elizabeth Moore," Drew told his boss. "He wants someone on her 24/7."

"Who have you got?"

He and Nick had their heads together, going over the list of possibles, when the intercom buzzed. Moments later Maggie Sinclair Ridgeway, code name Chameleon, breezed into the inner office.

"Hi, guys."

As always, Maggie brought her own high-charged energy field with her. The sheer force of her personality and bright, engaging smile affected the two men in different ways. Nick had first encountered her on the French Riviera years ago, during a mix-up of identities with a high-priced call girl. Drew had met her only after joining OMEGA but was in awe of her legendary exploits. The fact that she'd brought Adam Ridgeway, OMEGA's sophisticated and coolly ruthless former director, to his knees only added to her mystique.

Now the mother of three children and a tenured linguistics professor at Georgetown University, she juggled kids, pets and the demands of her husband's current chairmanship of the International Monetary

Fund with equal skill. The years had put a few character lines at the corners of her brown eyes, but nothing could dim their sparkle.

"Sorry to interrupt," she said with a peck on the cheek for both of them. "I just wanted to drop off some last-minute instructions for Nick."

When Lightning gave her a blank stare, she waggled her forefinger back and forth with vigorous determination.

"Oh, no! Feigning ignorance won't work. No way I'm letting you and Mackenzie out of babysitting for us this weekend."

"Is that *this* weekend?"

"Yes, it is. Adam and I have reservations at a resort in the White Mountains," she informed Drew. "We're going to hole up for two and a half days of uninterrupted bliss. Unless Nick and Mackenzie fink out on us," she added with a speaking glance at one of the potential finks.

Nick swallowed a groan. Even with a part-time nanny and a live-in housekeeper to assist, an entire weekend at the Ridgeway residence would require fortitude, endurance and protective body armor.

The kids were okay. Pretty darn terrific, in fact. And Nick had a soft spot for the Hungarian sheepdog Maggie had inherited after doubling for the vice president. The shaggy beast's sudden growl had provided the split second of warning necessary to save both Nick and Mackenzie from a vicious spray of gunfire by hired assassins.

It was Maggie's orange-and-purple-striped pet iguana that required constant vigilance. The damned thing had a yard-long tongue and the temperament of a pit bull with a thorn stuck in its muzzle. Nick and Mackenzie had driven home from the Ridgeways' more than once decorated with iguana spit.

"You're not going to try and weasel out, are you?" Maggie demanded, something close to desperation in her eyes. "You *did* promise. And you and Mackenzie *are* Tank's godparents."

The nickname produced a reluctant smile. All OMEGA operatives used code names when in the field. After considerable discussion, they'd unanimously agreed on Tank as a handle for Maggie and Adam's two-year-old son. The kid bubbled with energy and charged joyously at every obstacle, producing enough steam to bulldoze through a brick wall.

"I don't want to weasel out," Nick lied, "but Rigger's requested additional surveillance. Drew thinks he should go himself, which means..."

"...you'll have to bring someone else in to act as Rigger's controller and personally get them up to speed on the situation," Maggie finished glumly.

She knew how heavily tasked OMEGA's agents were. She should. She'd served as both a field operative and acting head of the agency for a few years. Brow knit, she tapped a forefinger against her lower lip.

"Rigger's working that op in Baja, right? Down at the tip of the peninsula?"

"He is, but don't get any ideas. Adam will skin me alive if you decide to help us here at the control center instead of joining him for a weekend of uninterrupted bliss."

"Actually, I was thinking of combining business and bliss." Her brown eyes gleaming, Maggie dug in her purse and extracted a cell phone. "There's a world-class resort just north of Cabo San Lucas. The Two Dolphins. Adam and I have talked several times about vacationing there."

"Maggie . . ."

"We're all packed. He's on his way home from the office as we speak. We could jump on a plane in a couple of hours. Given the time difference, we should touch down in Cabo San Lucas in time for dinner."

"You might want to think about this, Maggie. You might have to stay in the field longer than a weekend."

"God, I hope so!"

Her fervent prayer raised Nick's brows until he remembered how damned good she'd been. She'd given field ops up for the director's job, then traded that for motherhood and teaching. But her exploits in the field were still the stuff of legend among OMEGA operatives.

"I can manage five or six days with no problem," she said briskly. "Adam will have to rearrange his schedule, but that's doable. We'll ask Nanny to stay at the house with Mrs. Sorenson, so you and Mackenzie will have additional backup at night."

Nick made a last, feeble attempt. "Your husband might have something to say about the change in plans."

She gave him a pitying smile and punched in a speed dial number. "I'll tell Adam to meet me here so you and Drew can brief us both on the situation."

Half an hour later, the four of them were seated around the conference table.

"This," Nick said, sliding a dossier along the length of polished mahogany, "is Elizabeth Moore. She's a pilot for Aero Baja, under contract with the American-Mexican Petroleum Company. Rigger wants you to keep her under close surveillance."

Liz aimed a stream of water at the windshield of the Ranger. With the late-afternoon sun blazing down and the temperature hovering close to 110, both she and the helicopter benefited from the spray splatting against the Plexiglas.

She'd returned from the patch less than an hour ago and filed her postflight report. With nothing else to occupy her time, she'd offered to relieve Jorge of the chore of hosing the corrosive salt spray off the chopper. It was an easy task, one that left her mind free to roam. Whatever direction her thoughts started off in, however, they always banked into a steep turn and swooped back to the same point.

Joe Devlin.

Okay, it was impossible *not* to think about the man when she could still feel the effects of the night before. There was the occasional twinge from muscles unused to the kind of workout Devlin had given them. And the tender patch on her neck where his bristles had scraped. And the sudden tingle in her nipples whenever she remembered how he'd tongued them to hard, aching points.

Still, Liz couldn't quite believe she'd actually done what she'd vowed to during her ritual shredding of Donny's e-mail. She'd gotten naked with the very next man she'd met. It had taken several days and a visit to El Tiburón to make it happen, but happen it had.

Shaking her head, Liz aimed a jet stream at the forward-engine coupling. Who the heck was she kidding? She'd done a whole lot more than just get naked. She'd erupted like a modern-day Vesuvius. Both times. Devlin probably thought he'd struck oil. A hot, gushing stream of…

"Ms. Moore?"

The deep baritone sounded above the water's splash. Keeping the hose aimed at the rotor, Liz speared a glance over her shoulder.

"Yes?"

A figure stepped out of the hangar's shadow into the late-afternoon sunlight. Liz's heart did a nervous little jig until she noted he didn't walk with a limp. Nor was he wearing a purple silk shirt.

When she noted what he *was* wearing, her breath slid back down her throat. She hadn't been this close to such sophisticated masculinity since… Well. Never.

Devlin and the other oilmen she ferried out and back from the rig were brawny and tough and all male. This guy was Pierce Brosnan classed up several notches, if that was possible. Elegantly casual in a parrot-print polo shirt, pleated khaki slacks and tasseled loafers, he sported jet-black hair touched with silver at the temples and eyes a clearer and more compelling blue than the Pacific.

"The man I spoke to at the operations center—I think his name was Jorge Garcia—said I'd find you here. I'm Adam Ridgeway."

Shutting off the spray, Liz swiped her wet palm on her flight suit and returned his no-nonsense grip. "What can I do for you, Mr. Ridgeway?"

"My wife and I are staying at the Two Dolphins. The concierge told us Aero Baja does charter flights. We're thinking of buying some vacation property here and would like to hire you to show us the coast."

"Aero Baja does charters, but we have to schedule them around our flights for the American-Mexican Petroleum Company. AmMex is our bread and butter."

"No problem. All Maggie and I have to schedule around are our tee times." His penetrating blue eyes went past her to the helo. "I see you're flying the older model 214."

"She may be old, but she's got all new avionics."

"That's good to hear." A small smile played at one corner of his mouth. "Does she still drag her tail when you walk her off the pad with a full load?"

Well, well. He wasn't just a pretty face.

"Like a duck trying to take a squat," Liz admitted, making a swift mental reassessment. "Logged a few hours in a cockpit, have you?"

"A few. My wife's waiting at the office. Shall we go inside?"

Liz would have guessed the urbane Ridgeway would choose a sumptuous redhead or Chanel-draped blonde for a mate. The brunette perched on the corner of the desk looked far more intriguing. Comfortably chic in a gauzy white peasant skirt and white ribbed tank top, she'd pushed her sunglasses to the top of her head to sweep back her shoulder-length, honey-brown hair. It appeared she and Jorge had just shared some joke. Her cinnamon eyes danced with laughter and her rich chuckles suggested a woman who lived life to the fullest.

Liz liked her on the spot. She liked her even more when Ridgeway's voice deepened to a near caress.

"I see you've made yourself at home, my darling. As always."

Any woman who could evoke that husky note from a man like Adam Ridgeway had to be *very* special. Smiling, Liz held out her hand.

"Hello, Mrs. Ridgeway. I'm Liz Moore."

"Please, call me Maggie." The laughter still danced in her eyes. "Jorge's been telling me about the American who chartered you to take his family whale watching a few months back."

Liz groaned. She'd spent hours cleaning up vomit after that memorable flight. "You'd think a man with four kids prone to motion sickness would find another way to educate them about whales."

"Now, Lizetta," Jorge said with a grin, "the gringo swore he did not know their stomachs were so delicate."

"Our kids aren't with us on this trip," Maggie assured Liz. "And if they were, you wouldn't have to worry about their stomachs."

"True," her husband said with a wry smile. "Gillian would probably be hanging out the side hatch, Samantha would beg you to do loop-de-loops and Tank would want at the controls."

"Tank?"

"Our son."

"He's two," Maggie said blithely, as if that explained everything. "This is the first time we've left them for more than a day or two. Our friends are babysitting." She shared a quick glance with her husband. "I hope Nick and Mackenzie survive."

"They've got plenty of backup," Ridgeway replied calmly. "How does tomorrow afternoon look for you?" he asked Liz. "I checked the map and thought we'd head north first."

She flicked a glance at the grease board on the far wall. She wasn't scheduled to make her next run out to the rig until Tuesday. Unless she came up with an excuse to make one before then.

The thought wiggled into her head like a slippery little eel and wouldn't wiggle out. It snuggled right up to the image of Devlin sprawled in her bunk this morning. Unshaven. Smug. So damned sexy Liz wanted to climb back in and crawl all over him.

She was certifiable, she thought in disgust. Completely certifiable! One night with the man and she was already plotting another.

"Tomorrow afternoon is fine," she said crisply, "unless there's an emergency out on the rig and we have to make an unscheduled run."

"I understand we take second priority," Ridgeway replied. "Maggie and I will be out and around tomorrow morning. Here's my card with my cell phone number. Please keep it handy and call if you need to cancel."

Liz fingered the thick velum with its heavily embossed letters. They spelled out an impressive title—Adam Ridgeway, Governor pro tem, International Monetary Fund. Below that was a Washington, D.C., address.

Tugging down the zipper to her leg pocket, she extracted a plastic card case. Ridgeway's card slid in between her Baja Aero ID, her credit cards and several folded hundred-peso notes.

"We'll see you tomorrow," his wife said, slinging a straw tote over her shoulder. She abandoned her perch on the desk and started for the door. Halfway there she turned back.

"Oh, by the way... Rigger sent us."

Maggie hid a smile as Liz's brows shot up. Waggling her fingers in farewell, Maggie accompanied Adam out into the searing heat and tipped her sunglasses from the top of her head onto her nose.

"Nice going," she murmured as her husband escorted her to their rental car. "The chip embedded in your business card will allow us to track her every move."

"Amazing what they've come up with since our days," he replied, only half in jest.

"I like how you got her to tuck the card in with her ID. You haven't lost your touch."

Adam grinned down at her. "Feels good to be back in the field after all these years, doesn't it?"

"Damn good!"

Devlin got word that Chameleon and Thunder had tagged Liz shortly after he came off his twelve-hour shift. Stripping down, he hit the shower.

Chameleon and Thunder were both legends around OMEGA. Devlin knew Maggie better than Adam, having worked for her for a few months before she left to have her second child. But Ridgeway's reputation spoke for itself. Devlin couldn't have asked for better cover for Liz. Unless, of course, he provided it himself.

Grunting, he soaped down. The mere thought of all the ways he *wanted* to cover Elizabeth Moore flashed through his mind. He'd accomplished several different coverings last night. Next time he'd try a few more.

He had no doubt there would be a next time. Since meeting Liz on the beach what now seemed like a lifetime ago, he hadn't been able to get her out of his head. He'd figured their hours together in that cramped bunk would satisfy the lust she generated in him. He'd figured wrong. If anything, the feel of her sleek, supple body under his had fed a craving for more.

Her involuntary visit with Alvarez had thrown him a real curve, however. In addition to lusting after the woman, he was now worried as hell about her safety. Devlin had yet to link Eduardo Alvarez to the stolen passports. Or to his friend Harry, missing for several months. But Alvarez controlled the drug trade in this area with an iron fist. Odds were he controlled all other illegal activities. If El Tiburón had sold Harry's passport to the bastard who'd used it to run child prostitutes across the border, Devlin intended to have a piece of him.

First he had to establish the link, if there was one. They'd tracked the crew members that had rotated off the patch when Devlin had rotated on. All had arrived home safely and were still accounted for. Another batch was scheduled to rotate in three days, when Liz made her next scheduled run.

Devlin had already gotten acquainted with four of the men. He'd also planted tracking devices in their personal gear. If any of the four disappeared en route to their homes, the device might help locate them.

He had the next two days to tag the remaining two, both of whom possessed entry visas for the States. One was Portuguese and planning to visit a cousin in Massachusetts. The other hailed from Kuwait and had applied for a follow-on job at a rig off the coast of Louisiana.

Unfortunately, both men spoke limited English and Devlin's Portuguese was as fractured as his Arabic. He had the solution for the communications problem, however.

Toweling off, he dressed and dug a set of miniature earphones out of his desk drawer. The earphones were plastic, the kind that plugged into any iPod or MP3 player. Devlin unscrewed one of the tiny buds that served as an earpiece and inserted it into his ear canal before contacting Riever via his cell phone.

"Okay, Riev, I need you to sing to me in Portuguese."

"No problem, pal."

Knowing Devlin would be working with an international crew, OMEGA's electronics wizard, Mackenzie Blair, had adapted the miniaturized translator recently developed by the military for special operations forces dropped behind enemy lines. The tiny computer embedded in the earpiece used satellite signals to pick up spoken words, interpret them and feed an instant response. It wasn't as reliable as a real-live interpreter who could assess facial expressions and idiomatic nuances, of course. But absent a reliable man on the scene, the little bug worked wonders.

"Pode você ouvir-me?"

The device translated Riever's question and supplied Devlin an answer.

"Yeah, I can hear you," he replied in fluent Portuguese.

"Sounds like you're good to go."

"Roger that."

With the device buried deep in his left ear, Devlin went in search of Paulo Casimiro. He found the dark-eyed, curly-haired crane operator in the recreation center, wearing a look of desperation. Conrad Wallace had cornered the man and was expounding on a recent trip to Lisbon and the loss of a fistful of cash in the famed Estoril Casino.

"Two hundred euros," Wallace groused. "*Compreende* two hundred? That's, uh, *dos ciento*."

A quiet murmur sounded in Devlin's ear. "I think you mean *dois cem*," he then said to the AmMex rep.

"*Dos, dois,* whatever. The point is, those dealers at the Estoril were raking in the euros faster than I could shell them out. Damned dealers had to have stacked the deck. I tell you, they—"

Ruthlessly Devlin cut him off midstream. Courtesy was wasted on Wallace.

"I need to borrow Paulo for a few moments. I understand he's rotating in two days. Before he leaves, I'd like him to show me this new computer-aided offload system. I've heard about it, but haven't seen how it works."

It was a legitimate request. Crane operators on offshore rigs had a helluva job. The cab they worked in sat almost ninety feet above the surface of the sea, limiting their visibility. Fog, strong winds and rough seas could make the task of loading and unloading supply ships a tricky proposition at best.

At worst, the crash of a metal crane against a steel deck could spark a fire, as had happened just last year off the coast of Brazil. Almost a hundred men died in the series of explosions that followed. Three days later, exhausted rescue workers had watched with tears streaming down their faces as what remained of one of the world's largest rigs had tipped onto its side and sunk into the turquoise waters.

After that incident AmMex had followed the lead of other major oil companies and purchased a computer-based, sonar-sounding system that helped operators judge the crane's position relative to the boat deck. Besides having a professional interest in the system, Rigger figured asking about it was a good way to detach Paulo from Wallace and get him alone for a spell.

He figured right. Using pantomime and a few key phrases fed to him through his earpiece, he got his message across. The burly Paulo jumped to his feet and led the way out of the lounge. Devlin followed, making a mental note to have Riever dig into Conrad Wallace's financial situation. Losing a couple hundred euros at a casino was no big deal—as long as Wallace didn't make a habit of it.

In the meantime, Devlin had two days to get close to Paulo Casimiro.

Six

Maggie and Adam Ridgeway showed up at Aero Baja at one-fifteen the following afternoon. Liz spent the rest of the day with them, starting with a three-hour aerial tour of the coast north of Piedras Rojas and finishing with drinks at their private casita and dinner at the restaurant of their exclusive resort.

The following afternoon they flew south. A slight dogleg at Todos Santos took them to Eduardo Alvarez's walled compound. Liz made only one low-level pass. The heavily armed gate guards didn't appear to appreciate the outside interest. The two goons had their semiautomatics at shoulder level when Liz zoomed away.

"Interesting," Maggie commented through the

headset, twisting around in her seat harness to get another look at the compound.

"Very," Adam agreed.

They made a brief stop at the resort town of Cabo San Lucas, crowded with tourists off the gleaming white cruise ships lined up at the docks. Maggie tried to convince Adam she only wanted to pick up some souvenirs for the kids, but he insisted on buying her a magnificent silver cuff incised with a lizard set in turquoise, lapis and malachite.

Once back in Piedras Rojas, Liz invited Maggie and Adam to join her for dinner at El Poco Lobo. She'd gained enough insight into the aristocratic-looking Adam by now to know he wouldn't hesitate to chow down at a chipped Formica table on Anita's chicken, frijoles and rice. Still, she was surprised at how easily he blended in. While Maggie and Liz devoured hot, cinnamon-and-sugar-dusted sopaipillas dripping with honey, Adam joined the locals at the bar. Within minutes he was immersed in a deep philosophical discussion of the relative merits of football versus soccer.

Contentedly licking the honey from their fingers, Maggie and Liz lolled at their outdoor table in a breeze stirred by the swirling overhead fan. Cool and comfortable in a white cotton peasant blouse trimmed with colorful ribbons, another gauzy skirt and huarache sandals, Maggie tossed back the strong local brew with the same gusto she seemed to bring to every aspect of her life.

After two days in their company, Liz knew little

about their personal life aside from the fact that they had three children and lived in Washington, D.C. Curious, she drew a lazy circle on the Formica with her dew-streaked beer bottle. "How long have you and Adam been married?"

"Ten years next month. We worked together for some time before that. Those were, uh, interesting years." Her gaze drifted to the tall, broad-shouldered Americano at the bar. "These are better, though. *Much* better."

Ridgeway glanced over his shoulder and caught his wife's gaze. Smiling, he tipped his beer bottle in her direction. The look they shared sent a little ping of envy through Liz.

She'd been so sure she'd found her mate in Donny. Had sweated down here in Mexico all these months to build up their joint account and dreamed of buying the first of their planned fleet. All the while he was having fun with Bambang.

Bambang. God!

Her disgusted grunt brought the other woman's head around.

"Sorry. Did you say something?"

"No."

"What about you?" Maggie asked after a moment, picking up the conversational thread. "Do you have any particular males on your radar scope?"

"I had one. He dropped off a week or so ago."

Liz took a long swallow of beer and made an interesting discovery. The anger was still there, but fading fast. So was the self-disgust. But the hurt had completely evaporated. A certain roustabout had shoved Donny Carter right out of her heart.

"Another just popped up on the screen," she admitted with a half-embarrassed shrug.

Maggie arched a brow. "Would his name happen to be Joe Devlin?"

"It would." Shaking her head, Liz thumped the bottle back onto the table. "You'd think I would have learned my lesson. I fell for one slick operator and got burned. How dumb is it to jump into a bunk with another man less than a week later?"

Surprise rounded Maggie's eyes. "You and Devlin have made it to the bunk-jumping stage?"

"I didn't plan it."

"I'll bet he did!" Maggie retorted on a choke of suppressed laughter. "I know Rigger. He never goes into any situation unprepared."

Remembering the stash of condoms he'd had conveniently to hand, Liz pursed her lips. "See, that's the problem. You're obviously well acquainted with him. All I know is that he's big and tough and complicated."

"That pretty much pegs him. And most of the other men he associates with, my husband included."

Liz leaned back, letting the breeze stir the ends of the blunt-cut hair just touching her shoulder. "I don't suppose you're going to tell me exactly who you and Adam and Devlin work for."

"Adam is with the International Monetary Fund," Maggie replied gently. "As his business card indicates. I teach linguistics at Georgetown University. And Devlin is currently employed by…"

"…the American-Mexican Petroleum Company. Okay, I get the picture. I'm not cleared for that level of detail."

Drumming on the table with her nails, Liz shifted her gaze. The cantina was set on a slight hill, with red tile–roofed houses spilling down the hill on either side. Through the narrow slice between buildings she could just make out the cliffs that gave Piedras Rojas its name. The rocks glowed bright copper in the evening sun.

The scene was so peaceful, so idyllic. A small village perched on the cliffs overlooking the Pacific. A handful of cars parked in the narrow, cobbled streets. Dust swirling lazily in the slanting rays of the sun. Hardly the setting for danger and intrigue and murder.

"Devlin told me a little of what this is all about," she said, swinging her gaze back to Maggie. "It's pretty nasty stuff."

"Yes, it is."

"I might be able to help if you fill me in on…"

"*Hola,* Lizetta."

Grinning under his thick mustaches, Jorge waved and worked his way through the crowd. With him was a man Liz recognized as one of his many relatives. The fishing boat captain, she guessed from his denim shirt and the red bandanna knotted around his neck. The fishy tang of the docks that came with him provided another clue.

"Hello, Jorge. You remember Mrs. Ridgeway."

"But of course." The mechanic bowed over Maggie's hand with the grace of a matador. "Señora Ridgeway, this is my wife's cousin. I tell Emilio that Lizetta takes you and your husband up for charter flights. He wishes to know if you would like to charter his boat as well. The *Santa Guadalupe* is a very fine boat," he assured her.

"Very fine," the wiry Emilio echoed. "Clean and fast."

"We haven't talked about a fishing charter," Maggie said with a smile, "but I know Adam would enjoy it if we have time. Why don't you join us for a drink? I'll get him over to speak with you about it."

"She is a nice woman," Jorge commented as she went to relay their request for a cold beer to her husband.

"And very rich," Emilio murmured.

Liz said nothing. Tourism was the second largest legitimate industry in the area after tuna fishing. The locals could size up potential customers with a single glance at their shoes or watch. Then there was the rock atop the heavy gold band circling Maggie's ring finger....

When she returned with her husband and fresh drinks in tow, the talk turned to fish. Pacific striped marlin. Roosterfish. Sailfish. Tuna, dorado and wahoo. Liz sipped her beer, listening with half an ear, and let her thoughts slide back to her epiphany of a few moments ago. She was over Donny. She'd probably been over him for months and hadn't realized it. She ought to be grateful to Bambang.

And to Devlin.

Her thoughts turning inward, Liz hid a small smile. She'd have to show him just *how* grateful on her next run out to the patch. If she timed it right, she could catch him coming off his shift and...

"Ayyyy!"

Dismayed, Jorge made a grab for the beer bottle he'd sideswiped while demonstrating the size of one of his cousins-in-law's catches. The bottle flew off the table, spraying Maggie's blouse in the process, and hit the floor. The thick glass didn't shatter, but clinked around under the table a few times, spraying feet and shoes as well.

"*Excúse, señora! Excúse!*"

"It's okay." Smiling, Maggie raised the wet cotton a few inches off her chest. "No harm done."

"I am so clumsy," Jorge moaned as Emilio and Liz both bent to retrieve the bottle.

They came within a hair of knocking heads. She drew back just in time and left it to the fisherman to scoop up the bottle. When he did, a thin gold chain slithered out of his shirt collar. Dangling from the end of the chain was a three-inch-long shark's tooth capped with a gold filigree crown.

Liz froze, bent low in her chair. She'd seen a necklace just like that recently. Around the neck of Eduardo Alvarez, in the photo taken with his family aboard a sleek white yacht.

"That's quite a trophy," she commented. "Did it come from one of your catches?"

Emilio glanced down and muttered a curse under his breath. With a swift move, he stuffed the tooth back inside his shirt.

"*Sí,* I catch it."

Straightening, he plunked the bottle on the table and shoved back his chair.

"I must go," he told the Ridgeways. "You will contact Jorge if you wish to fish, yes?"

"Yes, we will."

While Maggie and Adam said goodbye to the still-mortified Jorge, Liz sat like a cardboard cutout in her chair. She had the sinking suspicion she'd just spotted the item of property El Tiburón was determined to reclaim.

Problem was, she couldn't decide what the heck to do about it.

She almost mentioned the tooth to Maggie and Adam before they parted at the cantina. Loyalty to Jorge kept her silent. He wasn't just her partner at work. He was her closest friend here in Mexico. She'd eaten dinner with him and Maria and their assorted relatives dozens of times and returned their hospitality at regular intervals.

She refused to believe the Aero Baja mechanic was involved in any way with the shooting on the beach. But he *had* brought Emilio to the cantina, and Emilio *had* acted really weird over the tooth.

Chewing on her lower lip, Liz drove through the

gathering dusk and parked under the leafy jacaranda tree. She kept her collapsible baton handy until she ascertained the massive trunk shielded no unwanted visitors, then climbed the stairs to her apartment.

The three rooms welcomed her with warm yellow walls and smooth tile floors. Since Liz had put every spare peso into the bank, she'd limited her decorating to inexpensive paintings by local artists and colorful handwoven rugs. Her only real indulgence was satellite Internet service.

She'd tried to convince Conrad Wallace that AmMex should cover the cost, since she used her computer to check weather the night before scheduled flights. Fiscally conservative as always, Wallace had countered that she should use the weather service at the terminal.

Tossing her purse onto the sofa, Liz hunkered down at the computer and booted up. When the screen lit up, she logged onto the net and typed "Eduardo Alvarez, El Tiburón" into Google's search box. A click of the mouse returned a surprising number of entries, but instead of scrolling through them, Liz aimed the pointer at the images icon at the top of the search screen.

She found what she was looking for almost immediately. The second image she looked at showed a black-and-white newspaper image of Alvarez. The photographer had caught him at an angle. His face was turned away, his upper torso twisted. The neck of his shirt had parted just enough to show a white triangle outlined against a mat of black chest hair.

Her stomach knotting, Liz zoomed in on the triangle. Yep, there it was, unique filigree crown and all.

She'd lived in Mexico for seven months, had hit the jewelry markets in Cabo and in La Paz. The tourists seemed to love shark's teeth necklaces, but the teeth were usually small and strung on leather rather than gold chain. Best she could recall, she'd never seen one as big or with such elaborate workmanship as this one. A master goldsmith had crafted the crown. The tooth itself...Liz didn't want to think about the size of the shark that must have come from.

Suspicion now hardened into certainty, she printed out the picture and exited the search mode. That was when she noted the envelope icon at the upper corner of her screen. Another click took her to her e-mail. One was from her mom, currently vacationing in Michigan with a gaggle of girlfriends. Another was a notice from Citibank confirming receipt of the latest payment on the loan she'd taken out for the Ranger. The third was from Donny.

Liz stared at the return address for a full minute, her finger hovering over the delete key. Finally she mouthed a gruff what-the-hell and opened the e-mail. She skimmed the lines, her jaw dropping in the process.

He'd made a mistake.

He loved her.

He wanted her to jettison the job in Mexico and fly to Malaysia on the next flight out. They'd get married as soon as she arrived.

"Right!" she hooted. "Like that's going to happen."

Fingers flying, she zinged off a pithy, two-word reply. She was still feeling the satisfaction of that terse response when she shut down the computer. The photo in the printer's tray sobered her instantly. Gnawing on her lower lip, Liz stared down into The Shark's flat, black eyes.

"Now what the heck am I going to do about you?"

After a fierce internal debate, she dug out Adam Ridgeway's card. He answered on the third ring, sounding curt, almost impatient.

"Ridgeway."

"It's Liz." She hesitated a moment, thrown off by his tone. "Did I catch you at a bad time?"

"What can I do for you?"

He'd dodged the question, but the creak of bedsprings and faint rustle of sheets provided their own answer.

Liz fought a grin. It wasn't yet nine o'clock, and Maggie and Adam had already hit the sheets. She had a pretty good hunch they hadn't been snoozing.

"I may have something, some information."

Adam's tone altered significantly. "What kind of information?"

She thought about the sophisticated electronics in Alvarez's study. And remembered that he'd known to the penny how much she owed Citibank. She wouldn't put it past him to have bugged her phone. Or have one of his goons parked down the street, manning a high-powered listening device.

"Why don't I drive over to the resort? I can be there in a half hour."

"That works."

Liz just bet it did. Guessing that the bedsprings would get a hard, fast workout, she hung up.

A quick shower removed the grime from the afternoon flight and heat of the day. Her hair still damp, Liz tucked the folded picture of El Tiburón into the back pocket of her jeans and slid her feet into flip-flops.

Night wrapped the coast road in breezy darkness. The surf foamed against the rocks, spinning lacy collars in the moonlight. What looked like a billion stars studded the sky. No clouds or storms on the horizon tonight.

Too bad, Liz thought with a wry smile. She was scheduled to ferry a replacement crew out to AM-237 first thing in the morning. She wouldn't have the excuse of a storm to delay her return flight.

The Two Dolphins Resort was perched on a curve of high cliffs some eight miles from Piedras Rojas. A spotlighted fountain with two giant bronze bottlenoses splashing joyfully marked the entrance to the resort. Flickering torches outlined the drive. With fragrant hibiscus crowding the roadside and eucalyptus trees touching branches overhead, Liz felt as though she was driving through a perfumed tunnel.

The main lodge of the resort sat in floodlit splendor at the end of the drive. From her visit the previous evening, Liz knew to circle the lodge and branch off on the graveled drive that led to Maggie and Adam's casita. Like the other bungalows at this high-priced getaway, the bougainvillea-draped cottage boasted a private pool complete with blue-and-white-striped cabana and deck overlooking the moon-washed Pacific.

One of these days, Liz thought as she parked beside the Ridgeways' rental vehicle, she might just treat herself to a vacation at a place like this. After she paid off the loan for that damned nonrefundable deposit. And reconstructed her bank account. And figured out just what the heck she was going to do when her AmMex contract came up for renewal again.

Time enough to worry about all that later. Right now the folded photo of The Shark was so hot she half expected it to burn a brand on her butt.

Soft golden light spilled from the windows of the casita. Liz crunched up the gravel path to the front door and let the dolphin-shaped brass knocker clank against the door. Maggie opened it, her hair a tousled brown cloud. She'd belted on a peach silk robe trimmed in ecru lace. The edges swished against the matching gown as she stepped aside.

"Hi, Liz. Come in."

The interior of the bungalow was as luxurious as the exterior. Her flip-flops slapping the tiles, Liz followed Maggie down a foyer lined with feathery potted ferns.

"Sorry 'bout the interruption."

"No problem. Actually, you aren't our only visitor."

Maggie swept a hand toward the male standing

beside Adam in the sitting room. Liz gaped at the unexpected sight.

"Devlin!"

"In the flesh, darlin'."

Flesh was right. Most of his was showing. Black Lyrca covered the little that wasn't. The short-sleeved muscle shirt clung to his chest and biceps like a thin coat of paint. The black shorts did the same on his muscular thighs. Both garments had obviously been designed to wear with the wet suit and scuba gear draped over a nearby chair.

"Don't tell me you swam all the way from the patch!"

"Only part of the way," he said, grinning. "I had a boat waiting."

"But...but..." Thrown for a loop by his unexpected appearance, Liz croaked like a tongue-tied macaw. "When did you get here?"

Adam answered that one. "About five minutes after you called," he said with just a hint of dryness in his aristocratic voice. "A little earlier than we expected."

He didn't look at his wife, but Maggie flushed and Devlin swallowed a snort of laughter. Still bewildered, Liz wanted more of an explanation.

"I don't understand. What are you doing here?"

"I wanted to be on hand to observe the crew rotating off the rig tomorrow morning. See where they go, who they talk to."

"So why didn't you just fly back with me when I picked them up?"

"Because we don't want them to know they're being observed," he explained. "Between us, Maggie, Adam and I are going to make sure the individuals who step off your helo are the same ones who continue into the States."

Liz was a little ticked they hadn't included her as part of the observation committee. She'd voice her opinion about that in a minute. Right now she was more curious about how the heck Devlin had orchestrated another disappearing act.

"Won't they miss you out on the patch?"

"Not unless there's an emergency. I worked a double shift yesterday. Twenty-four hours straight, with the next twenty-four off. I posted a sign in four languages on my cabin door. Anyone who knocks risks severe maiming or death. Maggie told me about your call," he said, shifting gears. "What's up?"

"This."

Reaching into her hip pocket, she extracted the printed photo and passed it to Devlin. When he unfolded the paper and recognized Alvarez's image, his brows snapped together.

"Has The Shark come after you again?"

"No. Although a couple of his resident thugs did aim Uzis my way yesterday."

Before Liz could explain about the low-level pass over Alvarez's compound, Devlin threw Ridgeway a swift glance.

"I thought you had her on a leash."

"We do."

"What leash?" Liz asked, frowning.

"Are the signals faulty? Did you lose her?"

"Hey! What leash?"

"The signals work perfectly," Adam said calmly. "Maggie and I were with her when it happened."

"What's this business about Uzis? How did…?"

Liz put her first and fourth fingers to her mouth. Her ear-shattering whistle spun Devlin around and had the other two wincing.

"*What* leash, dammit?"

Seven

Devlin had once strayed into a patch of quicksand. He'd been working a rig in a backwater Louisiana bayou at the time. The swamp was wet and boggy, crowded with marsh grasses, palmettos and moss-laden cypress trees. After stepping off a skiff onto what he thought was solid ground, he'd sunk to his kneecaps. As the echoes of Liz's shrill whistle hammered against his eardrums, he experienced the same sinking sensation.

"I was worried about you. I asked Maggie and Adam to tag you."

"Tag me how?"

Her voice was low and lethal. Bravely, Adam attempted to draw her fire.

"There's a microchip embedded in the business card I gave you. It tracks your every movement. If you'd strayed into unfamiliar or dangerous territory, one of us would have been there within minutes."

She didn't waste her fury on Adam. Turning her attention back to Devlin, she shot off so many sparks he could feel their white hot bite.

"Bastard. I actually—almost—trusted you."

Bristling, she dug a hand into the left front pocket of her jeans. Devlin kept his mouth shut when she produced a flat plastic case. Said nothing when she pulled out an embossed business card. But he almost blew it when she ripped it into halves, then quarters, and let the pieces flutter to the carpet.

Just in time he bit back the comment that she'd conducted a similar ritual the night they'd met. He didn't think Liz was in any mood to appreciate the irony.

"I want the truth this time," she demanded. "Were you three keeping tabs on me because you think I'm part of this stolen passport scheme?"

That one Devlin could answer unequivocally and without hesitation.

"No. I told you we considered the possibility. We also dedicated considerable resources to vetting you. Everything came back clean."

Her eyes narrowed to slits. "Was that what our little session in your cabin out on the rig was all about? You were 'vetting' me?"

The quicksand was up around Devlin's waist now. He could feel it sucking him deeper into the bog, but didn't look to either Maggie or Adam for help. They couldn't throw him a rope on this one.

"There's only so much I'll do for my country." That wasn't completely true, but the next statement was. "That particular session was for me and me alone."

He could see she wasn't buying it. He figured he had one last shot before he went under.

"You're smart, sexy and one hell of a pilot, Liz, but you're not in The Shark's league. I told you I was sending in some backup. You didn't object."

"Backup is one thing! Putting me under electronic surveillance without my knowledge or consent is another."

"I was worried about you," he repeated. It was his only real defense.

"Want to know what you can do with your worry?"

She hadn't given up the battle, but her voice had lost some of its steam. Relief rippled through Devlin. He might yet make it out of the swamp.

"How about we discuss that privately? After you tell us about this photograph of Alvarez."

The diversion worked, thank God. With a look that promised him some uncomfortable moments later, she stabbed a finger at the photo.

"See the necklace he's wearing?"

Maggie and Adam crowded around the picture. They made quite a trio, Liz thought as she struggled to get a grip on her temper. Adam as sleek as a panther with his black hair and half-buttoned white shirt. Maggie trim and elegant in peach silk. Devlin—the rat!—looking unrepentant and testosterone charged in that damned Lycra.

"That's a shark's tooth dangling from the chain," Liz pointed out.

"Apropos," Maggie commented as they passed the photo from hand to hand.

"You can't see the details, but a magnifying glass would show the tooth has gold filigree crown with a hook to loop a chain through. The filigree pattern is very intricate and very distinctive."

"We'll take your word for it," Devlin said. "So?"

"So I saw that same necklace tonight. On Jorge's cousin Emilio."

She speared a quick look at Maggie and Adam. Surprise and quick interest flared in their eyes. Devlin couldn't make the connection.

"Who are Emilio and Jorge?"

"Let's sit down," Adam suggested, gesturing to the love seat and easy chairs grouped around a hammered brass coffee table. "Liz can fill you in on the details."

Maggie dropped into one of the overstuffed chairs. Adam took a seat on the broad arm. Liz chose the love seat, then had to scoot over a few inches when Devlin crowded in beside her. The man tended to occupy more than his fair share of space, she thought wryly. In bed and out.

Sternly banishing the thought, she launched into an explanation. "Jorge Garcia is Aero Baja's chief mechanic. You saw him at the terminal the morning I flew you out to the patch."

He wrinkled his brow. "Short? Handlebar mustache? Grease under his fingernails?"

Amazed he could recall such detail about a man he'd glimpsed only briefly, she nodded.

"Emilio is Jorge's wife's cousin. He owns and operates a fishing boat. The *Santa Guadalupe*. Jorge brought him to the cantina to meet Maggie and Adam earlier this evening. He and his cousin-in-law thought the Rigeways might be interested in chartering the boat for some sport fishing."

"And this Emilio was wearing a shark's tooth necklace?"

"He was."

"You've got keen eyes," Maggie commented. "I didn't notice it."

"I spotted the glint of a gold chain," Adam said slowly, "but not what was attached to it."

"Remember when Jorge knocked over the beer bottle? Emilio and I both ducked down to retrieve it. The tooth slipped out of his shirt then. When I remarked on it, he got all flustered, stuffed the thing back inside his collar and—"

"—left faster than a gamecock with his tail feathers on fire," Maggie exclaimed. "Do you think this shark's tooth connects Emilio to Alvarez? Is it a gang symbol? A mark of the brothers?"

"I don't think it's a gang thing. The two goons who drove me out to Alvarez's compound weren't sporting any teeth but their own. No, this one is very distinctive." She paused for dramatic effect. "My guess is it's the personal possession El Tiburón's so anxious to recover."

She'd had plenty of time to puzzle this out during the drive to the resort.

"Alvarez told me his nephew was carrying something the night he was shot. Something that belonged to him. Something he wanted back. I'm thinking he gave the tooth to Martín. Or Martín borrowed it without his uncle's permission. Maybe he just wanted to flash it around. Maybe he was using it as a signal that he had his uncle's backing for whatever he was up to. In either case, my guess is Emilio lifted it off Martín's body. Or knows who did."

The other three exchanged glances. Their minds seemed to click on a level that didn't include Liz.

"It fits," Adam said. "Jorge works for Aero Baja. He has access to the AmMex flight manifests."

"He knows who's coming off the rig and when," Maggie murmured. "Jorge passes the information to his wife's cousin, who just happens to own a deep-sea fishing boat."

His face grim, Devlin picked it up from there. "Emilio approaches the target, takes him out on the boat, steals his passport and dumps him overboard. He then sells the passport to Alvarez, uncle or nephew. He even tries to make some extra on the side by arranging a meeting with an Americano reportedly willing to pay big bucks for information about the men coming off the rig."

His hazel eyes hardened to agate.

"I'm betting he didn't intend to tell me a damned thing. He probably arranged that midnight rendezvous with the idea of bumping me off and lifting my papers, as well. Except something went wrong. Martín Alvarez got wind of the meeting. Followed Emilio to the beach to see what he was up to, maybe intending to take him out. But Emilio got to him first."

Liz had to voice a protest. "Wait a sec! I see two flaws in your scenario. First, Jorge can't be involved in a scheme like that. I know him. He's not just my coworker. He's my friend."

"Harry Johnson was *my* friend," Devlin countered, his jaw tight.

"I'm just saying that Jorge and his wife are good people."

"What's the second flaw?"

"We still don't know for sure Emilio is part of the scheme. We don't even know he was the informant you were supposed to meet that night."

"Maybe not. But as you said, he either lifted the shark's tooth off Martín's body or knows who did."

The harsh edges to his face softened. He shifted on the sofa cushions, his thigh nudging hers.

"That was good work, Moore. Keep it up and we might just have to make you an honorary inductee."

"Into what?"

"Our little fraternity." Sliding a palm around her nape, he tugged her forward for a quick, hard kiss. "I'll drive you back to your place. Then Maggie, Adam and I need to get to work."

The kiss was delicious. The impetus behind it wasn't. Irritated all over again, Liz jerked away from his hold.

"Guess again, cowboy. You're not taking me home and tucking me into bed like a good little girl. I want in on what happens next."

The glint that sprang into his eyes suggested he'd been hoping she'd be more bad than good, but he countered her argument with one of his own.

"What happens next is just grunt work. You need your sleep. You have an early flight tomorrow, don't you?"

He knew damned well she did. And *she* knew he was doing his macho protective thing again, cutting her out of the action in the process.

"I can shave off a few hours. Or reschedule the flight to later in the day."

She figured the last option would make him squirm. The clock was already ticking. He couldn't stay off the rig too long before his absence was noted.

His face took on a stubborn cast and he looked ready to continue the debate when Adam stepped into the breach. "Liz is right. She's too much a part of this for us to shut her out now."

"I agree," Maggie said.

Their combined front forced Devlin to give a reluctant nod. Adam picked it up from there and reeled off a string of pseudonyms.

"As I think you know, Devlin's code name is Rigger. I'm Thunder. Maggie goes by Chameleon."

"Like in the lizard? The one that changes its color to fit its surroundings?"

"Like in the lizard. She's very good at changing colors, by the way."

His wife beamed up at him. "Thank you, my darling."

"We all work—or have worked—in various capacities for a government agency known as OMEGA."

Her mind whirling, Liz drove home through the darkness. Devlin sat silent beside her. He'd insisted on coming along, assuring her he'd find his own way back to the resort. She hadn't argued. She was still trying to absorb everything Adam had revealed. Code names. Undercover agents. OMEGA.

The acronym sounded as ominous as the tasks its operatives were apparently assigned. Liz knew a little about agencies hidden within departments buried in bureaucracies. Her father had retired from the military while she was still in her early teens, but he'd pulled two tours at the Pentagon. He'd rarely talked about his work there. What he didn't say, she now knew from her own military days, spoke volumes. Even today *she* couldn't talk about some of the special ops missions she'd flown.

Still... This stuff was right out of James Bond.

Chewing on her lower lip, she slanted Devlin a quick glance. He'd traded the black Lycra for a pair of shorts and a shirt borrowed from Adam. In the dappled moonlight filtering through the eucalyptus trees, he looked like what he purported to be—a tough, tanned roughneck.

His code name fit him like a second skin. He was an oilman first, an undercover operative second. Or was it the other way around? Liz couldn't separate the two. Idly she wondered if he could.

"You know," she said, breaking the silence, "it might help me understand what you're doing if I knew more than your name, rank and serial number."

"What do you want to know?"

"Where you were born might be a good start. Where you went to school. What you do in your down time. Why you list your brother on your next of kin form instead of, oh, say, a spouse. Little things like that."

"Let's take them in order," he said easily. "I hail from Bartlesville, Oklahoma. Got my undergraduate degree from Oklahoma State, my master's from OU. Down time I usually spend trout fishing with my brother in Colorado or tinkering on the '69 'Vette I've been restoring off and on for years. As for a spouse…"

His tone didn't alter significantly, but Liz caught an echo of old regrets.

"We called it quits just before I started working on the Corvette."

"Bad scene?"

"Could have been worse, I suppose. Time and distance had already numbed most of the hurt. Too many long rotations, too few happy homecomings."

"Didn't you ever consider taking a job ashore?"

"I did more than consider it. I sat behind a desk at corporate headquarters for two years. By that time the marriage was beyond saving."

"No kids?"

"No kids."

"Sounds like a lonely life."

"It is. The divorce rate for oil rig workers is almost as high as it is for military officers." Shifting, he wedged a shoulder against the door and slid an arm along the back of her seat. "What about you and what's-his-name? The sleazy bucket of slime I heard you excoriating the night we met. Why didn't it work for you two?"

"Same problem. Time. Distance. A Malaysian television reporter."

"He told you about her, did he? What a jerk."

She whipped her eyes off the road. "You knew about Bambang?"

"We had you checked out, remember. OMEGA is nothing if not thorough." His teeth flashed in a quick grin. "I didn't get quite that level of detail, though. Is Bambang really her name?"

"It is." Liz could laugh about it. Now. "Appropriate, wouldn't you say?"

His chuckles joined hers. She leaned her head back, feeling his arm warm and hard against her neck.

"I was pretty pissed that night on the beach."

"I kinda got that impression."

"Donny not only dumped me, he cleaned out our joint bank account."

"Sonuvabitch."

"My sentiments exactly. Funny thing is, he's now decided Bambang isn't the right one. I got an e-mail from him earlier tonight. He wants me to drop everything and jump on a plane to Singapore."

"I hope you suggested he take a flying leap."

"I wasn't that polite. Or that verbose."

"Good for you."

She thought about telling him he'd contributed significantly to her terse reply, but decided against it. No sense feeding the man's ego—or scaring him off. Particularly when she wasn't quite sure yet where things were going between them.

"Tell me again what the plan is for tomorrow," she said instead. "I want to make sure I have the sequence right."

Devlin worked his fingers under her hair and made a lazy circle on her neck. The pads were rough, raising little shivers where they rasped against Liz's skin.

"We've already got Riever—my controller at headquarters—checking out Emilio. While he's doing that, Maggie and Adam will use the pretext of chartering Emilio's boat to get up close and personal with him."

"He's scoping out Jorge, too," she murmured, feeling a surge of disloyalty to her friend.

"Yes, he is. We're counting on you to conduct a more-personal inquiry before you make the run out to the patch. Think you can do it without sending up a red flag? If not, Maggie or Adam can."

"I'll do it."

"Good enough. I'll be waiting when you return from the patch to count heads and conduct a visual ID." His fingers lost their gentle touch. "If Jorge or Emilio approaches any of them…"

"Emilio might," Liz said flatly. "Jorge won't."

"U.S. passports go for a big chunk of change in this part of the world. Your friend wouldn't be the first man to get caught up in something he couldn't get out of."

Liz didn't want to think of Jorge or Maria profiting from something so evil. Eduardo Alvarez, on the other hand…

"What about El Tiburón? Who's watching him?"

"He's covered."

She mulled that over for a half mile or so. The Pacific shimmered in the moonlight off to her right. Dead ahead, the lights of Piedras Rojas spilled down the black bulk of the hillside to the cliffs.

"What if Emilio and El Tiburón aren't connected?" she said after a moment. "What if Emilio's in this on his own?"

"Possible but unlikely. Harry rotated off another rig, remember. That suggests the operation involves more than one or two locals."

"True."

She chewed on that while the pinpricks of light grew brighter and closer. Moments later she pulled up under the jacaranda tree and cut the engine.

"My place is just up those stairs."

"I'll see you inside."

Liz hated the relief that rippled through her. Alvarez's two henchmen had really done a job on her nerves. The fact that she might have a line on the item their boss wanted back so badly only added to her jumpiness.

Thankfully, no one sprang out from behind the gnarled tree trunk or lurked under the stairs. She made it to her front door unmolested. Once inside, however, that situation changed dramatically.

Her palm was still slapping against the wall for the light switch when Devlin spun her into his arms. By the time he finished with her mouth and moved to her throat, her heart was pinging against her ribs.

"Any chance you might change your mind about letting me tuck you in?" he asked, nuzzling the soft spot just under her jaw.

She didn't want to make it *too* easy for him. "I have an early flight tomorrow, remember? And you have work to do."

"I'm a fast tucker-inner."

Eight

Devlin was as good as his word. He was fast. Very fast. He waltzed Liz from the front door straight to the bedroom, leaving a trail of discarded clothing along the way. Naked, she sank onto the quilted comforter.

He started to follow her down but she got her knees under her and rose up to meet him. Chest to chest, mouth to mouth, they strained against each other. His hands and mouth and stinging little nips soon had her in a fever of need.

She returned the favor, blazing a line of wet kisses and little love bites from his neck to his chest to his belly. He was as taut as a steel hawser when she took him in her mouth.

Then he pressed her back onto the mattress and

returned the favor. He tongued her sensitive flesh, alternating the strokes with a wicked suction that soon had Liz panting and arching her back.

The blinding speed of her climax took her by surprise. Sensation after sensation spiraled up from her belly, fast and powerful and searing in their intensity. Her last thought before she threw her head back and let them rip through her was that Devlin might be handy to have on hand every night. He was *one heck* of a tucker-inner.

She admitted as much sometime later, after he'd followed her over the edge. They lay sprawled across the bed, legs tangled, hearts pumping, perspiration cooling on their bodies. The taste of him was still on her lips. His head squashed her left breast. His arm was a deadweight across her middle. Idly, Liz played with the short, sun-streaked hair tickling her skin.

"That *was* fast," she remarked. "And pretty damned incredible."

"You won't get any argument from me." Tightening his arm, he drew her closer. "Why do you think I pulled a straight twenty-four-hour shift? My original plan was to wait until a few hours before dawn before slipping away from the rig. I was sorta hoping this might happen."

"Hoping, huh?"

A chuckle rumbled up from his chest, rich and unrepentant. "Okay, praying."

"I got the impression your early arrival surprised Maggie and Adam."

"I got the same impression."

Liz trailed a hand over his neck and shoulders, loving the feel of him. So warm, so solid.

So heavy.

She wiggled a little, trying to shift his weight. "You're smushing me into the mattress."

"I like smushing you." Despite the lazy reply, he eased to the side and propped his head in one hand. "I like it a lot, as a matter of fact. Maybe we should think about more smushing when this is over."

Her heart did a funny little flip, but caution lights started flashing.

"I'm not sure that's a good idea. We both learned the hard way long-distance relationships don't work."

"Could be those weren't the right relationships."

Much as Liz wanted to agree, there was no getting around the reality of their situation. Scooting up against the rickety headboard, she tucked the sheet under her arms.

"I fly charters for a living. You work offshore oil rigs. When you're not secret agenting, that is, which I suspect occurs on a frequent basis. We'd be lucky if we saw each other once every three or four months."

"Aero Baja isn't the only charter service handling the big rigs. We should be able to do better than every few months if we pick our locations."

"Why?" Liz was dead serious now. "What do we have going for us besides good, old-fashioned lust? And why do you think we wouldn't make the same mistakes we made the last time?"

"I'm older. You're certainly wiser. We ought to be able to stir experience in with lust and come up with… With…"

"With what?"

The word *love* stuck in Devlin's throat. It was too soon. Way too soon. If he laid something like that on Liz now, she wouldn't believe him. Hell, *he* could hardly believe the potent combination of worry, hunger and anticipation that had brought him off the rig hours ahead of schedule.

That alone told Devlin he had it bad. That and the fact he had to force himself to leave her, despite all that needed doing between now and dawn.

He'd fudged the truth a little when he'd described the upcoming night's activities as mere grunt work. Out of Liz's hearing, he'd shared a quick aside with Adam and arranged a rendezvous here in town. Together they planned to slip aboard Emilio's boat. Devlin suspected Maggie would insist on accompanying her husband, then argue about who should pull sentry duty while the other two poked around. Either way it looked to be a long night.

"Let's think about it," he suggested as he rolled out of bed. "Maybe we'll come up with the answer by the next time I tuck you in. Sleep well, darlin', and have a safe flight tomorrow."

Liz didn't think she would sleep at all. She figured worry about Jorge and repeated replays of Devlin's parting remarks would keep her awake through most of the night.

She dozed off soon after he left, however, and the next thing she knew dawn was filtering through the shutters. After a stand-up breakfast of coffee, juice and a power bar, she jumped in the Jeep and wove through the still-sleepy streets to the airfield.

Aero Baja's chief mechanic was already there. Zipped into a clean set of coveralls, he was gassing up the Ranger. The familiar stink of aviation fuel hung like a cloud on the hot morning air.

"'Morning, Jorge."

"Good morning, Lizetta." Smiling, he squinted up at the cloudless azure sky. "It is a good day for a run, yes?"

"Looks like. I'll go check weather and file the flight plan."

He had the bird gassed and ready to go when she returned. They fell into their normal ritual, with Liz performing a careful walk-around, Jorge marking off the checklist items as she completed them. They'd progressed from the front-engine coupling to the rear rotor before Liz dragged in a deep breath and launched her casual inquisition.

"I was surprised to hear Emilio is taking charters. I thought he was doing pretty well on his tuna runs."

"You know how it is. One day is good, the next not so good."

"I hear some of the tuna captains supplement their income by running drugs."

"I hear that, as well."

She feigned a surprised innocence. "But not Emilio. Surely he wouldn't get mixed up with something like that...would he?"

Mustache twitching, Jorge worked his mouth from side to side for several seconds. With each passing second, the deadweight in the pit of Liz's stomach grew heavier. Oh, God! Surely Jorge couldn't know of or be involved in drug smuggling. Or worse!

"I do not *think* Emilio would do such a thing," he said after a long moment. "But Maria..."

"Yes?"

"She says her cousin always wishes for more than he has." His burly shoulders lifted in a shrug. "So do we all, eh? Maria wishes for a new refrigerator. My grandson wants this thing called a Gamebox. You save to buy a Sikorsky so you may start your own charter service."

"What about you, Jorge? What do you wish for?"

His mustaches lifted in a wide grin. "I wish to be your chief mechanic."

"You got it," she promised with a ridiculous feeling of relief. She hadn't wormed much out of Jorge, but it was enough to ease the awful burden of suspicion. Whatever his wife's cousin might or might not be up to, it *couldn't* involve the mechanic.

"Let's get the cargo loaded before our passengers arrive."

* * *

She lifted off an hour later with the palletized cargo strapped down and the replacement crew of six buckled into the side-facing web seats.

AM-237 rose up to greet her, looming out of the sea like some mythical creature with the two giant cranes for arms and orange fuel flanges for a tail. Liz had radioed ahead to advise the crane operators she was on final approach so they could swing the monster arms out of the way. They were clear when she swooped in, timed her descent to the rise and fall of the platform and touched down.

The crew members coming off their month-long rotation were lined up on the pipe deck and eager to depart. Liz reviewed the manifest while the quartermaster and his folks unloaded the cargo. Paying close attention to both names and faces, she checked IDs against the computer-generated manifest.

One was an American, on his way home to San Diego. Two were foreign born but had visas granting them entry into the States. The other three planned to head straight for La Paz and connecting international flights to Europe and the Middle East.

Her chest tight, Liz screened the American carefully. Was he a target? Would he make it home safely or disappear somewhere en route, as Devlin's friend had? Would he even make it out of Piedras Rojas?

Devlin had assured her each of the six would have close surveillance on every leg of their journey. Still, Liz had to swallow the warning that hovered in the back of her throat as she watched them strap in.

She was about to climb back into the cockpit and power up when Conrad Wallace heaved his bulk up the ladder and onto the helideck.

"Hey! Liz!"

The brisk breeze off the ocean whipped his thin brown hair around his head like a hyperactive dust mop. Hanging on to the lifeline, the AmMex rep inched his way across the pad. Liz hoped to heck he hadn't decided to make a last-minute run back to dry land. She'd have to recalculate her fuel load and redistribute some weight.

"Almost missed you," he huffed. "I was down in the galley."

Swilling coffee and pontificating to anyone who'd listen, Liz guessed.

"What's up?"

"I need to mail this letter."

"Sorry, the mail pouch is sealed and I've already signed for it."

"I know, I know," Wallace groused. "The mail clerk sent the damned thing up before I got my data together. Just drop this envelope in the mail slot at the terminal."

She took the envelope, noting that it was addressed to some company she'd never heard of with a post office box in La Paz. She wasn't going to risk her license and her livelihood by slipping something through customs, though, even if it came from the company rep.

"I can't just drop it in the mail slot. It'll have to go through security screening."

"Sure, sure. No problem."

"See you next run, Conrad."

Nodding, he waved to the men inside the chopper and backtracked along the lifeline. Liz stuffed the envelope in her leg pocket, strapped in and flipped to the power-up checklist on her kneeboard.

Jorge was waiting when she touched down. Liz left him to secure the aircraft and hefted the mail pouch. Hard on the heels of her passengers, she entered the terminal.

The usual customs official processed them in, assisted by a second official Liz didn't recognize. She stood in line with the others, surreptitiously scanning the room. She knew Devlin was conducting a visual ID, probably via the camera mounted high on one wall. She could feel his eyes on her as she plopped the mail pouch onto the counter.

"Here you are. Oh, and this needs to go with it."

Wallace's letter joined the pouch on the dusty tile. The official gave the envelope a desultory glance.

"*Sí*, I will screen it."

Liz left the six oilmen waiting impatiently while the officials pawed through their bags and checked their papers. Exiting the customs area, she started across the terminal for the café. She'd taken only a few steps when a bent, arthritic woman swathed in layers of black hobbled forward. She clutched a knobby walking stick that tapped out an unsteady beat with each step.

Politely Liz went around her. Or tried to. A clawlike hand reached out and snagged her arm. Startled, she looked down into a seamed face framed by wispy white hair. Bottle-thick glasses magnified the woman's eyes into blurred brown orbs. Her voice weak and wavering with age, she asked for assistance.

"You are pilot, *sí?*"

"*Sí.*"

"Would you help me to find my bag? It doesn't come off the plane."

Liz threw a quick glance around the terminal. She wanted to track down Devlin, hear the results of last night's efforts, verify he had a visual on her passengers.

"*Por favor,*" the crone pleaded.

"Yes, of course. Lost baggage is right this way."

At the baggage claim area Liz looked in vain for a handler.

"I don't see…"

The grip on her arm tightened. "In there," the woman murmured in an entirely different voice, thrusting her toward a side door.

"Hey!"

"It's me. Maggie."

Her jaw sagging, Liz gaped at the seamed face.

"In here."

Still slack-jawed, Liz let Maggie tug her into a dusty, disused office. Adam was there, in deep conversation with a slender blonde in a leg cast and a gorgeous Latino. Devlin sat with his shoulders hunched and eyes locked on the screen of a high-tech laptop.

He was in black Lycra again. Her pulse jumping at the sight of all those interesting bulges, Liz skimmed a quick glance around the room. His wet suit and scuba gear were stashed in a corner. Stifling a pang of regret that they'd only have time for another parting, she returned the smile he aimed in her direction.

"Good run out to the patch?"

"Smooth as a baby's butt," she replied.

Her attention diverted, she watched in utter fascination as Maggie straightened and shed a good fifty years with just a simple rearrangement of her features.

"How the heck did you do that?"

Grinning, the brunette slid the bottle-thick glasses down to the tip of her nose. "It's simple. You think old, you act old, you are old. Same when you're playing a giddy young housewife or a tired IBM executive."

"Or a streetwalker," the hunk of a Latino commented, strolling over to join them. "That is how I met Chameleon," he explained, his smile devastating under a pencil-thin black mustache. "In a very dark, very smoky bar. I am Colonel Luis Esteban," he said, offering Liz his hand. "And this is my wife, Dr. Claire Cantwell."

"Code name Cyrene," Maggie supplied as the blonde stumped forward on her half cast. "Luis and Cyrene were supposed to be on their honeymoon. They flew in to help with the surveillance."

"We couldn't let you two have all the fun."

Smiling, Cyrene was about respond to Liz's question about her cast when Devlin scraped his chair back.

"Okay, team. Those six men are the same ones I tagged on the rig. I've activated their tracking devices. Check to see if you're picking up their signals."

The other four flipped up cell phones and punched various buttons. Liz felt distinctly left out when they acknowledged the signals and prepared to disperse. The blonde and her husband, she was informed, would follow the three men heading straight for the La Paz airport and see they boarded their international flights. Adam would trail the American, who had driven down from San Diego and planned to drive back. That left two—a Mexican electrician's helper who lived right here in Piedras Rojas and a Portuguese crane operator.

"You need to keep the Portuguese on your radar screen," Devlin said to Maggie. "He was issued a visa to visit relatives in the States. The visa's good for six months."

"I've got him covered."

Right before their eyes she went through a re-transformation. The glasses slid up, blurring the brilliance of her eyes. The lines of her face seemed to sag. Her shoulders slumped. Grasping the walking stick, she shuffled toward the door.

"What about me?" Liz asked Devlin when the others had departed. "What can I do?"

"You can tell me what Jorge had to say this morning." He checked his watch. "I've got a little time before I need to get back aboard the rig."

"How are you planning to accomplish that in broad daylight without anyone seeing you?"

"Through one of the subsea escape hatches."

She'd forgotten about the safety hatches. Some were designed to allow subs and other submersibles to dock to a rig and perform rescues in a catastrophic event such as a sinking. Others merely allowed crew members to egress the structure and swim like hell.

"What did Jorge say?"

"He said Emilio is always wishing for more than he had."

"Our friend Emilio has more than meets the eye. Adam and I shook down his boat at oh-dark-thirty this morning. He's running a seven-hundred-horsepower Caterpillar diesel turbocharged engine."

Liz whistled softly. "That's a lot of horses for a fishing boat."

"It is. Plus he's packed it with electronics. Radar, a new loran system, GPS—everything he needs to dodge coast guard patrol boats."

"You think he's running drugs?"

"I think it's a damned good possibility."

Devlin's jaw set. The ice in his eyes sent a little shiver down Liz's spine.

"The question I want answered is what else he's running. Adam and I planted hidden cameras. Next time Emilio puts out to sea, OMEGA will be watching. In the meantime…"

The hard edges softened and the cocky roustabout she knew emerged once again.

"In the meantime," he said, slipping an arm around her waist, "let's both do some thinking."

"About?"

He drew her closer, teasing her mouth with his. "What we talked about last night."

Nine

Despite her shuffling gait and sweltering layers of black clothing, Maggie had no difficulty keeping up with Paulo Casimiro. The big, curly haired Portuguese departed the Aero Baja terminal toting a duffel bag on his shoulder and, according to Rigger, a full month's pay in his pocket. His red-and-white-striped shirt made him an easy target. The electronic device Rigger had planted on the man made following him even easier. Maggie hobbled along, dropping well back at times. Other times, she'd hike her heavy black skirt, cut through back alleys and pick him up again when she emerged onto Piedras Rojas' one main street.

Lord, it felt good to be back in the field again!

After ten years of marriage, she adored Adam more than she would have dreamed possible and experienced a ridiculous gush of love at the mere thought of Gillian's cornflower-blue eyes or Samantha's infectious giggles. And Adam Ridgeway Jr. aka the Tank. So sturdy. So strong. Smelling of baby powder and the dirt he and their horse of a dog loved to dig in. Maggie missed the kids more with each passing hour, but had to admit being part of the action again sent a sizzle through her veins. Enjoying the adrenaline rush, she kept on her target.

He was booked on a flight out of La Paz tomorrow morning, reportedly heading for Boston to visit relatives before flying home. The man had plenty of time to idle away until then, but appeared to be in no hurry to squander his pay. He strolled down the street, savoring the scent of pork sizzling on charcoal braziers and the raucous salsa beat booming from the corner stand where an enterprising youngster hawked CDs and video games.

He made the mistake of stopping to purchase a CD. Like a Biblical plague, a swarm of other determined entrepreneurs appeared from nowhere, offering outrageous discounts on everything from hand-worked jewelry to hubcaps. The crane operator slapped a thorny palm over his back pocket to avoid losing his wallet and waded through the noisy throng. A determined quartet trailed him for several blocks.

"You come off the rig, yes? You buy tequila or rum to take home."

"This silver is from Taxco. Look, it is very fine workmanship."

"You want a woman, señor? My sister, she is beautiful."

Shaking his head, Casimiro plowed ahead. The eager salesmen dogged his heels.

"My sister, she has a friend. Many friends. You like two women? Three?"

"Taxco silver is the best, señor. Look! Look!"

In an effort to lose them, the Portuguese ducked down a side street. Maggie started to follow but stopped when a figure emerged from the shadow of a doorway. With the rolling gait of those used to a deck under their feet, he sauntered after the roustabout.

"Hola, señor."

Casimiro threw a glance over his shoulder. Mixing Spanish and a smattering of tortured Portuguese, Emilio caught up with him.

"You come off AM-237, *sí?*"

"*Sí.*"

"My friend works the rig." He slapped a hand on the roustabout's back, one deepwater man to another. "I have tequila on my boat. The *Santa Guadalupe*. She is just there, at the dock. I will pour you a drink, yes, and you tell me how my friend does."

Some yards back, Maggie slipped a hand into her skirt pocket. Her heart thumping, she palmed a cell phone. When she raised her hand again, a casual observer would have thought she'd lifted it to scratch the hairy wart on her chin.

"OMEGA control," she murmured into the speaker, "this is Chameleon."

"I'd better make tracks."

Devlin gave Liz a last, long kiss. He'd delayed his return to the rig as long as he dared to hear what she had to say concerning Jorge. He'd also tracked the movements off all six targets. Three were on a bus en route to the La Paz airport, with Cyrene and Esteban right behind them. The local had arrived home and was undoubtedly enjoying a reunion with his wife and kids. The American had picked up his car and hit the road north, with Adam following a few miles behind. Maggie had the Portuguese in her sights.

Much as Devlin hated to depart the scene, he had to get back to the rig. If these six made it home safely, the next six might not. OMEGA intended to keep him in the field until they broke this vicious ring.

Leaving Liz made the departure harder than he'd anticipated, however. The woman was now not only in his head. She was in his blood.

"When are you scheduled to make your next run?" he asked, retrieving his scuba gear.

"AmMex is flying in an on-site inspection team. I'm supposed to haul them out to AM-237 on Wednesday."

"Wednesday, huh? If I'm still on the patch, maybe you can arrange…"

His cell phone pinged, cutting him off in midsentence. Riever was coordinating the movements of all four agents from headquarters. That was his ring tone. Dropping his gear, Devlin flipped up the phone.

"Rigger, here."

"It's Riev. Chameleon's target was just approached by the local you had me check out, Emilio Garcia. She says— Hang on a sec."

Fierce satisfaction ripped through Devlin. Finally! A real break!

"That was Chameleon. She says the target and Garcia boarded his boat and went belowdecks. She's going to slip aboard, as well."

"Adam and I planted cameras on that craft last night," Devlin reminded him with tense urgency. "Get those activated, Riev."

"I'm receiving the visuals as we speak."

Devlin kept the phone to his ear and used the brief pause to fill Liz in. "Emilio lured the Portuguese crane operator aboard his boat. Maggie's going aboard as well."

"I've got Garcia and Casimiro on the screens," Riever reported, switching to broadcast mode to include both Rigger and Maggie on the transmissions. "There's someone else in the cabin. I don't... Hell! Whoever it is just whacked the Portuguese over the head with a marline spike. He went down like a felled ox. Chameleon, did you copy that?"

"I copy. I'm going below."

"No!" Devlin bit out. "Wait for backup."

He was already digging in his gear bag. Retrieving a belt with a lethal assortment of attachments, he raced for the door. A startled Liz chased after him.

"Hang tight, Chameleon. I'm on my way."

"Can't wait," Maggie replied in a terse whisper. "Emilio's firing up the engines as we speak. They'll have to come above deck to throw off the mooring ropes and clear the dock. I'll take them one at a— Uuuuuh!"

The small grunt was followed by silence that sliced into Devlin's heart. Riever broke the stillness with a taut transmission.

"Chameleon, this is control. Come in, please."

Devlin was in full sprint, the phone jammed against his ear. He burst through the rear door of the terminal into a blinding haze of light.

He and Riever weren't the only ones on the net, he discovered as he and Liz ran for the vehicle he'd parked at the rear of the building.

"Chameleon, this is Thunder." His voice as cold and sharp as a scalpel, Adam tried to contact his wife. "Come in, please."

Devlin strained to hear over the hammer of pounding footsteps. Maggie didn't reply. A second later Riever made a stark report.

"We've lost her signal."

"What about the cameras?" Devlin panted into the phone. "Are you still receiving visuals?"

"Roger. I'm showing Emilio at the controls. The other guy is tying up our target. Wait! Here comes a third. He's dragging something behind him. Something bundled in black."

Over the jackhammer beat of his heart, Devlin heard the hiss of Adam's indrawn breath.

"It's Chameleon," Riever confirmed after a second that seemed to stretch for hours. "Looks like she's out cold, but she must be alive. They wouldn't waste rope tying her up otherwise."

The vise around Devlin's heart eased a micrometer. He grabbed the vehicle's door handle and threw the web utility belt in the backseat. Liz jumped into the passenger seat.

"The boat's moving," Riever reported as Devlin jammed the key into the ignition. "We're tracking it via the signals from the device planted on the Portuguese."

Adam came on the net again. His years as head of OMEGA resonated as he assumed command of the situation.

"Notify the coast guard. Mexican or American, whoever's got a cutter nearby. Tell them to run an immediate intercept. And get some air cover. I'm returning to Piedras Rojas. Keep me advised."

Devlin snapped his phone shut. He didn't have time to provide Liz with more than the bare essentials. "They've got Maggie and are putting out to sea. Adam has requested air cover."

She whipped her head up. "We can manage that. Let's go!"

Liz was out of the car and running before Devlin retrieved his utility belt. The Aero Baja chopper sat baking on its pad, right where she'd set it down less than an hour ago.

Her mind churned as she calculated fuel, weight, airspeed and direction on the fly. She hadn't had to buck headwinds on the run out to the patch this morning. The cargo hold was empty. With only her and Devlin's weight to factor into the equation, she should have enough fuel to stay in the air for an hour, if necessary.

Scrambling into the cockpit, she initiated the power-up sequence. Devlin tossed his gear into the rear compartment before releasing the tie-down straps and kicking away the chocks. He scrambled into the copilot's seat just as Jorge erupted from inside the hangar. Swiping his hands on a rag, the mechanic rushed over to the pad.

"Where do you go?" he shouted above the roar of the engines.

Liz weighed the odds and came down firmly on her friend's side. She trusted this man. Besides, there was a lot of ocean out there. OMEGA had lost Maggie's signal. If they lost the signal they'd planted on the Portuguese, Liz might be able to lock on to the fishing boat's transponder or ship-to-shore communications.

"We're going after Emilio," she yelled. "He's just put out to sea with Mrs. Ridgeway aboard."

"Señora Ridgeway charters his boat? He says nothing to us."

Liz didn't have time to explain. "Do you know what RSS frequency Emilio transmits on?"

Devlin had said the fisherman had crammed his boat with electronics. Liz was betting the array included a Ratt Ship/Shore radio, the type used by most ships at sea to transmit and receive administrative and operational traffic. Shore stations transmitted on 5, 10 and 15 megahertz bands. Ships responded on frequencies in the 2, 3, 4, 6, 8, 16 and 22 megahertz range. Liz didn't have time to run through all of them searching for signals from Emilio's radio.

"Jorge, please! Mrs. Ridgeway's in trouble. What frequency?"

"Six-point-five. Sometimes eight-five." His face grim, the mechanic stuffed the rag in his back pocket. "I will come with you to help you look."

Liz darted a glance at Devlin, who gave a curt nod. Once Jorge was aboard and strapped in, the chopper lifted off the pad.

The tracking device Devlin had planted on the Portuguese crane operator continued to transmit, thank God. OMEGA headquarters vectored Liz on a course that took her north by northwest.

Using both hands and feet to work the controls, she pushed her bird to max airspeed. Ten pulse-pounding minutes later they picked up the lighter aquamarine of a boat's wake trailing through the cobalt-blue of the Pacific. Mere moments later they spotted the boat.

"There!"

Leaning over Liz's shoulder, Jorge pointed at the white speck. Devlin had filled him in on the details. He now knew what drove their desperate hunt for his cousin.

"That is the *Guadalupe*."

Nodding, Liz pushed for a few more knots of speed. The white speck grew to a fat-bottomed trawler, churning up a frothy wake. Its twin booms formed a V with the tall mast centered between them. The rear deck sported piles of rolled nets and a hoist that jutted up and out over the deck at a forty-five-degree angle.

"How close can you get me?" Devlin asked, straining forward in his harness to sweep the boat with narrowed eyes.

"As close as you want." Liz lined up on the rocking mast. "Getting you aboard her is another matter. I can skim alongside just above the waterline and let you swim for it or Jorge can lower you to the deck on a sling."

Either way made him an easy target should Emilio and friends object to being boarded. Liz tried to think of another option.

"Try the radio. See if you can raise them. Maybe they'll surrender peacefully if they know we're on to them."

Devlin flipped through the frequencies to six-point-five and keyed the mike. "Ahoy, *Santa Guadalupe*. This is Aero Baja 214. Do you read me?"

They waited for a response, static filling their earphones.

"*Santa Guadalupe*, this is Aero Baja 214. We're right off your stern. Do you read me?"

Liz held the chopper steady as a figure appeared on the back deck and trained binoculars at the fast-approaching chopper. The red handkerchief knotted around his neck gave a good clue as to his identity.

"That looks like Emilio."

"*Sí*," Jorge confirmed in a low growl. "That is my wife's cousin. *Híbrido!*"

A second figure popped out of the cabin. This one clutched a high-powered rifle. Emilio dropped the binoculars and stabbed a finger at the chopper. His cohort brought the rifle up to his shoulder. So much for a peaceful surrender!

"Hang on!" Liz shouted.

Gripping the collective, she prepared to take evasive action. Before she could jerk the controls, a third individual burst onto the deck. Streaming long white hair, she leaped forward and swung an odd shaped bat.

"That's Maggie!" Devlin strained against his harness. "Jesus! What's she armed with?"

Whatever it was, it caught the shooter up alongside his head. Stunned, the man staggered against the ship's rail. Maggie swung again and sent him careening over the side. His rifle went overboard with him.

She then turned her attention to Emilio, who dived for one of the long-handled gaffers lashed to the rail. With its sharp hook, it made for a lethal weapon.

Maggie fended off his attack with her own weapon while Liz swooped in as close as she dared. The skids were less than a foot off the water when Devlin dived in. Jorge splashed in after him.

Mindful of those rocking booms, Liz had no choice but to back off. Her heart jammed in the middle of her throat, she watched Maggie go down on the slippery deck. She scuttled backward, dodging a vicious swipe of the gaff and scissors kicking wildly to untangle the heavy skirts wrapped around her legs.

Liz didn't stop to think. Helicopters flew every which way but loose. Sideways. Backward. With the right pilot at the controls, they could do a pirouette while maintaining forward momentum. They could even turn on their sides and put out a rotor wash powerful enough to knock a full-grown man off his feet.

Which is exactly what it did.

Flying horizontal with the surface of the sea, Liz caught only a glimpse of Emilio as he hurtled across the deck and slammed into the cabin bulkhead.

Liz trailed the *Santa Guadalupe* back to Piedras Rojas' tiny harbor. She made a low pass, saw Adam standing on the dock and waved to him before zooming in for a landing at the Aero Baja terminal. Once there, she jumped in her Jeep and tore back through town to the harbor.

They were all still aboard the tuna boat, waiting for the Mexican authorities to arrive and take the suspects into custody. Maggie had shed her wig.

Paulo Casimiro was white around the gills, shaken from his near brush with death. Jorge nursed bruised and skinned knuckles, which no doubt accounted for the bloody pulp that used to be his cousin-in-law's nose. Devlin and Adam were conducting similarly physical and very intense conversations with two unidentified males. Sullen and restrained by plastic cuffs at wrists and ankles, the two pointed a figurative finger at Emilio.

"Not that we need their cooperation," Maggie said, combing her fingers through her honey-brown hair. "Emilio admitted he was paid to lure Paulo onto his boat, conk him over the head and steal his papers. The bastard bragged about it, in fact, after he had us trussed up like sardines."

"How did you get loose?"

"An old trick Adam taught me when we were both at OMEGA." Throwing her husband a fond glance, she lifted her skirt and waggled a laced-up granny shoe. "Always tuck a straight edged blade into your sole when you're going into the field."

"I'll remember that."

"Doesn't hurt to have a stuffed mackerel on hand, either." Grinning, Maggie pointed at the object wedged in the corner of the deck. "Emilio had it mounted on the wall inside the cabin. The thing packs quite a wallop."

"A fish? You knocked a couple of thugs on their asses with a *fish?*"

"Nothing special about that." Her brown eyes

sparkled with laughter. "You did the same to Emilio with a whoosh of air."

"Speaking of thugs…" Liz swiveled around to get a better look at the two men hunched beside the tuna boat captain. She didn't recognize either of them. "Do they all work for El Tiburón?"

"Evidently not. Emilio bragged about that, too. Said The Shark wanted nothing to do with the scheme, that it was too risky and would bring police from every country converging on this area. So his nephew, Martín, ran it without his uncle's knowledge. Emilio was one of his captains. Only, they had a slight falling out, which ended with a bullet between Martín Alvarez's eyes."

Liz let out a low whistle. Emilio had stepped in some serious doo-doo. Not only would he have the police coming down on him, he'd have to answer for flouting El Tiburón's authority in his own territory.

She knew which one *she'd* worry most about.

Ten

"We're still missing a key piece of the puzzle."

Devlin deposited his plate on the sturdy trunk Liz used as a coffee table. The remains of their microwave pizza littered the surface.

It was late, well past midnight, but a wide-awake Liz sat cross-legged beside him on the sofa. Still pumped from the wild chase this morning, she'd waited here at her apartment while Devlin and a small, select group of law enforcement officials conducted marathon sessions with Emilio and his cohorts.

The interrogations would continue for some days, but the rest of the OMEGA team had dispersed. Maggie and Adam had left for home. Claire and her new husband had resumed their honeymoon. Devlin would remain in the area a while longer. Although the Mexican authorities had promised to keep his ties to the U.S. Government quiet, he knew the information was bound to leak. Probably already had. He figured he'd blown his cover, but didn't intend to leave until he'd fitted all the pieces together.

"Emilio swears his only contact was Martín Alvarez," he told Liz, reiterating what Maggie had told her on the boat. "Alvarez supplied the names and photos of the targets and told Emilio when they were scheduled to rotate off the rig. He also picked up the papers after Emilio had…had disposed of the bodies."

The words sliced at Devlin's throat like broken glass. He had no doubt now Harry Johnson was dead. Emilio claimed he didn't know Harry, had nothing to do with his disappearance. He probably hadn't, as Devlin's friend had rotated off another rig farther south. Yet Emilio admitted Martín's instructions were explicit. Snatch the target. Take the papers. Weight the body with lead weights and feed it to the fish. He also admitted Martín did business with other boat captains along the coast.

Anxious to cut a deal, Emilio had supplied names of the captains he knew or suspected were part of the scheme. The Mexican authorities were rounding them up and bringing them in for questioning. Devlin planned to be present at the interrogations but he suspected they'd sing the same refrain Emilio had. Their only contact was Martín Alvarez.

"So why did Emilio go after Paulo?" Liz wanted to know. "With Martín dead, he wouldn't get paid for stealing the papers."

"He and Alvarez had set up the snatch before they got crosswise of each other. Emilio went ahead with it, figuring he wouldn't have any trouble coming up with another buyer. He was also hoping Martín's inside man—his source for information about the crew members rotating off the rig—would contact him directly when he learned of the snatch. Turns out Emilio planned to take over operations from Martín. That's why he lifted the shark's tooth off the body, by the way."

"He needed an authority symbol? Something to show he was now in charge?"

"Exactly. He had to be careful where and when he flashed it, though. Martín had warned him his uncle wanted no part of the scheme."

"Emilio-baby took one hell of a chance there." Liz's face screwed into a grimace. "Speaking from personal experience, I can tell you El Tiburón has access to all kinds of information. He would have latched on to Emilio sooner or later."

"We're lucky it was later." A tight knot of anger still twisted Devlin's gut, but he forced a smile. "We can chalk that one up to you. You spotted the shark's tooth and made the connection."

"Did Emilio still have it on him when they booked him?"

"Yeah, he did."

"What do you want to bet it won't remain in the evidence locker for long? The Shark has connections."

"Doesn't matter. We've got Emilio's confession on videotape. We don't have to have the tooth to connect him to Martín or the murder-for-passport scheme."

Frowning, Devlin went back to the missing link, the piece of the puzzle he had yet to find.

"Someone was providing Martín with information about the rig crew members. Names. Nationalities. Rotation dates. Someone with access to the AmMex personnel database."

The woman next to him gave a small hoot. "Their system isn't exactly secure. Any precocious eight-year-old could hack into it. I got in a few times myself to verify passenger data."

"Tell me something I don't know. Our experts found a dozen unauthorized accesses. We also screened thousands of e-mails sent via AmMex's satellite communications system over the past three months. None of them led back to Martín Alvarez."

"So the inside person passed the information to Alvarez by other means. In person, maybe, when he came ashore."

"Or by a message hidden in some object carried off the rig by an unsuspecting mule."

Liz made another noise, this one more of a choking gulp than a hoot.

"What?" Devlin asked.

"I haul a mail pouch out and back on every run."

"I know. Every item you hauled out and back since I arrived at the patch was screened."

"Not every item."

"What do you mean?" His brows snapped together. "Did you act as a private courier for someone on the rig?"

"Do I look stupid?"

Actually, Devlin thought wryly, she looked indignant as hell.

"I don't know most of those guys," she said, skewering him with a glare. "I wouldn't try to slip something through customs even for someone I *did* know. In this country, antics like that can earn you a one-way ticket to a very small, very crowded cell."

"Then what did we miss?"

"Nothing much, really. I probably shouldn't have even brought it up. Conrad Wallace had a letter he wanted to get in the mail, but he'd missed the pouch so I carried it back for him."

"Wallace, huh?"

Devlin turned the information over in his mind. After the AmMex rep had dropped that remark about losing big at the casinos, he'd had OMEGA comb through the man's personal finances. The queries had turned up a few questionable transactions but no major infusions of cash. This letter would most likely turn out to be a dead end, too. Still, it needed checking out.

"What did you do with the letter?"

"I gave it to the customs official at the terminal. I

assume he screened it before he dropped it in the mail slot with the pouch."

"Did you see who it was addressed to?"

"A company in La Paz. Marine Supplies, Incorporated, or something like that."

Devlin extracted his cell phone from the case clipped to his waist. "It's probably nothing, but I'll have our guys check this company and…"

He broke off at the slam of a car door. His glance sliced to Liz.

"Expecting someone?"

"No. You?"

Shaking his head, he pushed off the sofa and slid a hand into the gear bag sitting beside the trunk. His fingers closed around cold steel as footsteps sounded on the stairs, quick and fast. Devlin jerked his chin toward the waist-high divider between the kitchen and the living room.

"Get behind the counter."

Liz gave him a disgusted look and retreated to the kitchen, only to emerge a second later with her fist wrapped around the handle of a kitchen knife.

Devlin didn't have time to argue. Thumbing the safety on the Walther PPK, he planted his shoulder blades against the wall beside the door a half second before their uninvited visitor rapped against the thick panel.

Devlin made a chopping motion, signaling Liz to remain silent. Another knock followed the first. Louder. More insistent.

"Hey! 'Lizabeth!" The shout came through the panel, muffled but distinctly male. "I saw your lights. Open up. It's me. Donny."

Liz's eyes popped. She gawked at Devlin in openmouthed astonishment before reaching for the door latch.

"What the sweet Jesus are you doing here?"

"I got your e-mail." Her former fiancé leaned an elbow on the door frame and cranked his boyish charm up to full power. "Thought if I showed up in person I might convince you to reconsider."

A dimple creased his left cheek. A week ago that lopsided smile might have given Liz pause. Now it made her want to drill a matching dent in his right cheek.

"Not tonight," she said without batting an eye. "Not tomorrow. Not ever."

"Com'on, 'Lizabeth." Still confident, still cocky, he pushed forward and grabbed her arm. "You missed me. You know you missed me."

Stunned by his arrogance, Liz whipped free of his hold. "I did. For a long time. Now I don't."

"Bull. You can't turn it off that fast."

Devlin had heard enough. Shoving the PPK into its holster, he shouldered Liz aside.

"You heard what the lady said. You're history, pal."

The gutless wonder in the doorway blinked in surprise and backed up an involuntary step. Recovering swiftly, he thrust out his jaw.

"Who the hell are you?"

"I'm the man who's going to plant his fist in your face."

Grabbing Carter by the shirtfront, Devlin spun him inside, drew back an arm and let fly. Bone crunched against bone. Blood spurted from his nose. Carter crumpled like a sandbag that had lost its fill and groaned just once before passing out cold.

Liz was seriously annoyed. She couldn't believe Donny had the balls to show up like this. She would have knocked him on his keister herself once she'd recovered from her shock.

"I wanted to do that," she groused to Devlin.

"When he comes to, you can have the next shot."

"I will."

His eyes met hers over Donny's prone body. She saw the fierce satisfaction of a male who's routed a rival and intends to claim the prize. Stepping over Donny, he curled a hand around her nape.

"I hope you're not nursing any residual pangs for this jerk."

"What do you think?"

"I think… Scratch that." His fingers tightened, drawing her closer. "I *know* I want to be part of your life, Liz. We can work this business of separate careers. Make our schedules fit our needs."

"Are you sure?"

His grin appeared and put a stutter in her heart. "You resolved any and all doubts this morning, when you stood your chopper on its tail. I love your courage." He brushed her mouth with his. "Your incredible skill." Another kiss, longer this time. "Then there's your nice, tight ass."

He kissed her again, hard and deep, and it was all she could do to gasp out a suggestion.

"Why don't we continue the inventory inside?"

"Good idea."

He kicked Donny's feet out of the way and went to close the door. A sudden wash of headlights across the courtyard stilled his hand.

"Now who?" Liz muttered as a black Mercedes glided to a halt beside the vehicle Donny must have driven up in. She got her answer a moment later, when a familiar twosome jumped out of the Mercedes and did a quick sweep of the courtyard.

"Uh-oh."

Tensing, Devlin reached for the automatic tucked into his waistband. "Uh-oh what?"

"The ugly one is Short Guy. The gorilla in the lavender shirt and natty shoes is Wingtips. And that," Liz added when another figure exited the rear seat, "is El Tiburón."

Devlin hefted the Walther into plain view. Spitting curses, Short Guy and Wingtips scrambled for their weapons. Their boss stilled them with a swift order and calmly surveyed the two framed in the open doorway.

"There is no need for guns," he called up to them. "I merely wish to speak with you, Ms. Moore."

Devlin answered for her. "She's not talking to anyone until you and your two goons deposit your weapons in the dirt. Slowly. Very slowly."

The Shark shrugged and reached inside his linen sports coat. Using a thumb and index finger, he extracted an automatic and let it drop. His henchmen were too loyal to argue with him, but scowled as they followed his lead.

"May we come up now, Ms. Moore?" Alvarez asked politely.

Liz looked to Devlin for guidance. She wasn't ashamed to admit she was out of her league here.

"You may," he responded for her. "But your friends wait down there."

"As you will."

"No, *patrón!*" Wingtips followed his involuntary outburst with a spate of impassioned Spanish.

"Be quiet! Ms. Moore knows why I am here."

Liz didn't have a clue, but elected not to broadcast her ignorance as The Shark mounted the stairs.

As at their last meeting, he was elegantly dressed in pleated slacks and a dark shirt, paired this time with the linen jacket. The shirt was open down to the second or third button, affording Liz full view of the ivory triangle nestled against his chest hair.

"You got your tooth back!"

"Yes, I did."

"I *knew* it wouldn't remain in the evidence locker for long."

"You were correct."

Unperturbed by the gun barrel Devlin had sighted on the shark's tooth, the mobster reached the top of the stairs and gave the unconscious Donny a curious glance.

"Was this one bothering you, Ms. Moore?"

"You could put it that way."

"You should have told me. I would have taken care of him for you."

"Devlin here took care of him just fine, thank you."

Alvarez turned his black eyes on the OMEGA agent. "So you are Devlin. My sources have relayed interesting reports about your activities this afternoon."

Liz could see Devlin wasn't too thrilled that the mobster had a radar lock on him, but he covered it with a careless shrug.

"My sources have relayed a few interesting reports about you, as well."

"I should imagine they have." Raising fingers tipped by neatly manicured nails, he fondled the gleaming ivory triangle and turned to Liz. "My sources also tell me you are the one who spotted this on that pig Emilio."

"Well...er..."

Liz didn't want to take all the credit. Or blame, as the case may be.

"This is my good luck piece," Alvarez said quietly. "A shark attacked me when I was swimming out beyond the arches. I had only a small knife, but I put out its eye. After much effort, I killed it and dragged it to shore. I was very young at that time and very strong."

He wasn't exactly a ninety-pound weakling now. Liz kept the thought to herself.

"Ever since, this tooth has been... How do you say? My talisman. The sign of my authority. My nephew stole it and used it without my knowledge. I would have strangled him for that with my own hands had Emilio Garcia not deprived me of the pleasure."

She didn't doubt him for a minute.

"Instead," he said with a thin smile, "I must take my vengeance on Emilio, who conspired with my nephew against me."

"He's under police protection," Devlin bit out. "You won't get to him."

"Do you think not?" Alvarez asked politely.

Liz was trying to decide which one of them to put her money on when Donny decided to regain consciousness. Groaning, he struggled up on one elbow and put his other hand to his nose. When it connected, he winced and snorted a froth of blood into his palm. He stared at the gore for a few, disbelieving moments before fury propelled him to his feet.

"You sonuvabitch!" he snarled at Devlin, so beside himself with outrage he ignored the newcomer in their midst. "You broke my nose!"

"You're lucky that's all I broke. Now shut up and get out of my face before I— Oh, well. Never mind."

Donny sank like a stone again, this time from the swift chop Alvarez delivered to the back of his neck.

"He is not wise, this one." Those flat black eyes lifted to Liz. "Do you wish me to dispose of him for you?"

Liz entertained the notion for a second or two.

With a nasty little pang of regret, she stifled the thought. This was Donny, the man she'd once loved. Or thought she had. The suddenness and intensity of her feelings for Devlin were making her wonder if she knew what love was.

"I'll pass on that," she told Alvarez, "but thanks for the offer."

"As you wish." Dismissing Donny with cool disdain, he changed topics. "Those who know me will tell you I pay my debts. As promised, I have wired an electronic transfer to your bank and paid your loan in full."

"What!"

"I also wired the manufacturer. Your helicopter will be delivered next week. A Sikorsky 450L, I believe it is."

Liz got her breath back in a hot, fast rush. "I can't accept a payoff like that! Not from you!"

"The helicopter will arrive next week. What you do with it is your decision."

"I'll tell you what I'll do with it," she fired back. "I'll donate it to the antidrug task force operating in this region and suggest they fly close cover over a certain hacienda just south of there."

A glint of something that looked suspiciously like laughter appeared in Alvarez's dark eyes. "Perhaps we should renegotiate our terms."

Liz now knew how Alice must have felt after tumbling down the rabbit hole. Her ex-fiancée lay in a heap at her feet. The man who'd turned her life and notions of love upside down was nursing skinned knuckles and a 9 mm automatic. And a cold-blooded killer appeared to think she'd just delivered the joke of the century.

Breathing fire, Liz set him straight. "I'm dead serious, Alvarez. If you don't rescind all these wires you sent, you'll have a brand-new 450L buzzing your compound twice a day and three times every night. I'll fly it myself if I have to."

"Very well. I shall instruct the bank to cancel payment on the loan and cancel the delivery order."

He fingered the symbol of his authority again, considering, weighing, deciding.

"I am a man of honor, Ms. Moore. My own brand of honor, to be sure, but honor nevertheless. Perhaps you will accept this as reward for the return of my talisman."

She eyed the crumpled envelope he drew out of his breast pocket with the same suspicion a plump, juicy hen might give a python. "What is it?"

"Something my sister retrieved from a post office box her son had rented. She found the key to the box when she cleaned out Martín's apartment. I think you…" He included Devlin with a gracious nod. "Both of you will find the contents interesting."

Liz took the envelope gingerly and turned it over. The first line of the address leaped up at her.

"Look!" She waved the envelope two inches in front of Devlin's nose. "It's addressed to the company we were just talking about. Marine Supplies, Incorporated."

"Do you know this business?" Alvarez asked. "I do not. Perhaps because it doesn't exist. Or didn't, until my nephew established it via a post office box. I will leave the envelope with you. We shall consider my debt paid, yes?"

If he hadn't been a drug runner and a killer, Liz might have kissed him.

"Paid in full," she assured him.

"*Bueno.* I shall leave you, then." He stepped over Donny again, sparing him only a passing glance. "Are you sure you don't wish me to rid you of this one?"

"I'm sure."

Since Liz's fingerprints and DNA were already all over the envelope, Devlin gave her the honor of opening it. She extracted a bank deposit slip and a handwritten note with instructions for the amount to be deposited.

"Devlin!" Her voice shrill with excitement, Liz waved the note under his nose. "I recognize this scrawl!"

She should. She'd seen it only a week or so ago on a voucher authorizing a five-hundred-dollar advance on her pay.

"It's Wallace's. Conrad Wallace."

"You sure?"

"I'm sure. Wallace is your man," she said with dawning dismay and disgust. "The one providing the targets for Martín."

"That's what it's looking like to me, too."

Devlin's face could have been carved from granite, and his eyes were as cold as death. Liz wouldn't want to be in Wallace's shoes when the two met up again—which could be real soon. Consumed by a fierce, unrelenting urge to wrap her hands around the AmMex rep's neck, Liz posed a question filled with silky menace.

"What do you say we make a midnight run out to AM-237?"

"Sounds good to me. After I make a couple quick calls, we'll get rid of Carter here and head for the airport."

The mention of his name seemed to pull Donny from his second comatose state of the night. He gave a strangled moan and struggled up on one elbow, his expression a study in painful confusion.

"'Lizabeth?"

Shaking his head to clear it, he started to push to his feet. He was halfway up when Devlin moved into his field of vision. His eyes widening in alarm, Donny sank back to the floor.

"Smart move," Devlin said with savage approval. "You'd only end up there again, anyway."

"Who are you? What the hell's going on here?"

"All you need to know is that you're out of the picture, pal. Permanently."

Donny bobbled his head in Liz's direction. Gathering his courage, he curled his lip and sneered up at her.

"So much for all those e-mails about how you'd wait for me as long as it took."

"Funny thing about that. I did wait. I was under the mistaken impression that I loved you." Her gaze lifted to the man standing a few feet away. "Then I met a certain roustabout on a deserted beach. He's given me a whole different perspective on love."

Devlin banked his impatience and fury at Wallace long enough to deliver a swift, hard kiss.

"Hold that thought, darlin'. We'll pick up the discussion right here when we get back from AM-237."

Eleven

Less than two hours later Liz radioed the rig lit up like a Christmas tree in the distance.

"AM-237, this is Aero Baja 214. I'm five miles out and have your lights in view. Request you activate the helideck landing system."

"Roger, 214," the on-duty radio operator responded. "We'll turn on the welcome sign and send up the landing officer and tie-down crew. The duty officer wants to know what's up? Why this late night visit?"

"Tell the DO I'll advise him and the chief engineer when I land."

"Roger that."

Liz switched off the mike, gripped by the rage that had accompanied her across forty miles of black ocean.

"I still can't believe that bastard Wallace. The man acted as if every cent of the payroll came out of his own pocket and complained about any extra expense for the rig. The whole time he was feeding off the blood of his coworkers like a friggin' vampire."

"*I* can't believe we didn't find the account he'd set up in the Grand Caymans," Devlin returned.

He kept his eyes on the lights in the distance and tried to suppress the fury that strained against its chains. He could understand the miss. He didn't like it, but he could understand it. Even after he'd fed Riever the account number on the deposit slip, it had taken OMEGA's supercomputers three runs to trace the convoluted routing back to a U.S. bank account. The name on the account was fictitious, but the handwriting on checks written against that account matched that on the instructions in the envelope. It also matched the signature on a slew of digitized documents Riever had pulled from AmMex computers.

Come morning Riev would request videotapes from the bank, hoping for a shot of Wallace either making or withdrawing funds from the bogus account. A visual would provide another nail in the murdering bastard's coffin.

He'd need a coffin, Devlin thought savagely, ripped apart by memories of his last visit with Harry Johnson's fiancée. Eve and her young son had been so sure big, buff Harry would fill the hole in their lives…and so devastated by his unexplained disappearance.

Devlin clenched his fist, pulling at the skin of his bruised knuckles. He didn't notice the pain. Didn't focus on anything but the lights of the platform dead ahead. Wallace would be lucky if he made it off the patch without a toy bear stuffed down his throat.

"How are you going to handle him?" Liz asked, as if sensing his vicious thoughts.

"I'm hoping to God he puts up a fight," was all Devlin would say.

They lapsed into another silence for the last portion of the flight. Landings were trickier at night, but Liz had made enough of them to put her bird into a hover directly above the pad. Floods bathed the helideck in white light.

Clearly visible in his yellow vest, the landing officer waved her down foot by careful foot while the red-vested tie-down crew huddled behind the protective barriers at the far side of the pad to avoid the rotor blast.

The sea was calm tonight, and the deck appeared stable. Still, Liz had to ride the air currents and touch down just right to catch the deck at the peak of its gentle roll. Devlin had his harness unbuckled almost before the skids touched. Liz didn't want to miss any of the action, but she couldn't just jump out.

"Give me ten minutes," she told him. "I'll power down and secure the aircraft while you brief the duty officer and senior engineer."

"Good enough. I'll meet you on the bridge."

Devlin yanked off his headset and shoved open the

cockpit door. Ducking under the whirling rotors, he headed for the stairs.

Liz turned on the overhead lights and flipped to the power-down checklist on her kneeboard. She was reaching for the first bank of switches when one of the red vests sprang up from his crouch. Bent low to avoid the still rotating blades, he wrenched the passenger door open.

"Hey!" Liz yelled. "Wait until I—"

"Take her back up!"

Her stomach dropped all the way to the drill deck when she saw that it wasn't a tie-down crew man who scrambled into the passenger seat. It was Conrad Wallace, white-faced with desperation.

"Take her back up, Liz."

"The hell I will!"

Thrusting a hand inside the vest he must have lifted from the helipad crew locker, he whipped out a snub-nosed .38 and shouted over the whap of the blades.

"I know what happened this afternoon! On the *Santa Guadalupe*. It came over the marine police radio."

The hand gripping the .38 shook so badly Liz sucked in a razor-edged breath.

"Then I heard you were making an unscheduled run. A night run. Coming to get me. Take her back up, Liz."

She shot a glance out the windshield. Devlin had disappeared down the ladder. He was probably halfway to the elevators. The landing officer and rest of the tie-down crew were standing by, obviously confused. They couldn't see the revolver Wallace kept low in his lap.

"I'll shoot you! I mean it. I don't have anything to lose."

If she took him up, Liz figured he'd shoot her anyway once they touched down on shore. But there was a lot of ocean between the patch and dry land.

With every emergency maneuver and crazy acrobatic stunt she'd ever performed zinging through her mind, she gave the landing officer a thumbs-up to signal that she was lifting off again and dropped her hand to the throttle. The slowly dying engine revved back up to full power.

The change in pitch hit Devlin just as he was about to step into the elevator that would whisk him down to the crew deck. Head cocked, he listened as the engine's whine gathered sound and fury.

"What the hell…?"

The rumble grew to a full-throated roar. Devlin had logged hundreds of hours in choppers, flying out and back from rigs all around the world. He recognized the thunder of a liftoff when he heard it. Cursing, he spun around and sprinted for the ladder.

His head topped the edge of the pad just as the skids left the deck. He spotted Liz in the cockpit. Saw Wallace beside her in the passenger seat. Spitting out another venomous curse, he shot up the last few stairs.

The chopper's nose pitched down. It surged forward, gathering speed. His heart in his throat, Devlin exploded across the pad.

The Ranger cleared the deck. A yawning gap of black appeared between it and the pad. Black night. Black water twelve stories below.

Lunging, Devlin sailed through what seemed like a football field of empty space. One hand met only air. The other slapped metal.

Inside the cockpit, Liz felt the Ranger buck like a bee-stung mustang. The center of gravity shifted. The nose tilted. Forty-four feet of rotor blades tipped sideways and sliced dangerously close to the side of the rig. With a high-pitched scream, Wallace splayed out both hands to keep from being flung out of his seat.

That's what the bastard got for not strapping himself in, Liz thought viciously as she fought to keep her aircraft from going into the drink.

"Don't do it!" the AmMex rep shrieked, struggling to aim the gun in her direction without losing his precarious hold. "Don't take us down! I'll kill you! I swear I'll kill you!"

"I'm *not* taking us down."

She couldn't. Not yet. If the aircraft gyrated out of control... If she crashed into one of the flanges...

With nightmare visions of the Ranger exploding and the entire rig going up in a massive fireball erupting inside her head, she worked the pedals and collective. By the time she'd zoomed out over open water, she had a good idea what caused the drag on her right skid.

It was Devlin. It had to be Devlin. No one else would be insane enough to make that kind of leap.

Wallace reached the same conclusion a few seconds later. Twisting in his seat, he put a shoulder to the cockpit door and wedged it open a few inches.

Wind poured into the cabin and upped Liz's pucker factor yet another notch. Fighting the violent shear, she kept one eye on the altimeter and the other on Wallace. Then he shouldered the door open another few inches and stuck the revolver into the void.

"No! For God's sake, Wallace! Don't!"

Ignoring her frantic shout, he fired. Once. Twice.

"You'll hit the fuel tank, you moron!"

She'd hoped—*prayed*—that would scare him enough to pop back inside the cockpit. Either he didn't hear her over the scream of the wind or his desperation had made him crazy. It didn't matter. Liz wasn't about to let him take another potshot at Devlin.

The bastard had wedged the door open. Big mistake. Huge. Gripping the controls, Liz risked taking her foot off the right pedal long enough to swing it over the center lever.

"This flight is—"

Her boot connected with Wallace's back.

"—terminated!"

She put everything she had into the shove. The AmMex rep slammed against the door, springing it wide open with his weight, and pitched out.

Most people wouldn't survive falling out of a helicopter and smashing into the sea. Fortunately—or unfortunately—for him, Wallace constituted a minority.

Liz and Devlin were waiting when the rig's search-and-rescue crew hauled him back aboard. He stumbled onto the deck with a blanket wrapped around his shoulders, battered and bruised. The sight of Liz and Devlin started him babbling hysterically.

"I didn't know the real reason Martín Alvarez wanted names and photos of crew members rotating off the rigs! I swear, I thought he was just putting the touch on them."

"Yeah, sure."

Devlin wasn't the only one who refused to buy his line. The duty officer, the senior engineer, the search-and-rescue coordinator and a half-dozen roughnecks and roustabouts had all gathered on deck. Word of the AmMex rep's attempt to hijack the Ranger had flooded the patch like an uncapped gusher. Rumor had flamed into fury once the crew learned why.

Wallace knew he'd be lucky to make it off AM-237 in one piece. Panting, wild-eyed, dripping seawater from his nose, he threw a frightened look around the circle of hostile rig workers.

"Those men had just been paid! A whole month's salary. I thought— I was sure Alvarez just wanted to sell them drugs or...or fix them up with whores."

"You lying turd."

That came from the big, beefy Irishman Liz had ferried out to the patch with Devlin. His fists were bunched so tight the knuckles showed white as he shoved his way forward. Jaw locked, he turned to the engineer, who exercised overall responsibility for the rig.

"I'm thinking, sir, that you and Ms. Moore here should go below. Devlin, too, seeing as he's a police officer or something of the sort. The boys and I will be bringing Mr. Wallace along shortly."

The engineer looked to Devlin. His answer was to grip Liz's elbow and steer her toward the elevators. After a brief hesitation, the duty officer stalked across the deck and joined them.

They didn't make the return run to Piedras Rojas until the next morning.

By that time, Devlin had Wallace's full confession on record, and Doc Metwani had repaired most of the damage caused by his private session with the crew. Bruised, battered and cuffed with plastic restraints, Wallace huddled in a mass of shivering misery while Liz went to Devlin's cabin to advise him she had the Ranger gassed and ready to go.

The cabin door was ajar, the lockers open and the built-in shelves empty. Devlin stood beside his desk, his packed gear bag at his feet. His sleek little laptop was shut down and ready to slip into a pocket on the side of the bag. The toy bear that had slouched against the computer sat in the palm of his hand.

The pain in his eyes stirred an ache inside Liz's chest. She knew what caused it. Wallace had admitted that the list of targets he'd provided Martín Alvarez had included Harry Johnson.

"I'm sorry," she said softly.

"Yeah. Me, too."

He stuffed the toy inside his bag before reaching for her. The pain was still there, shadowing his face, as he drew her into his arms.

"You know that thought I told you to hang on to?"

"You think little things like getting hijacked and almost crashing into the sea would make me forget it?"

"I need you to hold on to it a while longer."

"Why?"

"It'll be a few weeks before we can pick up the discussion where we left off. I'll have to work Wallace's extradition and haul him back to States. Then I need to deliver the news about Harry to his fiancée."

Liz swallowed, fighting a sudden hollow feeling in the pit of her stomach. Was this the first of many times they'd have to put their lives on hold? The first of a hundred goodbyes? Would the absences stretch longer and longer? Would Devlin expect her to wait indefinitely, as Donny had?

Well, she'd learned her lesson there. She was done with waiting.

"Tell you what," she said, locking her hands behind his neck. "*I'll* haul you and that piece of garbage back to the States. And I'll go with you to deliver the news to Harry's fiancée, if you'll let me."

"You might want to think twice about that. It won't be easy."

"No, it won't. And it won't be easy turning what we have into something solid and rich and full. But you said it yourself. We can make it work. Combine careers. Pick our locations. Aero Baja isn't the only charter service handling the big rigs. I can fly for anyone—maybe even this organization you work for."

"You could," Devlin agreed. "I know Maggie and Adam will add their endorsement to mine." A smile slipped past the hurt in his eyes, creasing his tanned cheeks. "We'll have to put our heads together and come up with a code name for you."

The certainty swirling inside Liz's heart overflowed until she felt the warmth all through her body. This was right. So very right.

"Just our heads?" she murmured.

His laughter filled her soul. She'd spent all those empty months waiting for Donny. Or so she'd thought. Now she knew it was Devlin she'd been waiting for. Wherever their jobs took them, whatever deep blue seas needed to be crossed, they'd cross them together.

Epilogue

Six months later

It was the perfect spot for a wedding. The Pacific shimmered with a thousand pinpricks of dazzling light. The December sun was kind to the guests who had trooped down from vehicles parked on the road above, bathing them in gentle warmth while tinting the cliffs that thrust out of the sea at the far end of the beach to umber.

Rows of white chairs were set facing the turquoise sea. Subcommandante Riviera sat on the bride's side, stiff and official looking in his uniform. Jorge's wife, Maria and several of their children occupied the seats beside the police inspector. Anita Lopez and most of the regulars from El Poco Lobo filled the rows behind them. After much debate, Liz had extended an invitation to Eduardo Alvarez and his wife. They'd declined—to Liz's relief—indicating they'd be out of the country, but El Tiburón sent a congratulatory message and an offer to use his yacht for the honeymoon, which Liz politely refused.

Maggie and Adam sat on the groom's side with their three children. Coltish, long-legged Gillian had her father's black hair and killer blue eyes. Samantha was a giggling honey-haired brunette with her mother's lively personality. Tank had barreled through the sand immediately upon arrival and made straight for the water, only to be scooped up a second from total immersion by his vigilant father.

The protesting toddler wiggled impatiently in his designated seat beside Nick Jensen and his wife, Mackenzie. Next to them were Claire Cantwell and her husband. Claire's cast had come off months ago, but Luis Esteban still hovered over her as though she were made of the most delicate porcelain. On Claire's other side was a slender, auburn-haired woman who maintained a firm grasp on the hand of a three-year-old. Like Tank, the boy wanted to get to the waves in the worst way.

Devlin had debated whether to invite Eve and her son to the wedding. She insisted the pain of losing Harry had dulled in the long months since his disappearance and professed to feel only joy that Joe

Devlin found Liz while searching for her missing fiancé. Despite her assurances, Devlin thought she looked too thin and pale.

Apparently he was the only one who thought so. Liz's former fiancé had locked on to Eve at the rehearsal dinner last night and didn't appear at all ready to unlock. Devlin had been ready to rearrange Carter's face again when he showed up at the Two Dolphins, but Liz had felt more magnanimous—particularly since Donny had arrived with a check for the last of the funds he'd appropriated from their one-time joint account.

Not that Liz needed the infusion of cash. She'd already expanded her charter service to a fleet of three, with another helicopter on order. She and Devlin had been working the rigs along the California and Baja coasts for the past six months, with Jorge Garcia heading their shore operations. In the process, Devlin had used his cover twice for OMEGA missions—once to bust a ring specializing in the import of human organs for sale to desperate transplant recipients, once to infiltrate a renegade military group based at a San Diego naval base. Liz had provided air support in both operations.

They made a helluva team.

Devlin didn't realize he'd murmured the thought aloud until a mariachi trio hired for the occasion broke into a lively rendition of "Here Comes the Bride" and all eyes turned to the woman being escorted through the row of chairs by her mother and a beaming Jorge, his mustaches waxed to sharp points for the occasion.

"Yeah," his best man muttered over the beat of the music, "you do. Hope I get as lucky one of these days."

"Hope so, too, Riev."

Devlin voiced the words, but his mind, his gaze, his entire being were centered on Liz. She'd let her hair grow these past months, long enough to sweep up in a crown of blond curls banded by fresh flowers. Her dress was a simple sheath of creamy satin that left her shoulders bare. A smile tipped his mouth when he saw her feet were bare as well. Like the night they'd met, right on this very spot.

He took her hands in his, the smile spreading to his heart.

"Hello, darlin'. Ready to make this partnership permanent?"

Her eyes answered for her. Filled with love and laughter, they warmed every corner of Devlin's soul.

"I'm ready, cowboy."

* * * * *

MILLS & BOON
Desire 2 in 1

EXPECTING LONERGAN'S BABY by Maureen Child
(Summer of Secrets)

Sam Lonergan was home only for one summer – until a night of explosive passion with the sexy housekeeper gave him a reason to stay.

THE SINS OF HIS PAST by Roxanne St Claire

Does paying for his sins mean leaving Kendra Locke, the only woman he'd ever wanted, for a second time? This time, would she walk away?

DYNASTIES: THE ELLIOTTS
CAUSE FOR SCANDAL by Anna DePalo

Sensible heiress Summer Elliott had posed as her flamboyant identical twin and bedded a rock star. Now the shocking truth is about to be revealed and she has some serious explaining to do!

THE FORBIDDEN TWIN by Susan Crosby

Seducing your twin sister's ex-fiancé by pretending to be her is not the best idea... Unless, like Scarlet Elliott, you've loved him for years and he willingly succumbs.

SEVEN-YEAR SEDUCTION by Heidi Betts

Would one week stranded together by a storm be enough to indulge in a seduction that's been seven years in the making?

THEIR MILLION-DOLLAR NIGHT by Katherine Garbera
(What Happens in Vegas…)

Businessman Max Williams has millions at stake, but one sexy, sinful ex-showgirl has him risking scandal – and proposing a merger.

On sale from 16th February 2007

Available at WHSmith, Tesco, ASDA, and all good bookshops

www.millsandboon.co.uk

MILLS & BOON
Super ROMANCE

ALL ROADS LEAD TO TEXAS by Linda Warren
Home To Stay

With her three young half-siblings in tow, Callie is headed for the safe haven of Homestead. Keeping her identity secret until the children's abusive stepfather is brought to trial isn't going to be easy—especially with Sheriff Wade Montgomery paying so much attention to the town's newest residents.

THE RUNAWAY DAUGHTER by Anna DeStefano
Count on a Cop

Georgia has a drug problem. Tony Rivers and Angie Carter are deputies in the sheriff's department, and it's up to them to clean up their town. But when Tony's niece turns to him to help her hide a baby from his drug-dealer father, things get a bit complicated. And so do Tony's feelings for Angie...

A SOLDIER'S QUEST by Lori Handeland
The Luchetti Brothers

Bobby Luchetti just wants to forget the woman his brother stole from him while he was away serving his country. So he is happy to accept a mission to rescue Dr Jane Harker. As the danger —and his attraction to Jane—heats up, will this soldier finally find a love of his own?

MARRIAGE BY NECESSITY by Marisa Carroll

The last person Nate Fowler expects to see on his doorstep is his ex-wife—with a child no less, and a proposal of remarriage. When Sarah explains she has to have a life-threatening operation, and there's no one to care for little Matty but her, Nate agrees to go along with her plan. But what happens if Sarah survives?

On sale from 16th February 2007

Available at WHSmith, Tesco, ASDA, and all good bookshops
www.millsandboon.co.uk

MILLS & BOON

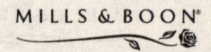

Two bestselling novels together in one volume for you to enjoy!

INSTANT FAMILY!

Featuring
The Tycoon's Instant Daughter
by Christine Rimmer

An Abundance of Babies
by Marie Ferrarella

2-in-1 FOR ONLY £4.99

MILLS & BOON

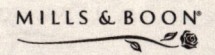

POSSESSED BY THE SHEIKH

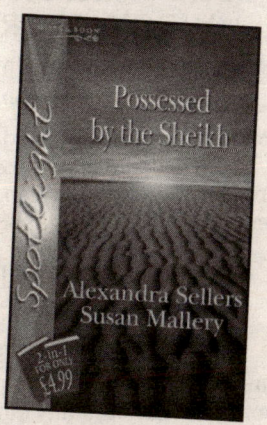

Spotlight

Featuring
The Playboy Sheikh
by Alexandra Sellers

The Sheikh and the Runaway Princess by Susan Mallery

2-in-1 FOR ONLY £4.99

**On sale from
16th February 2007**

*Available at WHSmith, Tesco, ASDA,
and all good bookshops*
www.millsandboon.co.uk

MILLS & BOON

SPECIAL EDITION

THE SHEIKH AND THE VIRGIN SECRETARY
by Susan Mallery
Desert Rogues

Kiley Hendrick wanted revenge on her fiancé for his infidelity – and becoming mistress to her rich, powerful boss seemed like the perfect plan. But Prince Rafiq was determined to make this virgin beauty his own!

FALLING FOR THE BOSS
by Elizabeth Harbison
Family Business

Evan Hanson only went to work for Hanson Media Group out of a sense of family duty. And when his first love, Meredith Waters, was hired old flames were rekindled. But would her secret agenda throw Meredith and Evan's own partnership into jeopardy?

AT THE MILLIONAIRE'S REQUEST
by Teresa Southwick

When millionaire Gavin Spencer needed a speech therapist for his injured son, he asked for MJ Taylor's help. As the boy began to heal, would MJ and Gavin give voice to their feelings?

Don't miss out!
On sale from 16th February 2007

Available at WHSmith, Tesco, ASDA, and all good bookshops
www.millsandboon.co.uk

MILLS & BOON

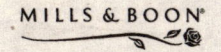

SPECIAL EDITION

CUSTODY FOR TWO
by Karen Rose Smith

Baby Bonds

When Dylan Malloy's sister died suddenly, he wanted to help her friend Shaye Bartholomew to raise his sister's newborn baby. He proposed marriage – but was it just to share custody or had Shaye too found a place in his heart?

DALTON'S UNDOING
by RaeAnne Thayne

The Dalton Brothers

Prim and proper Jenny Boyer's children found an unlikely role model in Pine Gulch's sexiest bachelor Seth Dalton – would Seth find an unlikely love match in Jenny?

A MOTHER'S REFLECTION
by Elissa Ambrose

Drama teacher Rachel Hartwell's latest role would be her most important yet: befriending her biological daughter after Megan's adoptive mother's death. But she hadn't banked on falling for her daughter's adoptive father!

Don't miss out!
On sale from 16th February 2007

Available at WHSmith, Tesco, ASDA, and all good bookshops
www.millsandboon.co.uk

MILLS & BOON

INTRIGUE

WARRIOR SPIRIT by Cassie Miles
Big Sky Bounty Hunters

When evidence hinted that a series of natural deaths were actually murders, Natalie Patterson was on the case. Sparks immediately flew with Brady Tomasini, the detective in charge of the case. But the killer wanted Natalie and he'd take out anyone who got in his way.

THE SHEIKH AND I by Linda Winstead Jones
Capturing the Crown

Kadir Al-Nuri is a sheikh willing to risk his life for peace. Cassandra Klein is his diplomatic aide, unwilling to let anything—or anyone—stand in the way of her career. Yet bullets weren't the only things flying when these star-crossed lovers met.

INVESTIGATING 101 by Debra Webb
Colby Agency: New Recruits

New recruit Todd Thompson skips basic training and jumps right into danger when he helps researcher Serena Blake investigate a horrifying case involving stolen identities and missing children.

THE WOMAN WHO WASN'T THERE
by Marie Ferrarella
Cavanaugh Justice

Agent Delene D'Angelo was thrown together with Detective Troy Cavanaugh by a murder investigation. Troy's attempts to woo Delene were met with disinterest and suspicion. Did she dare lower her guard when the stakes couldn't be higher?

On sale from 16th February 2007

Available at WHSmith, Tesco, ASDA, and all good bookshops

www.millsandboon.co.uk